Kitsune-Mochi

Laura VanArendonk Baugh

Æclipse Press
Indianapolis, IN

for my husband, Seeker Within
who has been ridiculously supportive and proud

Glossary

ani — elder brother, formal and archaic; with suffix, *ani-ue* (The twins each refer to the other as the elder, the rascals.)

ara — syllable of exclamation, such as "oh" or "ah" in English

ashiguru — foot soldier

ayakashi — any of several supernatural entities, similar to *youkai*

bakemono — any of several supernatural entities

bakeneko — cat spirit

-bouzu — often a playfully-derogatory honorific to a younger male

-chan — a diminutive or cutesy honorific mimicking a childish pronunciation of *-san*. Can also be used affectionately.

chichi — father, archaic formal (with suffix, *chichi-ue*)

chokuban — a square divination board based on astrological, astronomical, and seasonal influences

daijoubu desu ka — roughly, are you all right?

daikon — large, mild species of white radish

daimyou — territorial lord serving the *shogun*, during the shogunate

de gozaimasu, de gozaimashita — phrase to accompany and formalize other speech (*"yoroshiku de gozaimasu"*)

-dono — archaic formal honorific

doumo arigatou gozaimasu — thank you very much

fundoshi — loincloth

fusuma — opaque doors of wooden lattice overlaid with paper

futago — very roughly, "the two, the pair"

futagokyoudai — twin siblings

futon — sleeping mat

Genji & Kaworu — Genji Hikaru and his son Kaworu, famed philanderers of Lady Murasaki's fictional *Tale of Genji*

gochisousamadeshita — literally, "it has been a feast;" traditional polite phrase used at the end of a meal

gumo — spider

haha — mother, archaic formal (with suffix, *haha-ue*)

hai — affirmative

hakama — pleated leg garment

haori — men's jacket-type garment

happi — men's jacket-type garment

hime — princess or daughter of a high house

himo — belt, tie, sash

hitatare — a garment for the upper body, open in front and on the sides, with hanging sleeves

hitotsu-me-nyuudou — one-eyed priest, a *youkai* named for its appearance

hoshi no tama — "star-stone," a jewel or ball belonging to a kitsune

ichimonji — the first defensive position of *taijutsu*

itachi — weasel; some *youkai* legends feature weasels which move at the speed of the wind

itadakimasu — literally "I humbly receive," a polite phrase said at the beginning of a meal

jinmaku — camp curtains, a fabric wall used to define outdoor spaces

kai — a syllable of mystical release, empathy, or foreknowledge

kamikakushii — literally "hidden by gods or spirits," usually translated "spirited away," or abducted by *youkai*

kanji — written characters imported from China

kappa — predatory water *youkai*

kata — choreographed movement or form, often used in the practice of martial arts and dance

kawauso — river otter spirit

kekkai — mystic barrier

ki — spiritual energy

kimono — literally "clothing," but most often referring to the long body robe

kisama — a rude form of address (making Genji's "Ki-sama" rather borderline!)

kitsune — fox spirit

kitsune-bi — foxfire, a cool supernatural flame

kitsune-mochi — fox possessor, a human who bound or used *kitsune*

kitsune-tsuki — state of being possessed by a fox spirit

koku — unit of measure, enough rice to feed one person for one year

konbanwa — good evening

kosode — loose garment with smaller sleeve openings

kuji-in — "the nine syllables," mystic mantras used in religion and martial arts for defense, attack, meditation, and magics

-kun — honorific to address one of lower status or, often, a young male

kuso — from the verb "to stink" or "to smell foul," a profanity

-me — a disparaging form of address

mon — crest, a heraldic symbol

mononoke — general term for supernatural entity, usually harmful

naginata — polearm, a staff with a long curved blade at the end

nozuchi — a thick, snake-like *youkai*

odaiko — great drum

ofuda — a paper strip on which has been inked a spell, used for sealing or dispelling spirits

ohisashiburi de gozaimasu — it has been a while, or very colloquially, "Long time, no see."

oji — uncle; may be used literally or figuratively (as with the

English equivalent)

ojii — old man

okugata — form of address to or referring to the lady of the house

oni — large, strong *youkai* often compared to western trolls or ogres

onmyoudou — system of knowledge and mysticism which includes aspects of yin-yang, feng shui, astronomy, astrology, natural sciences, divination, calendar-keeping, etc. At one point a valued and vital government occupation with high position.

onmyouji — one who practices *onmyoudou*

onore — a first-person pronoun which may be used pejoratively as a second-person pronoun, now archaic

origami — art of paper folding

ougumo — great spider

oyakata — form of address to or referring to the lord of the house

rou — long raised wooden decks of corridor and rooms, connecting the *tai no ya* and *tsuridono* in a *shinden* house

sake — rice wine

-sama — respectful honorific

samurai — warrior caste

-san — less formal honorific (likely evolved from *-sama*)

sara — the depression in the top of the *kappa*'s skull which must remained filled with water, or the *kappa* weakens

sensei — teacher or master (of an art)

seppuku — ritual suicide

shakujou — priest's ringed staff

shikigami — spirit assisting an *onmyouji*, often using folded paper or similar constructs

shime-kazari — folded paper strips used to spiritually purify an area shinden — primary building in a *shinden-zukuri*, the single-story style of house and estate popular among Heian nobles. At this transitional period, the iconic tower strongholds had not yet come into existence.

shirikodama — in folklore, a ball-like concretion of life energy found at the top of the rectum

shishi-odoshi — "deer-chaser," a water-powered bamboo noisemaker to startle grazing animals from the garden

shouji — door or room-dividing screen. Today, *shouji* are generally of lattice and rice paper, but at this time, *shouji* were wood overlaid with paper like what is today called *fusuma.*

sumimasen — thank you, for an action ("thank you for taking the trouble")

sunoko — a deck or open veranda running along the rooms and serving as corridor in a house. Today, *sunoko* refers more often to raised wooden slatted flooring often used as mats or steps.

taijutsu — literally "body technique," martial art focusing first on body combat before weapons

tai no ya — an "opposed house" or pavilion attached to the *shinden*, or primary structure

tama — cut stone or gem

-tan — a diminutive or cutesy honorific mimicking a childish pronunciation of *-san*

tantou — dagger

tatami — woven mat

tengu — mountain spirit often seen as a bird-headed man, or a man with bird-like characteristics such as a long, beaklike nose. Usually dressed as a *yamabushi* and carrying a *shakujou* and feather fan.

tono — lord, honorific

torii — gate at shrine

tsuridono — open pavilions at the end of the long *rou*, often extending into the garden or pond

uchiwa - fan

-ue — honorific, formal

ushi-oni — ox *youkai*, often a bull-headed humanoid but can appear in other forms

-wan-wan — Murame is not only using obnoxiously childish language (-chan and -tan) but is also referencing a dog's bark; in Japanese dogs say not "bow-wow" but "wan-wan."

wataridono — corridors, open with rooms along one side, linking the *shinden* and *tai yo na*

yamabushi — mountain priest, traveling ascetic

yoroshiku de gozaimasu/gozaimashita — a polite phrase of introduction

youkai — any of many supernatural entities

you-ki — spiritual energy

youkoso — welcome, in a context of distant or special travel

yuki-onna — snow woman, a beautiful *youkai* which appears to travelers lost or struggling in snow and devours them

yuurei — a type of ghost

zen — low, individual table

zouri — woven sandals

Author's Note

This story takes place in Not-Japan.

This is an important note, because it affects everything one will read here. Were this an actual Heian/Kamakura transition period piece, some details would have to be changed for the sake of strict accuracy, from the language the characters use to the attributes of the *youkai* featured here. The supernatural creature of the eighth century is a very different creature than that of the eighteenth, and nearly unrecognizable when contrasted with that of the twenty-first.

Folklore changes, of course, and in the last century or so particularly, the inhuman have been sanitized and de-fanged like never before. This phenomenon isn't unique to Japanese folklore — Western fairies and elves were feared for centuries before they became Tinkerbell and Legolas, and the fearsome vampire's most distinguishing traits have in recent decades faded from mist-walking and hypnotic compulsion to emo self-absorption. We still remember older characteristics, but we remember for the space of a few hundred years, not a thousand.

The denizens of Japanese folklore have similarly evolved, and I have chosen the creatures we have come to expect — the river predators referenced in period writings were very unlike modern *kappa*, yet what modern reader would be pleased with a *kappa* who did not like cucumbers? — and thus I have used primarily more recent incarnations of *youkai* myths.

Similarly, I have used more modern Japanese. The honorific *-san* probably did not come into general use until the

Edo period, for example, but it appears frequently here. Again, this is to prevent disrupting or confusing the modern reader.

I have set Gennosuke and his people slightly ahead of known history, but their very nature means their origins are misty. Also, I have blurred contemporary customs and features, blending aspects of Heian and Kamakura eras because, after all, eras do bleed into one another rather than abruptly and distinctly changing, especially in a more rural house such as Naka no Yoritomo's. I feel what is presented is well within possibility, just as we might still listen to '90s pop music even in the twenty-first century, but if a scholarly reader feels otherwise, please remember that this is Not-Japan.

Thank you, and please enjoy!

"You don't know about me without you have read a book by the name of *The Adventures of Tom Sawyer*, but that ain't no matter."

— *The Adventures of Huckleberry Finn*, by Mark Twain

This novel is a sequel to the novelette *Kitsune-Tsuki*.

CHAPTER ONE

"KAGEMURA no Shishio Hitoshi would never have deserted his duty. If he cannot be found, he must be dead." Naka no Yoritomo fixed unyielding eyes on Tsurugu. "How has this happened?"

Tsurugu bowed low. "I am sorry, *tono*. I cannot say."

Naka no Yoritomo's voice darkened. "I have paid well for an *onmyouji* so I would know exactly the dangers we face. I brought you to learn if a *kitsune* were present, and I set Shishio Hitoshi to assist you. Is this how my generosity is rewarded?"

Tsurugu Kiyomori had not come for the gold, but that was not for Naka-dono to hear. "*Onmyoudou* gives many insights and a great deal of power, *tono*. It does not make us like the gods themselves."

The *daimyou's* voice quieted. "Tsurugu-sama, I have lost my eye, my hand, my shadow." Tsurugu's gut tightened. "What happened to him?"

"I cannot say."

"You cannot say? Or you do not know?"

Tsurugu swore silently.

"Tsurugu-sama, I do not know even whether Shishio-san was lost to a *bakemono* or to a rival house, whether the danger is political or supernatural. I must have information, if I am to protect my house, my people, my bride."

"Be patient a short time, *tono*, and I will try to have an answer. With your permission, I will come again in one hour."

He retreated to his room and seated himself before the *chokuban*, the divining board marked with stars and directions and lunar mansions. He would need no *onmyoudou* to answer the *daimyou's* question, but it would be good to make an appropriate show for the servants.

He worked the desultory divination, his hands knowing the motions on the *chokuban* while his thoughts wandered. He had liked and respected Shishio Hitoshi, had even been his friend in an odd way, and he had never wished him harm. Even at the end, if there had been any way to speak reasonably to him, if Shishio had not tried to attack once more —

His fingers stuck on the *chokuban*, and Tsurugu looked down, startled. He blinked and reset the device, turning the stars to align with the myriad other markings, but the result was the same.

Was it *karma*, already?

He was still staring at the divination results when a sound at the door caught his attention. It was one of the *daimyou's* pages, trying to look self-important while peeking at the divination materials. Tsurugu held up a hand to forestall the prompt. "I'm ready."

When he returned, Fujitani no Kaede was seated near her husband, screened from Tsurugu's view with only a bit of multi-layered train artfully displayed. He knelt, bowed, and then straightened to answer them. "*Oyakata-sama, okugata-sama*, I have something to report of your lost servant."

"Please, speak."

Tsurugu bowed again, an excuse to hide his face. "He died at the hands of the *kitsune* you feared. He discovered it and fought it and was killed."

Yoritomo was surprised. "But — *kitsune* do not often kill."

"No, they do not." Tsurugu could hear unsteadiness in his voice. "But he had trapped this one, and it seems it had no other chance to escape. It killed him and bore away his corpse. I am very sorry."

"Rise, Tsurugu-sama, there is no need for apology in this. It was not your doing that Shishio fell in his duty." The *daimyou* frowned. "Though it is unlike him to have acted alone, without informing me — or asking you to join him, when you were brought specifically to counter the *kitsune*."

"He may have come upon the creature while it was trapped or weakened, *tono*, perhaps changing forms or otherwise hampered," came Kaede's rich voice. "He might have thought the opportunity too rare to lose."

Tsurugu nodded. "If the creature had no other escape...." Though humans killed the trickster spirits, *kitsune* did not often kill humans. It was almost unthinkable. Nearly unbearable.

Naka no Yoritomo sighed. "Still, a mistake, and one which has cost us all. Tsurugu-sama, do you wish to add something?"

Tsurugu clenched his fists, fearing what the *daimyou* had seen in his face. "No, *tono*. It is only — he was my friend."

Naka no Yoritomo nodded. "We will honor him."

Dismissed, Tsurugu fled to his room, where he hugged his knees close and pressed his face into them. If Shishio had not been stopped, they would all have suffered, even died — Tsurugu, the twins, Hanae, and Fujitani no Kaede herself. He had done what was necessary. He could not allow harm to come to Kaede-dono, and it was foolish not to protect his own life. What had been done was now done.

And he had new matters to occupy him.

He waited until evening, when fireflies came out to play among the yard's carefully arranged stones. Tsurugu rose, bound his *hakama* to his legs so the fabric would not sag damply with dew, and went out into the night. They would meet in the far reaches of the garden, in the artful wilderness beyond the house. There were few secrets within a house of moving walls.

The twins were there already, rolling in the grass in their play. One glanced up as Tsurugu approached, and his brother promptly pinned him. "Unfair!" yelped the one in the wet grass.

"*Konbanwa*, Kiyomori-sama," greeted the upper youth. He slid from his position of advantage and leaned lazily upon his reclining brother.

They had, in private moments, little appreciation for the delicacies of rank, though at least Tsurugu had been accorded his proper honorific. "Up, you two," Tsurugu admonished mildly. "You're soaking."

The twins rolled up from the flattened grass with wide grins. Genji and Kaworu — Tsurugu had facetiously named them for the irresistibly handsome philanderers of the popular novel — were identical to the casual human eye. They were Fujitani no Kaede's servants, brought to the household when she married Naka no Yoritomo. They were excellent dancers as well, despite their lowly status in the household, and almost never seen singly.

"While we are alone...." Tsurugu withdrew from his clothes a plum-sized ball, iridescent in the moonlight. He let the *hoshi no tama* roll over his fingers, toying with it. "Which of you lost this?"

Genji held out a hand. "It is mine, Ki-san."

"See that you do not lose it again. And do not call me Ki-san."

"Ki-sama, then."

Tsurugu cuffed him. "There are limits, Genji-kun."

Genji made a face. "My *tama*?"

"Tsurugu Kiyomori-san," called a lilting voice, "please finish your business, so we may join you without recalling that one of these had carelessly lost something precious."

Genji retreated a few steps, tucking the ball safely within his clothing. He and Kaoru bowed as Kaede-dono, followed closely by her maid Hanae, came to join them.

Tsurugu bowed as well. "*Konbanwa*, Kaede-dono." He straightened. "And the *tama* was not found by anyone who knew its nature. There was no danger of it betraying us."

"Only through good fortune." Kaede looked at the twins, rumpled and damp. "*Ara*, what a disheveled mess you look. This will never do when—"

"*Okugata-sama!*" A voice rang through the garden, and a torch flared beyond a line of trees. "Kaede-dono! *Okugata-sama!*"

"I am here alone," Kaede ordered in a hushed tone.

Tsurugu nodded, and there was a brief blur of colors as his vision shifted. A moment later, he was a fox, disappearing into the hydrangeas and flattening himself to the ground. A few paces away, two pale young foxes slipped into the darkness.

Hanae draped a robe across the ground; safe with her mistress, she had no reason to hide. Kaede sank upon the robe. "Here I am," she called. "Who's there?"

There was a crash of foliage as someone came nearer, raising the torch. "Kaede-dono! We have—"

"Stay where you are!" snapped Hanae with uncharacteristic authority. "Your lady is unveiled."

Kaede raised a silk sleeve to conceal herself from the torchlight, as ladies of rank were not to be viewed by servants or strangers. "I came out to gaze upon the moon, and to think upon a poem. Has my lord called for me?"

"I beg your pardon, Kaede-dono. You were missed, and there was an alarm.... The *kitsune*...."

Kaede rolled her eyes behind her sleeve. "The *onmyouji* has given me a charm which he promised would protect me for this evening. I thank you for your concern, but I am perfectly safe."

"We could not find the *onmyouji* when we went for him."

Even behind her sleeve, Kaede had the presence of mind to resist glancing at the flowering bush hiding Tsurugu's fox form. Kaede always had great presence of mind. "It is possible he went out as well, for it is a lovely night. You may find him yet, and soon if you keep up this racket. Tell my lord Yoritomo-dono that I am found, that I am safe, and that I beg him to join me in my room shortly."

"Yes, my lady." The torch moved away.

Kaede lowered her sleeve; her *kitsune* had the intimate privilege of looking upon her. "Come, we must finish quickly."

Three foxes slid from hiding places and faced her, becoming human once more. The twins were grinning; Tsurugu would have to warn them against teasing the searching servants before returning to the house.

"Very briefly," Kaede said, "Midorikawa-dono is coming."

Tsurugu heard an intake of breath, almost too soft to note, and when he looked, the twins' grins had vanished. "When?" he asked.

"In a fortnight or so. I will tell you when he's come."

As if they would need telling.... The arrival of Midorikawa-dono would stir every *youkai* in the mountain. And with the warnings he had seen.... Tsurugu would be kept busy, for the *daimyou*'s household would surely notice the increased supernatural activity.

"Now go, and leave no suspicion." Kaede gestured.

Tsurugu bowed. Beside him, the twins became pale foxes once more and slipped into the darkness. He did not worry that they would find trouble. The news of Midorikawa-dono would have quelled their taste for excitement.

CHAPTER TWO

to the west, domain of Sanjou no Takeo

OGASAWARA no Manabu hurried into the room and knelt on the *tatami*, pressing himself forward in a deep bow. He drew a slow, ragged breath. *"Tono."*

Sanjou-dono sat upright on his dais, his face a rigid mask. This was worrisome. The *daimyou* was an expressive man, given to wild gestures and curses which vented steam from the kettle and averted an explosion. "Ogasawara-san, face me."

Ogasawara did, schooling his distress into polite passivity. "How may I serve you, Sanjou-dono?"

The mask cracked as an eyebrow twitched. "Now you wish to serve me? Why now, Ogasawara-san? Why not two weeks ago, when Naka no Yoritomo must have sent this man on his errand? Why not yesterday morning, when he crept into my house, past all defenses?" The mask broke further. "Why not yesterday evening, when he entered my wife's room to kill her and my unborn heir?"

Ogasawara's fingers dug into the *tatami*. "He was stopped, Sanjou-dono. And, if I may add, at great personal cost to myself."

"Great cost," snorted the *daimyou*.

Broken bits from the *tatami* splintered into Ogasawara's fingers. "With respect, Sanjou-dono, it was my wife who leapt between the assassin and the *okugata-sama*. It was my wife who died."

"There are no secrets in my house; she was no loving wife to you."

You are wrong — she was everything to me. We were unhappy, yes, arguing, yes, but — we still loved one another. And now I can never apologize, I can never tell her I love her, I can never make it right.

Sanjou no Takeo took Ogasawara's silence for assent. "Why did you not predict this, Ogasawara-san? Why did you not warn us?"

"*Onmyoudou* is not so simple." Ogasawara tried to moderate his voice. "It is not possible to predict exactly that an assassin will come at such and such an hour. I had indeed warned of a possible danger from the east, and the lady was securely in her chambers because I had told her it was an unlucky date for her and she should be cautious."

"It was your own warning which placed my pregnant wife so predictably within his grasp." Sanjou's face hardened. "We have no need of an *onmyouji* whose *onmyoudou* is useless or dangerous. You are banished, Ogasawara no Manabu, from my domain."

Ogasawara stared. "But—"

"If you are here when the gate closes at twilight, you will be executed for a traitor. If you are seen within my borders this week, you will be flogged out of them. If you are seen within my borders after seven days, you will be put to death."

Ogasawara gulped and bowed. "Sanjou-dono, is there nothing I can do to—"

"Earn my trust? After you have allowed an assassin into our very chambers?" Sanjou barked a cold, derisive laugh. "Bring me the head of Naka no Yoritomo's bride, if you wish. Visit him as he has visited me. That is your just duty now."

Ogasawara pressed himself forward, careless of his dignity as he blinked hot tears from his eyes. "Sanjou-dono, I beg you — do not be so hasty. Let me serve you, let me bury my wife—"

"Go! Or I shall have you flogged from this place this very hour."

Ogasawara's chest spasmed and he drew himself up. "As you command, *tono*."

He was halfway to the door when Sanjou-dono spoke again. "But for all that she did not love you, she did you one excellent favor in her death — because my heir is not dead, you have not died this night. Perhaps that will give you some comfort as you remember her."

Ogasawara did not trust himself to speak, and he had little left to lose by not answering the *tono*, so he clenched his aching jaw and left without response.

狐

Ogasawara lay still against the tree, his limbs too heavy to move. He was weary with travel — three days of pushing his servant Hideo to greater speed, ducking off the road at each sound of approach lest it be *daimyou*'s men, sleeping in chilly thickets rather than inns to avoid being identified — and more weary with grief. Dear Matsue's body had been removed for cleaning and preparation, and he had not been able to find her before Sanjou's twilight ultimatum. He had not been able to say goodbye.

They were near an inn but safely hidden off the road. Hideo had set down his load and unpacked, and when he'd thought Ogasawara distracted with his musing, he had quietly left. Drinking, no doubt, but Ogasawara wasn't alarmed. Hideo was an ox, strong and lazy and not particularly bright. He would unwisely drink his little money away, but he would not betray his master.

Ogasawara rubbed his face. He should eat something, he knew. The flight was grueling and his grief had left him without appetite, and his condition was beginning to suffer. He should have gone with Hideo, if only for a meal.

He shivered; he had feared drawing attention from the road with a fire. It was an unlikely chance that some random patrol of Sanjou's men should be the ones to see and investigate their camp, but the potential consequences were worth avoiding. But the night was cooling fast, and perhaps it was late enough to risk flame, as most travelers and soldiers would be off the road already.

He had just coaxed a small fire to life when he heard Hideo returning. "Did you happen to bring me dinner?" he asked, feeding sticks into the fire.

Hideo rubbed his hand across his mouth and blinked. "Er, no. Didn't think to."

Ogasawara regarded him dubiously. "I can see that thinking would come hard now," he observed. "Don't think you can sleep this off in the morning."

Hideo shook his head slowly, more like an ox than ever.

Ogasawara sighed and stood. He still had to look up at Hideo. "Must have been a cheap inn. I didn't think you carried enough to drink so much." Hideo had lost much of his savings the previous week in a gaming session. "Or did you play for it?"

His foot came down on something in the low grass, and an icy chill pierced him in uncanny certitude. He reached slowly down for the comb, mother-of-pearl blossoms reflecting the low firelight in a soft gleam.

Hideo's eyes widened in his bovine face. Ogasawara turned to their supplies and opened a wooden box he had packed nearly empty — there had not been much to fill it. It had held a silken *himo*, a fan, a few combs. Now it was empty.

Hideo started backward, raising his hands in placation or defense. Ogasawara made a series of savage gestures and snapped a command, and two inhuman figures dropped from nothingness to either side of Hideo, seizing his arms and forcing him to kneel. Hideo shook his head, suddenly sober. "No, great master — be merciful!"

"Merciful?" Ogasawara could hardly form words. "When you have stolen my only mementos of my dead wife?"

"I needed a drink," pleaded Hideo. "It's hard, running like this, and you don't know how I needed it."

"It will be harder still with your back plowed like a field," snarled Ogasawara. He flipped open a second box, and a stream of paper unfurled into the air. Hideo blinked, his mouth working silently. Ogasawara raised his hand, and the paper spiraled into a long form, wrapping tightly into a flail. Little strips protruded from its length where pieces had twined together.

Hideo shook his head and tried to clasp his hands in supplication, but the figures on either side held him firm. "No, please — great master, I will earn their cost, I will—"

"You cannot buy back a memory!" shouted Ogasawara. "On his face, and bare him."

Hideo was pressed forward, his arms wide and shoulders driven hard into the ground. He dragged his face to one side, but his clothes were pulled loose and thrown over his head, leaving only the narrow *fundoshi* about his hips and between his buttocks.

Paper was versatile but strong, and twisted tightly it made a formidable weapon. The alcohol betrayed stoic Hideo and he cried aloud as the flail bit into him. Ogasawara lashed him with the fury of the theft, and the betrayal, and the exile, and the death of Matsue. He moved mechanically, hardly aware of what he did, blindly repeating his actions as he wept for all that was gone.

At last, he dropped the flail, and it uncoiled into rumpled, stained paper. He gestured, and the figures holding Hideo released him and vanished. Ogasawara wiped tears from his eyes. He had done too much, but there was no help for it now. "Get up."

Hideo did haltingly, pulling his *juban* and *kimono* back over his head and clenching his jaw as they brushed his weeping flesh. The cries had shamed him, almost as much as the beating itself. He had probably not been flogged before.

"Don't think you can sleep this off in the morning, either," Ogasawara warned darkly. "Dawdle under your pack, and I'll put a ring in your nose and prod you down the road like the ox you are, you understand?"

"Yes, Ogasawara-san."

Ogasawara took a fresh sheet of paper and wrapped it carefully about the comb before tucking it into his own robe. Then he kicked the uncoiled flail's paper, too soiled to be reliable for future use, into the fire.

狐

Ogasawara did not dream, but he lay so deeply in his memories that it seemed a dream. Hideo's rough breathing fell away, and the cicadas' cry swelled until the roadside clearing became a street lined with trees bearing tiny green fruits, lit by moonlight.

"Ogasawara-san!"

Ogasawara turned and saw Ryouichi waving to him. *"Konbanwa."*

"And a good evening to you, too. Where are you off to?"

Ogasawara smiled. "It is a lovely night for romancing, don't you think?"

Ryouichi grinned. "Indeed. I am off to see my beautiful Lady of the Moon. And you to your Lady of the Fan?"

"Indeed." Ogasawara shared a knowing grin in return. "A welcome respite after a harrowing day."

"Ugh." Ryouichi clapped Ogasawara on the shoulder. "I am sorry, my friend. I hope your mistress brings you more pleasure than your wife brings you misery."

Ogasawara only nodded. After a moment he thought to reply, "And may your Lady of the Moon be kind to you."

"Thank you. Well, this is my turn, and we part here. Good sailing!" Ryouichi laughed and went down a tree-lined avenue.

Ogasawara turned left, went one block, and then turned left again. He withdrew a mask and tied it over his face. It was the fashion to not know, or to allege one didn't know, the identity of one's lover. Then he slipped to a familiar window and hopped up.

Matsue had lost no time in transforming herself; she had layered *kimono* upon *kimono* until she dragged with draped fabric like an expensive courtesan. Her hair was pulled to one side, giving a glimpse of the nape of her neck beneath the erotically-layered garments. Ogasawara's pulse quickened.

She turned toward the window, sensing him, obscuring her powdered face with her signature fan. "Come in, my dark lover."

It was embarrassing, how much he wanted her already. He cleared the window and moved toward her on the *tatami*. "My golden darling. My love. My princess."

She laughed. "Flatterer. Come to me."

This night, they made love first, finding one another in the voluminous fabrics. Once finished, their disguises still carefully in place, Ogasawara sank into her silken lap, letting her tug back his hair which had come loose during their play. "How is it with you, *uchiwa-hime*?"

"I am glad you came to me this night. I had a most tedious evening with my husband."

He knew. "Really? What has the rascal done now?"

"Sanjou-tono is holding a banquet at the next new moon."

"I have heard something of that."

"Oh, you have? Then you must be something of the *daimyou*'s court?" Her tone was teasing, playful.

"No more than you yourself, who also know of it," he returned. "And what of this banquet?"

"The *daimyou*'s wife is having a new set of *kimono* for the event," she said, "and when I asked my husband for money for the same, he refused."

Ogasawara turned his masked face into her soft, warm hand. "Is he so cheap?"

"He can be generous, at times, but at the moment he thinks I am only selfishly seeking new clothes. He doesn't realize that this is another game of politics."

"How is that?"

"The *okugata-sama* is having new *kimono* to mark this as a great event. If I do not honor it in the same way, I denigrate their banquet and bring dishonor upon both myself and my husband."

"But the ladies will be behind screens all the evening," he protested gently. "The *daimyou* will not see their new clothing, even if he could somehow guess it was new."

She laughed. "You are as foolish as my husband. Do you

not think the *daimyou* has means to know what the ladies do behind their screens? Have you forgotten the *daimyou*'s own wife is there herself, at the least? And she is most intrigued by her guests."

She ran fingers over his forehead and back along the temples, and the last of the fight's tension fled beneath her touch. "I see. Your idiotic husband is fortunate to have such an insightful wife. It is a shame he cannot see far enough to value your observation."

"I still hope one day he might be taught."

"If anyone can manage him, it would be my *uchiwa-hime*," Ogasawara said lightly. "I wish you luck in your effort."

"I thank you for your kind wishes."

"And take this, also." He withdrew the packet from his robe. "I have heard that jealousy can sway an obstinate man. Try this trinket to catch his eye."

The comb was polished to a smooth, glassy gleam, but it was the mother-of-pearl blossoms that caught the eye and sparkled in the candlelight. She gasped and cooed over it and let him pull it through her hair.

She was still in her many-layered robes, and he breathed her intoxicating scent with every inhalation as he leaned over her exposed nape. By all the gods, she had the most entrancing neck of any woman alive. She shifted her fan and glanced up at him.

He rolled into her, tipping her backward upon the *tatami*, and pressed his face into the hollow beneath her ear, against the warm pulse of her throat. He spoke to her, telling her all the things a man could never tell the wife he fought, but which he could pour out to his understanding mistress, his beautiful mistress, his laughing, teasing, fulfilling mistress.

He stayed late, and only escaped through the window when dawn was threatening. He took a walk to give her time to bathe and dress, to order the servants to clear the room and bring breakfast. The breaking dawn was invigorating and lovely, even as he walked near the fish market. He breathed the salty, fishy air and idly wondered what sort of spirits might live beneath the bridge, feeding on offal and drunken fishermen.

When he returned to his house, all looked as usual. Matsue sat before a *zen* plated with breakfast, nodding politely as he entered. "Good morning, husband."

"Good morning." He sat beside her, and she served him. Her movements had none of the terse, barely-suppressed energy she had displayed at dinner. The new comb was beside her.

"I hope your business went well last night," she said mildly, playing the part of ignorance. "It kept you very late."

"I was investigating certain political rumors," he answered, selecting a clump of rice. "And, speaking of politics... I have been thinking, Matsue-san, that you should have new *kimono* for the banquet. You should be seen to do it proper honor."

"Thank you, husband," she answered with perfectly-feigned surprise.

"Not too costly, though," he cautioned. "I cannot afford to let you play at being the *hime* of a great house. But—"

"Not to worry, husband," she interrupted. "I know just how to go about it, so that we will look far more lavish than truth." She smiled.

Someday, they would be able to resolve their differences as man and wife rather than only as lovers. Even now, their fights were gentling, anticipating a dispassionate resolution — well, not so dispassionate, but less antagonistic. Someday.

The cicadas above sang for their mates. One crawled across Ogasawara's hand, drawing his mind to the present. He looked down at the insect, recalling delicate poems of cicadas, brief life, empty shells, new birth. He reached to cup the singing insect and gently plucked it from his arm. Matsue had often sat outside to listen to their soothing song.

Someday... and only two weeks later, Matsue was dead. He would never embrace her unmasked, never hold her again at all.

CHAPTER THREE

"AREN'T they a pretty pair!"

Seated on the wooden decking of the *sunoko*, their backs to the speaker, the twins Kaworu and Genji made no discernible response, yet Tsurugu suspected they were inwardly laughing. He shook his head and continued to pack the little coffer, nesting colored stones gently.

"Best to leave them be," advised another servant's voice. "They're in finer beds than yours."

A derisive snort. "I might have guessed."

The twins did not speak among humans, except privately with Kaede-dono. It was striking how many assumed those who did not speak also did not hear.

"The *okugata-sama* brought them with her when she came."

"And our lord does not — oh, do you suppose...?"

Tsurugu was not looking, but he had seen the knowing nod directed at the twins often enough. "Whether they be for her or for him, no one can say, but I myself can count there are two of them." They laughed together as they moved on.

Genji smothered an inappropriate snigger, and Tsurugu turned to see Kaworu's cheeks round and then smooth as he suppressed a grin. Tsurugu himself gave a quiet sniff of derision. Kaede-dono held Naka no Yoritomo entirely, requiring no assistance to attract or to pleasure him — and she would countenance none. Since her arrival, there had been no other in the *daimyou*'s bed.

Nor anyone else in hers.

Invitations — formal, veiled, and obscenely explicit — came often to the brothers, but they denied all with a mute glance of apology. And the rumors protected them, as no one dared to force the *daimyou*'s favorites.

In truth, Tsurugu knew the brothers occasionally thought of accepting. They did not relish the thought of being catamites, but some of the ladies were quite lovely, and there would likely be gifts. But Tsurugu had promised dire consequences if they did not keep to themselves, and the wrath of an *onmyouji* was not to be flaunted lightly.

He closed the coffer and straightened. "Carry this for me, as I have work outside the walls."

The twins took the baggage and followed him, servants assisting the *onmyouji*. They passed another cluster of servants talking. "Did you hear of the messenger chased all night by a *yuurei?*" asked one. The others made sounds of appropriate horror. "Seems he'd stepped on the place she died."

Tsurugu doubted that particular tale. Humans were always more inclined to see the larger entities than the smaller. But it was possible a few lesser *youkai* were moving as Midorikawa-dono approached, much as birds took flight as a wolf or boar passed, and were now squabbling with one another as they crossed territories or startling the occasional human for entertainment. There would be no serious worry until later, most likely.

The west, and the south…. The power stirring to the east was Midorikawa-dono, no doubt. But the *chokuban* had shown him danger in the west and the south, and he could not guess what that might be.

The twins waited until they were safely out of earshot before speaking. "As long as they're not thinking of *kitsune*, we could go out and play, yes? I could make an admirable *yuurei*. I might haunt the hot spring and take their clothes, making them run naked through the brambles."

"Genji-bouzu, how many tails do you have?"

"One, Ki-san."

"Would you like to live long enough to gain more?"

Kaworu stifled a chuckle. Genji shifted the box in his arms, a little sulky. "What would it hurt?"

"If no one believed there was really a *yuurei*, then it would do relatively little harm," Tsurugu allowed. "But if someone called for an exorcist, that would be a considerable inconvenience."

"And what of it?" asked Kaworu. "That's the reason we have you as an *onmyouji*."

"And you, Kaworu-bouzu, how many tails have you?"

"One, Kiyomori-san."

"And would you like to keep it?"

The twins laughed, more amused than rebuked.

Tsurugu decided on a location not far from where the stream slowed after descending the hills. "Let's settle there, and perhaps with a glimpse into the art, you will see it's a bit complex to waste in defending your pranks."

They unpacked the materials beneath a wide shade tree that would conceal their activities from the house's walls. No one would think much of Tsurugu going out to practice his arcane skills, but it would be very odd if he were seen instructing the mute twin servants.

Tsurugu set out five colored stones. "Earth, metal, fire, wood, water. Do you recall the order of the creation cycle?"

Kaworu frowned in concentration. "Water nurtures Wood, and Wood fuels Fire." He set the three stones to form a semi-circle.

"Fire yields Earth," volunteered Genji, placing another. He paused. They had done little formal instruction with Tsurugu. "That leaves Metal."

Tsurugu reached to finish the cycle and space the stones evenly. "Earth holds Metal, and Metal carries Water. There is of course more than just aligning these elements; they are merely a conduit."

"There are other cycles as well," said Genji eagerly.

"Of course, but we will start with only this one." He raised an eyebrow at the youth's unspoken protest. "Come now, did Toyotsune-san begin your training with live steel? No? Then neither shall we, metaphorically speaking. It is better to start with generating energy than exhausting or destroying it. Now, be sure you're seated properly, for balance will be as vital here as in your *taijutsu.*"

They folded themselves into proper positions and presented reasonable appearances of scholarly attention.

"*Onmyoudou* is the way of *on* and *myou*, which is in all things. Wood and fire are *myou*, and metal and water are *on*. But keep in mind, things which are *myou* have *on* in them, and things which are *on* contain *myou* as well."

Genji nodded. "Like earth."

"Ah, you do remember some things. Yes, earth is balanced."

"And," Kaworu added, "trees are *myou*, like fire, but they have more *on* than fire, because they represent growth and rebirth."

Genji elbowed his brother and fixed over-bright eyes on Tsurugu. "As you were saying, *onmyouji-sama*?"

Tsurugu inhaled, exhaled, and set his eyes on the five colored *tama*. "The creation cycle produces energy. Let's start there."

狐

By evening, Genji and Kaworu were exhausted, hardly able to keep the five elements in mind. Though they had ordered their breathing and chanted and focused, neither had managed even a thumb-sized *kekkai*, or barrier, which Tsurugu-sama had said would be the most immediately useful thing to learn. Now, getting to their feet, they found they were stiff and physically weary as well as mentally fatigued.

"Carry these materials back," instructed Tsurugu, "and then go to practice your *taijutsu*. That will help you recover more quickly than anything else, no matter how you'd rather nap."

"A drink first, I think." Kaworu stretched, easing the stiffness of long concentration, and then, wiping his damp forehead, he started for the stream.

He reached a slow-moving eddy and knelt, scooping water in his hands and bringing it to his mouth. It was cool and only faintly fishy. He dipped his hands for a second drink.

Fingers coiled about his wrists and jerked sharply. Kaworu pitched forward, barely catching breath before he went underwater. He twisted his legs beneath him and kicked, but the grip on his arms was immovable and it drew him down, down—

Someone else grasped his hair, then his shoulder, and then the grip shifted beneath his arm and pulled upward. Kaworu kicked out and connected with something hard and slick, unyielding. He writhed and saw for the first time a shape before him. More hands clutched him. With a rush of panic he twisted again, desperate to reach the surface.

And then they were moving up, and Kaworu's head broke the surface. He threw back his face and gasped deep, sucking precious air before he could be drawn down again. But the hands beneath his arms held firm and pulled him against the bank.

He blinked water from his eyes and looked at the *kappa* still holding his wrists. It was smaller than his human shape, the size of a child. Its beak was only a hand's breadth from his face. Kaworu pressed backward against the bank, digging for purchase with his heels, and Tsurugu leaned over his shoulder to face the *kappa*.

The *kappa* turned from Kaworu to Tsurugu. "This one came to me."

Kaworu tried to turn his arms to break the hold on his wrists, as he'd been taught, but the *kappa's* solid grip pinned his wrists together. Genji's hands shifted about his torso to grasp Kaworu more securely, bracing him against the bank.

"This one is not yours," Tsurugu answered. "Return him to me, if you please."

The *kappa* clacked its beak angrily. "I am hungry, and I have caught him in my own domain."

Kaworu kicked again, but again he struck the *kappa's* turtle-like shell and the creature hardly seemed to note the blow.

Tsurugu shifted forward and began to chant. The *kappa* looked wary, and then it jumped as the water began to move out of the current's natural flow. The *kappa* hissed and glared at Tsurugu. "You wish to match strength?"

"No, *kappa-sama*," replied Tsurugu. "I wish to have this boy returned. But I would not deprive you; we will bring in return two cucumbers to make your meal."

The *kappa* blinked and brightened. "You will barter for him?"

"He is worth it to me, yes."

"Three cucumbers."

"Three cucumbers, then."

The *kappa* nodded. "Your bargain is acceptable, *onmyouji-sama.*"

His hands still on Kaworu's shoulders, Tsurugu bowed low. "Thank you for your kind understanding."

The *kappa* bowed in the water, showing the lilypad depression at the top of his head. "Thank you for your kind generosity."

The pressure on Kaworu's wrists ceased, and he scrambled backward against the bank. Genji pulled hard and he fell back on the grass, winded and shaken.

"I shall expect the cucumbers this evening," said the *kappa*, and then it sank into the water, its blue-green hide vanishing instantly into the mud and plants and current.

For a moment, Kaworu couldn't speak. They had not known of a *kappa*, and he had nearly died. It was Genji who said, "I don't know that the cook will give us cucumbers tonight."

"You'd better thieve them, then," Tsurugu said, "loath as I am to encourage your mischief. But you daren't break faith with the *kappa*. Their memories are long, and you cannot avoid water forever."

Kaworu imagined that sharp beak tearing flesh from his drowning body.

"And bear in mind," Tsurugu continued, "that tonight's offering is only for this day. Be cautious when you approach the river next time."

"*Hai*, Tsurugu-sama. I will bring the cucumbers."

"Couldn't you have stopped him?" demanded Genji.

Tsurugu shook his head. "I would not have let him have Kaworu — but Kaworu cannot always be sure of my help. And in fairness, the *kappa* caught his prey, just as you would take a rabbit, and a bargain is a better end if we do not wish to make enemies. And for all their hunger, *kappa* are skilled bonesetters; what if you should need his help one day? Bring him the cucumbers and be careful."

狐

Kaworu crept to the river, listening tautly to every breeze's sigh and flexing reed. *Kappa* came onto land as well as their preferred water, and the mark of the webbed grip was still clear upon his wrists.

Despite his best efforts, he had found only two cucumbers remaining in the household's stores. He had searched longer than was wise, and had hidden beneath a table once when someone came to investigate the faint noises he'd made, but in the end he had found only two. He dared not fail to bring his offering, but he feared meeting the *kappa* and having to explain the shortage.

He had not been able to ask Tsurugu-sama for help. The *onmyouji* had gone out alone to ward away an approaching *bakemono*. Genji had been conscripted for additional chores when a few *samurai* unexpectedly visited Naka-dono, and Kaworu would have been required as well had he not ducked out of sight and fled to the storerooms. He was on his own to face the *kappa*.

He was nearly at the river's edge now. He stopped, his heart racing. He did not want to go nearer the water. Cucumbers were the one food *kappa* enjoyed above all others, but mightn't individual *kappa* have individual tastes? This one could prefer flesh to fruit. More, he might decide to take both, garnishing Kaworu with cucumber.

"Kappa-sama?" he called into the dark. There was no sound but the soft current, no matter how he strained to hear the splash of someone leaving the water. Still, a water creature might slide from the river without betraying himself. *"Kappa-sama*, I am leaving your cucumbers here." He set the fruit at his feet. "There are only two, *kappa-sama*, but I will look for another…." He heard nothing. "I bid you good evening."

There was no one watching, and so he felt only a bit ashamed that he returned to the *daimyou's* house at a steady trot.

CHAPTER FOUR

GENNOSUKE ran. His feet skimmed the ground, weaving through children and carts and baskets and village detritus, and he raced through the village with the wind roaring in his ears as if to obliterate the words that still echoed there.

Has sent no word. Has answered nothing. Has not been seen by Naka no Yoritomo-dono. Presumed dead.

Gennosuke leapt from a ridge and slid down an uneven slope, crouching to keep his balance and then flailing as he lost it. He tumbled, somersaulting once, and came to a rough halt. He lay still, winded and hurt, and wished it had been more. He could still hear, still feel.

Presumed dead.

The Kagemura did not give up their people lightly. If they had lost hope for Shishio Hitoshi, it was probable that even without a body to confirm it, he was indeed dead.

Oji-san....

Harume-sama had broken the news as gently as possible, showing a kindness to the boy who was a son in all but fact, but there was no easy way to hear such a thing. And now, far from the village and shielded by the slope, Gennosuke wept.

And he made a pact, if only with himself. Shishio had been serving in the *daimyou's* own house. Somewhere in the *daimyou's* household, someone knew what had become of the shadow-warrior Shishio Hitoshi, how his life had ended. Gennosuke would find that person and know it as well.

狐

Ogasawara bowed. "Cousin, I have come to ask your help."

Chikahiro-sama returned a smug little smile that made Ogasawara's neck burn hot. "I supposed as much. We have had news."

Ogasawara nodded. "Then you know what happened — you know I am not at fault and am in dire need. The *daimyou* has promised my death."

Chikahiro scratched his chin reflectively. "I don't see that any particular action on my part is necessary."

Ogasawara stared. "But surely the family — you will not allow one of our own to be slaughtered!"

Chikahiro beckoned a serving boy, who approached with a tray of fruits. "As I hear it, your life is forfeit only if you are still within the *daimyou's* lands. I need lift no finger to save you when you may save yourself. And if a cousin, a twig from an off branch, is too stupid to save himself—" he selected a peach — "well, that is a shame, but not my shame. Off branches may be pruned."

Ogasawara clenched his fists. "I can still be of use to you, Chikahiro-sama. I am a good *onmyouji*, you know that, and—"

The peach in Chikahiro's hand squelched out a little spray of juice. "Is this how you think to win my aid? By reminding me you won the position of *onmyouji* to the *daimyou?*"

"I — everyone knows that as scion of the main branch, you were required to stay in the main house...." Ogasawara's voice trailed off, knowing it was a futile protest. The Ogasawara were *onmyouji* as other families were warriors or doctors or farmers or *daimyou*. When Chikahiro's grandfather had chosen Ogasawara over his cousin to enter the *daimyou*'s household, all had known the true reason was not that Chikahiro had to remain for his role as future head.

Ogasawara swallowed the last of his battered pride and pressed himself flat to the floor. "Cousin, look, I am begging you. Hide me, or give me money that I may save myself. I left with nothing. I am at your mercy. I will do what you ask, only help me."

Chikahiro wiped peach pulp down the serving boy's *happi* and turned hard eyes on Ogasawara. "Get out. Get out and die for the *daimyou* or live in exile, I don't care, as long as we never see you again."

Ogasawara's stomach spasmed. "Chikahiro-sama—"

Chikahiro threw a small bag which skittered across the polished floor past Ogasawara. "There — money for your travel. All will hear I have done right by you. Now go."

Ogasawara's body clenched in rage. With few weapons left and nothing to lose, he met Chikahiro's eyes and snarled, "You were always jealous of me, weren't you?"

Chikahiro laughed, showing bits of peach on his teeth. "Jealous of your skill, perhaps — but jealous of you, cousin? Never."

Ogasawara snatched the little bag and fled, ducking his head not in respect but to hide the treacherous tears burning his eyes. Fury shook him as he stomped out the *sunoko* and down the steps, shoving past a few servants who stared in recognition and curiosity. Hideo was waiting beside his tiny pack. "We're going!" snapped Ogasawara, and he turned toward the east gate.

The little bag was strangely light. He waited until they were well into the street, away from Chikahiro's borrowed eyes, before he opened it and shook out a single copper piece.

Chikahiro could not have bagged the coin during their brief conversation. He had planned this devastating and fatal insult from the moment he was told of Ogasawara's arrival.

Ogasawara shoved the coin into his sleeve and pushed through the street, clenching his fists and grinding his teeth. Rage would suppress the desperation threatening to overtake him.

They would regret this, Sanjou no Takeo and Chikahiro both. His *daimyou* and his cousin. He would survive this, and he would return and destroy them.

No, he would do better — first, he would destroy the man they both feared. He would break Naka no Yoritomo-dono, and thus at once he would avenge dear Matsue and demonstrate to Sanjou and Chikahiro his power. They did not fear him now, they would.

He would kill Naka no Yoritomo's wife as Naka had tried to kill Sanjou's, and then he would kill the *daimyou* himself. It would not be impossible for a lone, unsuspected *onmyouji*; Naka no Yoritomo considered himself unreachable. But Ogasawara would overturn them all.

五

CHAPTER FIVE

IT was not normally Kaworu's duty to carry tea to Tsurugu, but this evening it fell to him. As he entered and knelt to arrange the serving items, the *onmyouji* did not so much as look up from his *chokuban*. Kaworu listened for a moment, but no one outside was near enough to hear him. "Is something wrong, Tsurugu-sama?"

Tsurugu nodded, still frowning at the divining board. "Yes. Yes, I'm afraid so."

Kaworu lifted the teapot. "Would it help if I brought *sake* instead?"

That brought a faint smile, and Tsurugu at last lifted his head. "Thank you, no."

"Is it something to do with...."

"With Midorikawa-dono's coming? I'm not certain, but I don't think so." He nodded toward the board. "Midorikawa-dono will be coming from the east, and by what I see, we will face trouble from the west." He reached for the teacup. "And the south."

"Both?"

"That is what I do not understand. The primary danger is from the west, but there is something more in the south. A smaller matter, but there."

A chill ran through Kaworu. "What will you do?"

"I will watch, of course. And I will meet it." He gestured at the board. "And this matter of the south is not so threatening, merely an inauspicious direction. I will search it out and deal with it. We cannot face two directions at once." He smiled, as if that resolved the matter.

Kaworu tipped his head and frowned. "Wouldn't it be more apt to avoid the south, if it is an inauspicious direction?"

"Under usual circumstances, yes, of course. But with Midorikawa-dono coming and this mystery in the west, I do not wish to be distracted by anything unknown."

"Can we help?"

Tsurugu laughed, but not unkindly. "A few hours of study does not make one an *onmyouji*, Kaworu-bouzu, and I will not risk you in this. When an enemy must be fought, or danced away, I will send you."

Kaworu's ears would have flattened, had they not been the silly mute human shape. "Kaede-dono likes our dancing."

"And rightly so, and I am sorry if I seemed to take it lightly. Consider it thus: if I played at dancing as you do, I would be a fool ten times over."

Kaworu grinned.

"And if you played at *onmyoudou* against an opponent, you would not be a fool, but dead."

Kaworu sobered. "I understand."

Tsurugu held out his cup for Kaworu to refill. "I will go tomorrow and see what lies to the south. It is not worth the risk to Kaede-dono to leave it unexplored."

Tsurugu remained in his human form as he traveled south. He was the only one on the road, no one would have seen his transformation, and his fox form could have moved more rapidly over the terrain, but he carried too many items to want to bother with his fox form. His fox magic was inherent and effective, but it had particular strengths. *Onmyoudou* had other strengths, but for all that it was a path of nature magic, it was a human construct and required human paraphernalia.

As he trotted south, his thoughts went to the west. The divination had been quite clear; there was danger in the west, and it was coming toward them.

The trouble was, it was difficult to know what danger that might be, or even *whose* danger it might be. Tsurugu had the unwieldy task of reading for Kaede-dono first of all, and Naka no Yoritomo, and all the little band that was his ersatz family, Hanae and Genji and Kaworu. Further, it was difficult to guess whether this danger would come into the *daimyou*'s household to assassinate him, or whether it would remain in the village, harmless unless Genji should sneak out to terrorize a superstitious peasant. At times, a little knowledge was downright inconvenient.

And this was why Tsurugu jogged south, though the divination had advised this was an inauspicious direction. As this danger seemed the lesser, he would meet it, identify or dispose of it, and leave himself to think only of the greater westerly threat.

It was difficult to say whether his fox instincts or *onmyouji* sensitivity noticed first, but he came to a halt and looked around, sniffing the air without thinking. There was a darkness here, an unseen aura that bespoke an unseemly presence.

The breeze came across the rice field, bearing a scent of — not decay, exactly, but illness. Wrongness. Tsurugu froze;

stillness could be an asset.

As he waited, watching, a motion caught his eye, and he was able to detect in the reeds a pestle-shaped creature like a fat serpent. Tsurugu would have nodded to himself if he had dared to move — a *nozuchi.*

Nozuchi were predatory *youkai,* more dangerous to rodents and humans than to a fox with any sense. Tsurugu had only to walk away and he would be safe. Even if the *nozuchi* saw him, they were notoriously slow. He could easily avoid it entirely.

But the thing was in a rice field, and that meant it would likely devour a child, or cripple or kill a farmer. The things had wicked bites which took fever easily.

Tsurugu took out an *ofuda,* a rectangular paper painted with a spell, and began to prepare his mind. It would not do to send it to eat the children at the next field; he would need to banish the *nozuchi* from the region.

The pestle-snake writhed, turning, and began to wriggle toward him. It moved more like an inchworm than a serpent, heaving its ungainly body upward and dragging itself forward. Tsurugu shook his head. "This is to no good end, *nozuchi-san.*"

A dog came out of the bushes, wagging high with its nose hard on a trail of some sort, and then went rigid as it jerked its head toward Tsurugu. Tsurugu felt a growl stir deep within him, unfamiliar in his human shape. The dog began barking, its body jerking with each sound, feet skidding on the ground with the force of its barks. Tsurugu's lip curled in simultaneous dislike and disgust.

The *nozuchi* had not moved since the dog had appeared, and after a moment the dog seemed to gain confidence facing the fox. Its eyes fixed on Tsurugu, it started toward him, darting forward and back, fear disguising itself in aggression, slowly making progress. Tsurugu wished for a staff or other weapon to drive it off; he did not want to be reduced to changing forms and running before the *nozuchi* he meant to exorcise.

The dog, barking jerkily at Tsurugu, its shrill voice echoing off the hills, came level with the *nozuchi*. And the wide snake-like body opened and yawned, displaying a mouth too impossibly large for its shape, and the dog had only the barest instant to yelp in terror as it was drawn into the cavernous mouth. The quiet was sudden and disturbing, after the barking, and Tsurugu thought he could hear bones crunch as the *nozuchi* swallowed.

Tsurugu was mildly relieved by the dog's disappearance and discomfited that he was now under a sort of obligation to the *nozuchi*. He made a tiny bow in its direction. "Many thanks, but I still have business with you."

The *nozuchi* pulled itself upright, as if to inchworm forward again, but this time it seemed to draw together and then unfold. A man stood in its place, its face nearly featureless in an expanse of sagging skin, clad in the rotting robes of a monk. When he spoke, his voice was rusted and rotting as well. "What business could you have with me?"

The fine hairs at the back of Tsurugu's human neck prickled, as if he were trying to raise hackles he didn't have. "What did you do, that you were cast out? What did you do, that you became this?"

The thing that was no longer a monk grinned, too wide and too toothy. "I do not recall what I did first. But what I did last was devour them."

Tsurugu's hackles tried to rise higher, prickling all down his spine. This was no common *nozuchi* — this would be more difficult. And now he knew, more urgent; such a creature could not be allowed to remain near the *daimyou's* household. "You chose poorly in coming here, *nozuchi-san*."

The spiked grin parted and grew wider. "Not so poorly as you, *onmyouji-san.*"

CHAPTER SIX

GENJI and Kaworu were summoned in the morning,
after they had run their usual chores. Kaede-dono was outwardly
composed as ever, but there was a vein of tension within her
musical voice. "Tsurugu-sama did not return last night."

"From the matter in the south?" Kaworu asked.

Kaede-dono nodded. "I want you to go out and look for
him. Find him and see what assistance he might need, if any."

Genji looked thoughtful. "But if he wanted us, he could
have sent a — one of his — a messenger."

"A *shikigami*?" Kaede smiled in catlike amusement. "Say
it."

Genji screwed up his face in concentration. *"Shhhh...
Shuki... shah.... Siki. Sukikigami."* He grinned.

Kaede-dono laughed; a *kitsune* could not form the
syllable *shi.* "You never fail to entertain with your efforts. But
no, I have received no *shikigami.* That may mean he has been
too occupied, or the *shikigami* did not reach us safely, or he did
not think to send for help, or even that he is unable to send. But

whatever has delayed him, I charge you to find and assist him. Return before he is missed by too many."

The brothers nodded agreeably. There were worse chores than leaving the estate and wandering the countryside. And if they found Tsurugu-sama in good time, they might take a more leisurely return, perhaps stopping by the hot spring low on the mountain. No one else would be losing morning hours to the spring, and they might have it to themselves.

A tree grew very near the east wall, and an enterprising and athletic youth might leap from one to the other. Genji and Kaworu heard the servant Jirou calling them for more tasks, but they slipped through the *wataridono* unseen and bolted for the wall.

狐

They paused above the rice fields, looking over the green fields and the village. Genji wrinkled his nose. "Something has been here."

"A *bakeneko*. Or a *nozuchi*." Kaworu sniffed. "I think, anyway."

"Whatever it was, it was strong."

They reached the crest of the hill and looked down at the torn ground before them. A half-splintered tree leaned to one side, its leaves still fresh, and there were several long rips in the grass and rice.

Genji turned to scan the trees before speaking again. "Do you think — you know...."

"He's fine. Of course he's fine. It's just, it was powerful, and he wanted to rest before returning."

Genji nodded. "You're right. He's a strong *onmyouji*, for all his jokes."

Tsurugu no Kiyomori had told them of Abe no Seimei, the legendary *onmyouji* who, it was said, had his mother's *kitsune* blood to thank for his unusual ability. Tsurugu chuckled over the fact that his mother also was a *kitsune*, but lacking a complementary human parent, he had to work harder to master *onmyoudou*. Despite his jests, he was a competent practitioner.

Even with both *onmyoudou* and native fox magic, however, the creature, whatever it was, would have been a formidable opponent. Kaworu wondered if the faint dark haze were his imagination, influenced by Tsurugu's occasional explanations, or a true lingering miasma. They descended, looking about at the abandoned battlefield, and began climbing the next hill.

"What's that?" Genji pointed to a bit of paper, fluttering in a standing tree. The branches about it were broken and twisted. He trotted to the tree and tore the paper free.

It was an *ofuda*. Kaworu could not read the spell, unfamiliar and obscured with smeared blood.

The twins looked at one another.

"We should separate," Genji suggested, "to cover more ground." He glanced uphill. "I'll go that way. But — we should keep talking. So we can hear one another."

The shifting breeze interrupted him as a new scent was carried down the hill. Kaworu's stomach wrenched and he looked at his brother. Genji was already glancing at him for confirmation. They started together, sprinting uphill.

There was a clearing at the top of the ridge, the grass short over the rocky surface. A dark stain discolored the earth and rocks, far too wide, and in its center lay a crumpled heap of soaked fur.

The brothers hesitated only a second before easing toward the fallen fox. "Is he...?" At death, all *kitsune* reverted to a mundane fox shape, regardless of what they had been.

"He's alive!" Genji's voice carried a grateful relief that

would have embarrassed him, had he heard it. "He must have changed because of the injury, maybe because he lost too much blood. There is... an awful lot of blood." He looked at Kaworu. "I'm not sure how to move him."

"We have to carry him back. He needs help, more than we can give." Kaworu swallowed. It felt difficult to breathe.

"We'll never get him inside," Genji protested. "We can't carry a fox into the *daimyou's* house! If he's seen, it will draw suspicion on us all."

"We can't leave him, and there's no one but Kaede-dono to treat him."

Genji paused, and then he began to strip his outer clothing. "Can you manage him?"

"With your *kosode*," Kaworu said, guessing at his brother's plan. "He's small enough like this. I can hide him, if I can blot the blood." He took the jacket. "You'll be all right?"

Genji grinned. "Don't worry about me."

They wrapped the wounded fox gently in the *kosode*, trying not to break open the partially clotted wounds, and Kaworu cradled the silent figure against his torso, mostly hidden within his blousing clothing. Why was Tsurugu so still? Shouldn't he wake, with all their handling? The thought frightened him.

They started toward the *daimyou's* house, moving at a gentle pace for fear of harming Tsurugu. It would have been easier to carry him in Kaworu's arms, but even here on the road there was a risk of being seen.

Finally they were outside the *daimyou's* gate. "You have him secure?" Genji confirmed.

Kaworu nodded. "Be careful, *ani-ue*."

"Not to worry, *ani-ue*." Genji grinned and started through the gate at a run. He ducked his head and rammed his shoulder against a worker as he passed. Two men turned to shout after him. There was a crash as Genji disappeared inside the wall, and more voices were raised in protest.

All eyes were on Genji's wake. Kaworu pressed his arm close to support the motionless fox form and slipped discreetly inside the gate.

He clung to lesser paths. Servants were not normally challenged, but he would not risk anyone noting his hidden contraband. At last he was inside the *shinden*, and he moved directly to Kaede-dono's quarters.

Hanae-san's eyes widened upon seeing Kaworu alone. But Kaworu could hear other ladies further within, and Hanae-san could not ask the urgent questions. Instead, she gestured to one side. "I shall tell the *okugata-sama* you have come as ordered," she said more clearly than necessary. "Wait there."

Kaworu bowed his head and fretted at the delay. He sat low and hoped for the usual invisibility of a waiting servant. Inside, he heard Kaede's voice rising and falling as she spoke amiably to the other women. Finally she made an excuse and Kaworu felt a quick rush of gratitude. Tsurugu had not stirred within his *kosode*.

"Come quickly!" snapped Hanae, safely out of the ladies' hearing. Kaworu rose, one hand cradling the fox against his body, and moved as smoothly as possible into the room indicated. Hanae closed the *fusuma* and turned back. "Did you find him?"

Kaede-dono herself entered from the other side of the room with unladylike haste. "What did you find?"

For answer, Kaworu eased the limp bundle from his clothing. Fresh blood marred Genji's *kosode*, but the fox was still warm and breathed faintly. Hanae uttered a little shriek.

"Silence!" snapped Kaede. "Bring water and medicine. How badly wounded is he?" She knelt beside the fox and began to tease back the fabric, cautious of opening the injury.

"We found him thus, Kaede-dono."

Kaede nodded without looking at him, concentrating on the injured fox. "You did well to bring him this far. I trust no one saw him?"

"No. *Ani-ue* provided distraction as I carried him."

"Good. Go now, and fetch your brother before he draws too much upon himself." She looked up as Hanae carried in a medicine box. "We will see to Tsurugu-sama."

CHAPTER SEVEN

TSURUGU lay shivering on his mat, insensible. The
bleeding had slowed again to seeping, a relief after the cleaning,
and his other minor injuries had been treated. But the
incoherent shaking remained, and it worried Kaede more than
she dared admit. Her medical knowledge was competent, but if
the injury were spiritual as well as physical, she could do
nothing. And wasn't that perhaps possible in *onmyoudou*?

She had grown to rely on Tsurugu, and she liked him
well. And how would she explain to Midorikawa-dono that she
had lost his *onmyouji*?

Hanae watched the shaking fox, open worry plain in her
expression. "Is he cold?"

Kaede shook her head slowly. "I don't know; this is
beyond me. But he has lost much blood, and he might well be
cold with the loss." She glanced at the servant. "Warm him. It
cannot hurt and may help."

Hanae nodded anxiously and slipped from her *kimono*.
Naked, she slid beneath the blankets and clothing and wrapped

herself gently about the wounded fox, cradling him to her. Though she was a fox as well, it was hardly a romantic encounter; Tsurugu was insensible, badly wounded, and dangerously near to dying in Hanae's arms.

Kaede closed her eyes. Midorikawa-dono would arrive soon, and *mononoke* and *youkai* were already stirring. They would grow only more obvious in the next days, and demands would be made to send the *onmyouji* to calm the area. He would be missed soon.

狐

Kaworu normally disliked the crowded servants' area, but tonight he was anxious for something to keep his thoughts from Tsurugu's cool, damp body. Genji was scrubbing vegetables, ears sore with the cuffs he'd taken when he was caught. Kaworu would sneak him his meal as soon as Jirou forgot to keep a watch.

No one knew of the *onmyouji*'s injury, but still the talk was of the *youkai* dangers without. "It's the *kitsune* again," one man insisted. "It's back — if ever it left."

"Food is missing or sullied, equipment is broken — there's more mischief than we can lay at the feet of one *kitsune*," protested another. "There must be a group of them here."

Kaworu's throat tightened, and he could not swallow his rice. None of them had done harm. Even his and Genji's occasional pranks had been harmless, and nothing directly attributable to *youkai* influence. *Kitsune* were mischievous by nature, of course, but they had tempered their tricks here. Even now, Tsurugu lay near death for protecting this house and its people. They had only served Kaede-dono and, by extension, the *daimyou*'s household.

But the servants blamed *kitsune*, and if anyone began

looking for a group of *kitsune*, instead of one, half their camouflage would be lost.

"Natsume-kun saw terrible figures on the road. He thinks there are *bakemono* and *mononoke* about."

"But he was unharmed. Would a *mononoke* have left him whole? It was an illusion, a *kitsune* illusion, so they might wreak the more havoc."

"What if someone in the village is a *kitsune-mochi*?" asked a woman. Kaworu's stomach clenched. "A fox-keeper might have many foxes to make trouble. Wasn't there a girl there, not long ago, who had doings with *kitsune*?"

"She ran away," another woman dismissed.

"She was mad, possessed," contributed a man from the corner. "She said the traveling priest had tied and taken her, but he explained it was *kitsune-tsuki*. They tried everything to drive the fox out of her."

"Why not ask her yourselves?" A man laughed coarsely as he snatched a girl's wrist. She pulled and twisted, but he was stronger. "Here she is."

Kaworu stared with the others as the man pushed up her sleeve, revealing scattered scars. "Look where they burned her to drive out the fox! More than once, they had to try, and who's to say she doesn't still have it?"

"Let me go," pleaded the girl, tugging at her arm and twisting. "Please, let me go!"

The girl had never had a fox spirit in her, Kaworu was certain of that. There had been no *kitsune* but themselves since Kaede-dono had come to the *daimyou*. But he could not intervene, even if there were a way to somehow convince the suspicious servants.

"What is it? Why do the *kitsune* always return where you are? Are you not *kitsune-tsuki*, but *kitsune-mochi*?" A woman twisted a handful of the girl's hair, making her cry. "Are you trying to ruin us all?"

The girl was neither fox-possessed nor a fox-user, but Kaworu could do nothing. Within the *daimyou*'s house, he was only a pretty mute belonging to the lord's wife. He and Genji had a certain power within the house, but none he could use here.

He stood and carried his bowl outside, fleeing the shouting and the hall.

CHAPTER EIGHT

GENJI stirred and stretched, nudging Kaworu. They found it difficult to sleep in the usual human posture — on the back, helpless to either spring to one's feet or to warm cold extremities — and often found themselves bumping one another through the night. They were littermates, and they did not mind so much as humans might.

Kaworu grumbled good-naturedly at his brother, pushing him away before stretching his own limbs. Humans never stretched enough; that was perhaps part of the reason they could be so clumsy.

Genji dressed and then, with a glance at Kaworu, slipped out the door. As long as one of them was in the servants' area, they would not be missed. Genji would go to Kaede-dono's room and learn of Tsurugu's condition, whether he had improved or — but he had made it through the night. Of course he had lasted the night.

Kaworu shook himself and dressed, then rolled the *futons* and tucked them neatly away. He wanted an early start.

Along with their chores today, they might have additional tasks to help Kaede-dono care for Tsurugu, seeking medicinal herbs or petitioning at the shrine of Inari.

He had nearly finished wiping the wooden planks of the *sunoko* when Genji returned. Kaworu looked at his anxious face and wanted to ask, but chubby Jirou was scowling at him, so he remained quiet. Genji gave him a glance as he passed and went inside, and after a moment Kaworu set down his rag and made to follow.

"Oh, no, you don't!" Jirou started across the little yard, pleased in finding a justified outlet for his anger. "These boards are still dusty, and there are footprints behind you." He leaned close, over-enunciating too loudly to the youth who did not speak. "Clean it!"

Kaworu made an appeasing gesture and bobbed deferentially. Jirou was still angry about Genji's tear through the estate the day before, and he couldn't tell the brothers apart. He would shout willingly at either of them. Kaworu worked on the boards until Jirou looked elsewhere, and then he slipped inside.

Genji was waiting for him. He answered the most critical question first. "He's alive. He's ill, but he's alive."

Kaworu nodded. "Does he need anything?"

"Kaede-dono wants something to fight blood poison. We should slip out to search." He wrinkled his nose. "And review our *kata*. They will arrive soon."

The words hung in the air a moment, as weighty as those defining Tsurugu's condition. Then Genji shrugged, shedding the weight as easily as dropping a robe. "Well, time enough this afternoon."

It was mid-afternoon before they slipped over a wall and escaped into the distant trees. The twins might risk wrestling and games by night in the *daimyou*'s garden, but serious practice required greater secrecy.

After a couple of hours, sweaty and tired, they separated and started into the forest. Kaworu slipped into his fox shape, trotting through the hill's brush and listening to the world around him. As much as he loved aspects of the human world, it was impossible to forget this was his native place, his own world.

He lifted his head, sniffing. There was little danger here; no *bakemono* or more natural predator awaited. He trotted on, questing for medicinal herbs.

He had not gone far when he came across another scent — human, female, and excited or frightened. He concentrated for a moment. It was occasionally difficult to correlate those he encountered as a human with those he encountered as a fox, when his senses were wholly different. This scent was vaguely familiar, someone he had likely met in the *daimyou's* household. It should have been uninteresting, but for the remoteness and the fear-scent. It was well away from the path to the hot spring for soaking, and no one going to an appointed tryst would be so afraid.

He trotted after the scent. It was strong, as were all fear-trails, and easy to follow. He stopped occasionally to check for herbs in likely places, and once he dug a clump from the earth, but he let himself be loosely guided by the scent trail. He had to choose some route, after all, and he was curious.

He came upon the dilapidated hut beside a trickle of snowmelt, thin now in the advancing season. The human had taken refuge inside. Kaworu crept through the late growth and approached the rotting hut, listening. At last he reached one of the many gaps in the walls and peered inside.

It was the girl from the servants' dinner, the one accused of *kitsune-tsuki* or *kitsune-mochi.* She was bruised, and her clothing was dirty as if she'd been on the ground. She was holding her knees to her chest and rocking.

Kaworu watched her a moment, and then he quietly withdrew, taking up the herbs he'd found. He trotted away, following the snowmelt until it joined the stream below.

Genji was sunning himself, stretched on his side. He rolled to his feet as Kaworu approached, kicking a bundle of herbs. "There you are! I've been waiting."

"I've found these, at least." Kaworu dropped his own herbs. "Go on without me. I want to look after something."

"Another *youkai?*"

"Something else. I'll explain later. But take these to Hanae-san."

"Right. Be careful!"

Genji set off for the house at a lope. Kaworu turned away and, careful to skirt the stream, started for the village.

CHAPTER NINE

MURAME held herself and rocked for a long time. She
had returned to the *onmyouji's* empty hut because there was no
place else to go — the village had turned against her that spring,
and the *daimyou's* house was supposed to be her refuge. Now
that the rumors had followed her there, she was without options.

But the hut had fallen into deep disrepair, even more
than the disadvantages she had remembered. It looked as if it
had been abandoned for years, not months. She suspected now
she had seen magic when she came before. She clutched her
knees and rocked. Even magic could not help her now. And the
onmyouji would not come again.

She was cold, and hungry despite her distress, and she
knew she should seek firewood and food. There might be
berries ripening in the autumn woods, or nuts. But the tasks
seemed too large and too difficult, and she could not bring
herself to rise.

Something moved in the hut's fallen doorway, and she
glanced up with a start, half-expecting to see someone from the

house come after her. But something else was there, and she stared in disbelief.

The fox took another step, edging into the room, and laid down the dead fowl it carried. It looked at her with an unnaturally steady gaze.

She stared at the animal, her heart pounding in her chest. *"Kitsune?"* she whispered.

The fox was a pale color, almost amber. Its ears tipped back as she spoke.

She swallowed. "I have been driven out because of you, foul *kitsune*. I have lost everything."

The pale fox dropped its head and nudged the dead fowl.

"And now you have killed a bird from the village." Realization dawned on her. "You have brought it to me? You have done what they blamed me for, and brought it to me?"

The fox's ears flattened. It did not move.

"They said I was responsible for everything — and if I eat that chicken, I will be what they have said!"

The fox glanced at the chicken, and then it nudged it again, shoving the bird a bit closer.

Murame rubbed a hand across her aching eyes. "But, if I am to be blamed anyway, why not reap the little good? If a dozen lost chickens are put to my name, I surely may take one." She rubbed her face again. "And I never would have had this chicken if they had not done such things to drive me out."

She half-rose and then hesitated, looking at the fox. It shifted, moving away a few steps to sit on the very edge of the rotting floor. She stood and, stiff with bruising and emotion and nerves, jerkily crossed the small room to collect the dead bird. She kept her eyes on the fox, feeling for the chicken, and then retreated. The fox in the doorway licked its lips once and glanced away.

Murame began to pluck the chicken, her eyes still on the fox. The feathers hardly seemed to add to the litter of the hut. "You're not much of a *kitsune*, are you?" she said after a moment. "You have only one tail."

The fox's ears rotated backward in an expression that must have been embarrassed annoyance. This struck her as funny and she laughed, surprising herself.

The fox wrapped its single tail about its feet and licked a couple of times at its shoulder. Murame laughed again, relaxing marginally. "Fine, fine. Now if only you could carry wood as well."

She scanned the room for cooking implements — she had used some while here before, but how many had been real? She had known much of the *onmyouji's* help had been magical, but she had not realized how much.

She didn't notice when the fox disappeared, sliding silently away as she unearthed utensils and brushed out leaf litter and droppings. She felt a small pang of — something, upon noticing he had gone. Aside from the *onmyouji*, the *kitsune* was the first to offer help in her accusations. Shameful, when the very creature responsible for her misery was her only comfort.

She was cutting and tearing the bird into a freshly-rinsed pan when she heard a short, falling cry from outside. It was repeated twice more — a high-pitched sound, like the scream of a ghost. Murame froze, remembering the report of an angry *yuurei*. Twilight had come while she worked, and she could not guess what waited in the woods.

The cry came again, and it was near, just behind the hut. Murame leaned to one side and carefully peered through the insubstantial wall.

The fox sat atop a small pile of branches and deadfall. As she watched, it called once more, looking at the hut.

She rose and went out, circling to the rear. "You — brought wood," she said, startled and embarrassed and grateful together.

The fox gave a couple of hoarse barks and bounded off the wood. Murame bent to collect some — how had the slight fox brought two great armloads of wood? — and started back to the hut.

The fox was sitting in the door again, but she stepped past it and set the wood beside the central pit. She started a fire — at least that was simple, with so much leaf litter and such — and then turned back to the fox. She hesitated, and then she gestured to the entrails and refuse. "Would you like these?"

The fox's ears pricked forward, and then its tail twitched and it looked away. Murame didn't understand the reason, but the meaning was clear enough. "Not good enough for you, then? Or aren't you staying for supper?"

The fox stood and then, unexpectedly, dropped its forequarters and head as if making an attempt at a bow. Then it turned and loped into the twilight.

狐

Kaede dined with her husband that night.

"You look tired," she said with concern. "What has taxed you this day? Did the *samurai* bring some trouble with them?" The question was an honest one, but also served a purpose; it was difficult to speak lightly with him while her mind whirled with Tsurugu's tenuous condition and the impending arrival of Midorikawa-dono. She needed him to speak for a while until she could fabricate a calm, untroubled demeanor.

Naka exhaled slowly. "Not directly, but yes. Ayumu-dono walks a knife's edge, neatly parting his allegiance between Sanjou no Takeo and myself. He may cut himself one day, but for now…. Some of the others are looking to him, and I know

what they are thinking. But he has done nothing overt, and —
no, my love, I'm sorry. You need not be troubled with such
heady matters." He smiled at her. "I'd rather forget such things
for now and think only of you."

She smiled, flattered and irritated.

He took a piece of *daikon* and chewed. "Tell me a
poem?"

Kaede clenched her fist, hidden within her voluminous
sleeve. "One moment…." She scraped her brain for a theme, a
metaphor. Poems were the trade of conversation, the ever-new
display of wit and skill, and a poor poem would be like serving
spoiled fruit.

> "A singing stream trails
> Beneath my wide-arching bridge.
> I stand like a rock
> Unmoved over tumbling froth
> My eyes fixed…."

She faltered, realizing the last line would carry an extra
syllable. *Careless.* And the whole had been sloppy and too plain.

Yoritomo-dono touched the furrows forming between
her eyebrows. "That's unlike you. Are you well, my love?"

She hated deceiving him, hated not being able to discuss
it all with him — but she would never risk losing him, and that
meant keeping all hints of the foxes from him. "I am tired and a
bit unwell, yes, but it is nothing serious. Only, I think I shall
retire early this evening."

He nodded. "Be careful of yourself. There are strange
reports, so if you suspect anything more than an autumn fever,
don't hesitate to call the *onmyouji.*"

Kaede's pulse quickened. The *onmyouji* was lying
insensible and half-bloodless in her room. "Yes, of course,

tono." She touched his arm. "Good night, my love."

When she returned to her room, Hanae was again lying with the fox, holding him close. "How is he?" Kaede asked.

As if in response, the fox gulped air and moaned. Hanae looked at her. "He stirs at times."

"Kaede-dono," breathed the wounded fox, his voice hoarse. "Kaede-dono...." He made a sound and choked.

Kaede's breath caught. "What has he said?"

Hanae glanced down self-consciously. "He calls for you."

"Always for me?" Kaede made a sharp gesture. "He dreams he is reporting to me, telling me of the *mononoke* he met." She flicked her hand at Hanae. "If he can speak, he needs no more warming. Out and leave him be. Bring some broth and noodles for him."

"Yes, Kaede-dono." Hanae slid from the bed and dressed.

Kaede went to her needlework and stared at it dully, wondering how she could focus her mind and hands. She left the embroidery and went to the medicine box. She would give Tsurugu something in the broth to make him sleep more soundly.

CHAPTER TEN

Kaworu shifted his weight on the tree branch and frowned to himself. Would his human or fox form cause more disturbance in the chickens below? He thought to take a bird from a different flock than the previous day, both to reduce suspicion and to ease the burden on the villagers, but he wanted as little telltale noise as possible.

Then his eye fell on a nearby bucket and he smiled to himself. It would actually be quite simple, after all.

He dropped from the tree and took up the bucket. It was empty, and it was the same bucket that had been sitting nearby for hours or days, but the chickens reacted with hopeful anticipation, clustering close to him and clucking in happy voices. He made a few gestures of tossing, and chickens scattered to follow his gestures, searching for feed. He sprinkled invisible feed about his feet, and a few ran close to his *zouri*. He scooped up a bird — not one of the layers, but a young rooster — and nestled it into his arm as he set down the bucket. The other birds clustered close around the bucket, confused and questing, and he held the captive bird quiet and still. None shrieked in alarm as they had the day before, making him run for cover with his prize.

Chickens were dumb.

He walked away, feeling smug, until he was safely out of easy sight, and then he paused and looked at the bird. It looked back at him and tried to flap, finally alarmed, but he held it steady. He frowned; he wasn't quite sure how to accomplish this next task as a human.

He transformed to his fox form and killed it cleanly. Then, taking it by the neck and slinging it over his shoulders, he trotted away toward the hut in the woods.

The girl was surprised to see him, but not too surprised. She blinked at the chicken. "Another?" She rose and took it from where he left it, a short distance from him. "Thank you." She began to pluck the bird. "Will you stay this time?"

Of course he did not answer.

"But for all your kindness, we don't know one another," she responded, as if to her own question. "I am Murame." She glanced at him. "And what do I call you?"

He could not have answered even if he had wished it.

"Kitsune-san, then, you remain."

He watched her, uncertain why. There was nothing more he could do for her. He dared not carry wood again, lest she watch this time and recognize his human form.

"I am afraid of becoming what they say I am," she said after a moment, "but I do very much thank you for your help."

He should return, help Genji with their chores and ask after Tsurugu-sama. He stood, made his awkward fox-bow, and then loped into the darkening forest.

"Where do you go in the evenings?"

Kaworu glanced at his brother, startled by the question. "I..." He had not thought to keep the girl a secret, and indeed he kept nothing from Genji, but it was awkward to explain her. "I am — doing a good deed, of sorts. Near the shrine."

Genji raised a skeptical eyebrow. "Relieving travelers of trinkets and snacks is hardly a good deed."

"No — this is different." Kaworu scratched at the back of his neck. "I am delivering food. To a hermit. Of sorts."

Now Genji was even more skeptical, and his grin displayed his amusement. "What sort of hermit?"

Kaworu surrendered. "A girl." At Genji's interest, he quickly added, "A village girl, a servant."

Now Genji's grin turned knowing. "What Tsurugu-sama doesn't know won't hurt either of you, eh?"

Kaworu shook his head. "No, not like that. I've taken her a couple of chickens from the village, that is all."

"From the village?"

Kaworu shrugged. "They are the ones who drove her out, they accused her falsely of *kitsune-tsuki*. They should be the ones to support her."

"Ah, this is Tsurugu-sama's girl." Genji stretched his arms overhead. "He won't be pleased."

It was easier to speak as if Tsurugu-sama were away, rather than lying still in Kaede-dono's room. "He'll have nothing to complain of. She's never seen me as a human."

"Of course not. It's dark in the mountain forest." Genji grinned. "Go ahead and stay late. I won't tell."

Kaworu tossed a balled cleaning rag over his brother's head. As Genji looked up to snatch it, Kaworu dove into him and they rolled across the ground, laughing.

"You *futago-me*!" shouted Jirou from the end of the *sunoko*. "Quit roughhousing, and back to your work!"

They separated and rolled to their feet in smooth

motions; they hadn't realized anyone was so near. But it seemed Jirou hadn't heard them speaking.

There was a flurry of barking from the gate, and as one Kaworu and Genji stiffened. Dogs! But they were on the far side of the estate, and if the twins kept themselves occupied with chores here....

And then someone shouted, and a frantic barking came across the courtyard. Without hesitation Genji and Kaworu moved, splitting and dashing for a roof support and a tree respectively. From their heights they could see the dog bolting across the garden, barking nonstop as it cast about. A trio of shouting men followed and tried to corner it, but it was too quick and intent on its scenting. Near the gate, two more men held back a lunging, barking pair.

"Get down!" called Jirou. "Go help catch that dog!"

Genji pointed, tracking the dog's progress.

"Get down here!"

Kaworu grasped a tree branch and leaned tentatively. The dog darted around one of its pursuers and leapt onto the *tsuridono*, the pavilion at the end of the long *rou* to the main buildings, scrabbling for purchase on the slick deck. It caught its footing and dashed toward the house.

Kaworu's heart froze in his chest. They hated and feared dogs, and they were safely out of reach here, but the wounded Tsurugu-sama would be utterly helpless, and Hanae-san would be trapped. Even Kaede-dono could not protect her servants from a hunting dog.

Kaworu leapt from the tree and hit the ground in a crouch. Behind him he heard his brother land, and they dashed after the dog with all the speed they could manage. They could not overtake the dog, but they might draw near enough to distract it, to lure it away and trap it in another room.

If it turned on them before they had found an escape

route....

The dog was unfamiliar with the estate, and it slowed to sniff at a *sukiwatadono*, a covered bridge connecting two houses. Kaworu didn't slow, wonderingly madly if they dared pounce on it. Would they have a chance, in their human shapes? But then the dog took off again, and they continued their pursuit, nearer now but still without hope of capturing it before it reached the inner *shinden*.

The dog whipped around the final corner and disappeared again from sight. Someone cried out in surprise and there was a sound of many pieces hitting the floor. The brothers rounded the corner, leapt a spilled basket, and ran on in the direction the servant was staring.

The dog hit the *wataridono* and went silent, catching the fresh *kitsune* scent. It was running directly for Kaede's quarters. They would never catch it in time.

There was a crashing sound, as the dog shouldered through the *shouji* which marked Kaede's rooms. Hanae screamed. Kaworu's breath caught in a way that had nothing to do with his sprint.

There was a yelp of surprise and pain, and Genji swore under his panting breath.

They burst into the *wataridono*, sliding on the veranda — prepared to do what? Seize the dog? Drag away Tsurugu as it pursued Hanae? — and froze. Beyond the smashed *shouji*, Kaede-dono and Hanae pressed against the wall behind Tsurugu's *futon*. Tsurugu was half-risen, braced on one arm with the other outstretched toward the dog, which rocked back upon its haunches with a wary, surprised expression. Between them spun a faintly visible five-pointed star, as wide as the *futon*.

The dog barked a couple of times and then rushed forward. It struck the spinning star as if a wall, yelping and backing away. Then it began barking furiously, dashing a short distance back and forth but no longer trying to advance.

Men pushed their way up the corridor and shoved the brothers aside, swearing. The dog glanced over his shoulder and began barking even more intensely, darting back and forth as if seeking a way past Tsurugu's shield. The dog's keeper lunged for it and snatched a handful of skin on its back, stumbling to the floor. The dog yelped and the man grabbed it with both hands before wrapping a rope about its neck.

Genji and Kaworu hurried out of the way. The dog's keeper cuffed the animal several times, making it yelp again, and then began dragging it backward. It barked once more, almost forlornly, toward the *onmyouji* and women, and he gave the rope a jerk and pulled the dog after him.

Kaede-dono drew a visible breath. The other men exchanged glances, unsure of what to do or say. Tsurugu dropped his arm and the star spun out of existence.

"Out of my way!" Naka no Yoritomo ran into the *wataridono*, followed by armed guards, and batted aside the destroyed *shouji*. "Kaede-dono!"

"I am well, my lord," she answered. "I was protected by the *onmyouji-sama*." She raised her sleeve to shield her face from the others.

Genji and Kaworu eased closer; everyone seemed to be fine, indeed. Tsurugu was fully dressed, without a hint of bloodstain — though that was fox magic, not reality.

The *daimyou* looked to him. "Yes?"

Tsurugu bowed his head. "Forgive me, *tono*; I fell as I ran. I am only glad I arrived in time."

The men who had pursued the dog began edging away.

Naka no Yoritomo nodded toward Tsurugu. "We are all most glad you were able to arrive so quickly. Are you injured?"

"A moment, *tono*, and we shall see." But Tsurugu's voice betrayed him, shallow and strained.

The *daimyou* turned and pointed to the men disappearing down the veranda. "Take them — and the one with the dog. I want them beaten for this dangerous affront to my wife."

The men began to protest, but the guards hurried them away. Tsurugu drew a leg slowly beneath himself, and Genji darted forward to offer his shoulder as a crutch. Together they stood, and Tsurugu bowed his head before the *daimyou*. "My lord."

"Take your ease, Tsurugu-sama," said Naka no Yoritomo. "Go and see the physician, if your discomfort persists. You have our thanks."

Then he turned to Kaede-dono and, heedless of those watching, embraced her. The remaining guards fanned slightly and turned away from the damaged *shouji*, as if they waited outside a closed room. Tsurugu and Genji started away, moving very carefully.

"*Tono*," said Kaede, "please take me from this room. I am — frightened here, at least for this moment."

"Certainly," he murmured, and he gestured to Hanae, who promptly went to collect a fan, another robe, and any other items Kaede might want in her lord's quarters. Another gesture sent the guards back to their posts. The *daimyou* and the two women went away, leaving Tsurugu and the brothers alone.

"Bless her," he breathed, leaning heavily upon Genji. "I don't think I could have fooled anyone for long."

"Tsurugu-sama!" Kaworu grinned happily. "You're alive and well!"

"Alive, anyway," Tsurugu agreed flatly. "Hardly well. I woke at the barking, or I'd be less well."

"You stopped it," Genji said with a faint awe. "You stopped the dog."

Tsurugu managed a weak smile. "Do you see why I tell

you to practice the art?"

Kaworu got beneath his other arm and they started down the *sukiwatadono*, moving very cautiously. The secondary building, the *tai yo na*, had emptied before the *daimyou*'s anger, and they shuffled on to the *rou*.

The stairs that divided the *rou*, permitting gate traffic to pass through the long wing, were hardly worth a thought on most days. Now their descent was slow and painful, as each step jolted Tsurugu, but supporting him seemed to cause as much pain.

They paused, Tsurugu panting as he leaned on them, and looked across to the upward stairs leading to the *onmyouji*'s quarters. "*Kuso*," swore Tsurugu frankly.

Genji looked at them. "Can't we carry you as we did before?"

"How else?"

"No — not just now, but when we found you. *Ani-ue* carried you in a *kosode* to sneak you to Kaede-dono."

Tsurugu blinked and then chuckled weakly. "I wish you'd mentioned that before the stairs. Yes, I will gladly be shamed by your carrying me, if it means I am spared."

They were sheltered by the wall, and there was no one to see. Tsurugu took his fox form and Kaworu gently gathered him. From there, it was a far easier trek to his quarters.

There was blood on Kaworu's sleeves when they arrived, but Tsurugu seemed less distressed. "Now," he said, taking his human shape, "set out my *futon* and let me sleep again."

Kaworu went for the *futon*. Genji seated himself near the door, to watch and warn Tsurugu in case anyone came.

"Merciful goddess," groaned Tsurugu as he eased himself to the floor. Kaworu thought him merely swearing in pain, but the *onmyouji* continued, "That was only the lesser danger. What comes from the west?"

CHAPTER ELEVEN

THE leaves were a brilliant gold on the mountain, and it seemed the pale fox formed out of them like a spirit.

Well, he *was* a spirit, at that.

Murame turned to face him, fighting a smile. "Welcome, *kitsune-san*. How are you this day?"

The fox had a fowl again, but not a chicken this time. It was one of the forest birds, slung over his shoulders so that it did not drag. He deposited the dead bird and looked at her.

"Thank you," Murame said with real enthusiasm. Her day's scavenging had produced nuts and berries, but nothing more. She rose, carrying the bird into the little hut. "Will you stay to share it?"

The fox never stayed. She wasn't sure why that was; she couldn't recall any warnings or superstitions about dining with a fox. It seemed only that he wasn't interested — but what fox would not be interested in his own catch?

She glanced at the fox, who sat still outside. He wouldn't stay, then. "I wish you good hunting, then, if you won't let me feed you." She laughed. "Of course, I wouldn't be feeding you. It is you who are feeding me. And I thank you."

The fox made its odd little bow.

"I wish I had something to call you," she said, pushing together kindling. If she started the fire now, the water would be boiling by the time she plucked the bird. Many would have eaten it raw, fresh as it was, but she had a taste for boiled meat. "I feel…" She stopped herself. *I feel we're nearly friends* was a ridiculously stupid thing to say to a *kitsune*, even one which brought her meat and vegetables.

The fox, when she glanced at it, hadn't seemed to notice her lapse, or at least she could read nothing in its vulpine expression.

"Well, I'll have to call you something. If you won't give me your name, *kitsune-san*, then you will be… Ki-chan."

The fox's ears rotated outward, giving him an expression of annoyance.

"No? Ki-tan, maybe?"

The ears flattened further.

Murame laughed. "No, wait, I have it! An adorable puppy like you must be Ki-wan-wan!" She cupped her hands and mimicked ruffling a dog's ears.

The fox's lip curled in a little growl and it turned away.

Murame shook her head, still, laughing. "No, come back, I'm sorry. That's cold favor for all you've done, I know. It's only that I want a name for you."

The fox hesitated, and then it turned and bounded onto the hut's floor. Gently it tugged the fowl from Murame's grasp and settled on the floor with it, where it placidly began gnawing off the bird's head.

Murame sat down at a respectful distance. "Does this mean you're staying for dinner?"

The fox freed the head with a final crunch and took it,

sitting upright and wrapping its tail around its paws in a gesture of polite attention. Murame was startled at how obvious the fox's mimicry of human postures had become to her.

She took back the bird, tearing the skin. She could be polite, too. "Well, then let's eat. *Itadakimasu.*"

狐

Kaede shivered, cold even within her many layers of silk, and Yoritomo-dono poured more *sake* with his own hand. "Here, drink. You mustn't take cold, and the weather is changing early this year."

Kaede drank, the *sake* warm in her hands and burning inside her. They had sent the servants away and were gazing at the autumn moon together, just the two of them. It was a precious moment, the moonlight and the stream and the garden and Yoritomo warm beside her, smelling of himself.

He turned his face back to the sky, bright with cold light. "It is beautiful." He was quiet a moment, and then he spoke.

> "Moonlight glistens on
> Rippling pond and running stream,
> Silvers all the path,
> Runs deep, shines clear, and turns to
> Ash before my love's bright eye."

He looked at her, his face feigning sober intent but his eyes smiling, and Kaede laughed aloud. "I should mock such an unskilled poem," she said, "but I am too in love with the poet."

"You have low taste," he said, his voice warm with hidden laughter. "How you have fallen in your second marriage."

Kaede took a drink instead of answering, and he sobered. "Kaede-dono — I do not mind that you had a previous husband.

You are precious to me as you are."

"As I am?" Kaede looked into the *sake*, her reflection blurring in its surface. As she was? No widow, no Fujitani, only a medicine-seller's daughter in borrowed trappings, and a *kitsune-mochi*. She had used no magic to win Yoritomo's affection, but no one would believe that after she had lied over so much else.

"As you are." Yoritomo took the *sake*, draining it, and pulled her close, warming her as he looked up at the moon again. "That you had a husband once before meant that I had a chance to win you now, even being such a rustic instead of one of the polished and favored lords your family might have preferred."

Kaede made herself smile. "They would have had no choice. I would have had you, regardless of what they might have said."

He snorted. "Defied your family? You would have dared? For me?"

"Yes," she said, and now her voice was firm with truth. They had not been the Fujitani, but they had been formidable enough — and she had defied them, had fled them, and had made a way for herself as no one could have imagined. And now she sat at the side of Naka no Yoritomo, who for all his present self-deprecation was yet a powerful and noble *daimyou*.

He smiled and turned his face into her neck. His nose was cold. "I would go to war for you."

Yes, she had defied them, and she was now the *daimyou*'s wife. And unfashionable as it might be, she loved him. "I hope you never must. But if war comes, I will fight with you and for you."

He chuckled into her hair. "What women they breed. Come, it is cold here, and we can warm ourselves inside."

Gennosuke made himself breathe, flushing the tension through his body before it was noticed. All the youths kneeling in crisp rows wanted to hear their names called, but Gennosuke had a particular hope.

Only three names remained.

"Ushimaru-kun."

The boy to Gennosuke's left stood and bowed.

"Sakura-san."

A girl at the far end of the row bowed. Gennosuke's stomach twisted. He was better than Ushimaru, he was, and what if his name were not the last to be called?

"Susumu-kun."

Susumu jumped to his feet as Gennosuke's shoulders dropped. That was it. There would not be another selection through the rest of the winter. His eyes burned. Without leaving the village, he would have no chance to explore the *daimyou*'s household for the secret of Shishio-oji-san's death.

He felt Harume-sama's eyes upon him and he looked down at his knees. The grey-haired woman regarded him a moment, frowning, and Gennosuke willed away the traitorous flush of heat that crept over him. Harume-sama was too aware that he was eager to win an assignment, and she likely knew the reason.

Let me prove myself, Gennosuke thought. *I want to find what happened to* oji-san, *and you want to test me. Let me go.*

But the steel-haired woman said nothing, and they were dismissed from their neat rows. Gennosuke did not rise as quickly as the others, and he clenched his fists on his thighs. He would go. If he were not chosen in the spring, he would leave the village and go on his own. For his *oji-san*'s sake.

CHAPTER TWELVE

COLD had fallen sharply on the hills these last few days, and Murame could not warm the dilapidated hut enough. Despite the meat and rice and vegetables the fox supplied — upon which she relied, loath as she was to admit it — and the wood she often found in the morning, she could not stay warm.

Now the fire had burned low, darkening the hut, but she did not rise from her thin *futon*. She was curled tightly on her side, her arms and knees drawn against her chest. She would grow colder as the fire faded, but she would grow colder if she moved the few robes she had, losing precious heat to the air. The broken walls and roof held little heat, anyway, and it would not be long before she could do nothing against the coming winter. This night was already bitter; without proper shelter or better clothing, she would die.

She shivered, making a small sound of despair. She did not want to die, not so uselessly as freezing in a shack. Why hadn't she asked the *kitsune* for clothing?

What was she thinking? Had she really come to think of

the *kitsune* as her provider? Did she even think to direct it to her needs? Had she become the *kitsune-mochi* they believed her?

She shivered, exhaling against her own chest to conserve warmth. She didn't care. She would accept their accusations, if only she could keep warm.

The fire popped, startling her, and she opened her eyes to see a branch sliding into it. Half-lit by the flames, she could see the fox biting at the wood, awkwardly pushing it.

"I thought animals were supposed to fear fire." Her voice was thin and shaking. She had not realized how dangerously cold she'd become. "You've never come this late before."

The fox released the branch, now burning, and came toward her. She did not move; the animal no longer alarmed her. It lay down, facing her, and extended its neck gently, sniffing at her.

"Here to check on me?" She didn't like speaking, all lost warmth. She eyed the fox's fluffy coat with sudden envy. "What I would give for your pelt."

His ears rotated, and then he crawled forward. Murame watched, strangely detached, as he nosed up the edge of the robe that lay over her and wriggled beneath it. "You're cold, too? I'm afraid I won't be much help."

But the fox turned within the robe and lay against her, pressed to her folded arms, and she realized he meant to share his own warmth. She closed her eyes, concentrating on the smooth fur against her arms, and tried to imagine it wrapped about all of her.

They lay close for a few moments, but even with the fox's fur beside her, Murame could not stop shivering. She dared not sleep this night, she realized, and she would be glad to survive it.

The fox stirred and crawled from the robe, leaving her

colder with his departure. He was not enough to save her, but still she missed him. He pushed at the fire again, feeding the fresh wood entirely into it, and then padded into the darkness.

She closed her eyes and shivered violently. She could not feel her legs.

The robe shifted as something moved at her back. The fox? But then it drew near her, larger than the fox, and a human arm reached about her.

A man's arm.

Murame screamed and jerked away, catching at her robes. But the arm caught her and pressed her down upon the *futon*, facing the fire. "Please!"

Cold and weak and numb, she could not escape anyway. She lay on the *futon* and shook, tears frozen in her eyes.

"Please," the voice said again, "lie still. I will not harm you — I will not hurt you."

There was nowhere to flee, even if she got away from him, only the dark forest and the bitter cold, full of dangers as real as a man upon her.

"I know what you said, why they accused you of madness," the voice said quietly. "I know what you fear. Please — I won't hurt you. I only want to warm you."

Realization came to her, and she caught her breath. "Are — are you the *kitsune-san*?"

"I am."

His human form! She tried to turn to face him, but the arm pressed down like iron. "No! No, you mustn't look at me. Not as I am."

She hesitated, half-turned and still half-blinded by the fire. "But, *kitsune-san—*"

"No. I will stay, but you must not look at me." Something moved over them, and she felt more robes settle evenly upon her. "Please."

Her fox had never harmed her. And keeping her eyes from him was a small price for warmth. But, still, no matter what her mind said, her body feared him. She lay tense and rigid, and her trembling was now only partly from the cold.

"It's all right," he said softly. "It's only a fox, sleeping beside you."

She closed her eyes. "It's only a fox," she repeated in a whisper. "It's only a fox."

His body was long, and he lay close without pressing to her, without ever quite touching her. She could feel the heat of him, and she craved warmth.

She slept.

狐

A sound woke Murame, though she could not say what it was exactly. The fire had dwindled again, but she was warmer than she had right to expect. Sunlight streaked through the hut's many openings. True to his word, the fox-man behind her was close, but he had not pressed himself upon her in the other fashion.

The sound came again, with accompaniments — a rustle, and a snapping branch, the breathing of a horse, a creak of saddle leather.

The figure behind her jerked with sudden awareness and he swore. He wriggled against her back and then the pale fox leapt over her, clearly visible in the early morning light, and ran for the damaged rear wall.

Something glinted in the slanted sunlight and the fox yelped, skidding to a halt. He dashed in another direction, and this time Murame saw a five-pointed star form faintly in the air, spinning upright, and the fox recoiled again. He whirled, apparently seeking an exit, and then dropped to the sagging floor, belly and chin pressed flat.

A figure appeared in the doorway, illuminated by the morning light. Murame, half-risen to watch the panicked fox, kicked off the robes and knelt. *"Onmyouji-sama."*

Tsurugu-sama barely glanced at her; his eyes were on the fox lying before him.

Terror rushed through Murame. "No!" she protested bluntly, crawling forward. "Don't kill him!"

Now Tsurugu-sama looked at her, dubious surprise on his face. "What?"

Without the fox, she would starve. Without the fox, she would have frozen. "Don't hurt him. Please. Only — I'm not...." How could she plead for the fox, found in her hut, while protesting she was not *kitsune-mochi?*

Tsurugu-sama turned back to the fox, who had not moved. Its ears flattened, and the white-tipped tail shifted against its side.

The *onmyouji* sighed. "I will not kill him," he conceded, and Murame's heart seemed to trip in her chest. "But I cannot leave him here with you."

She could hardly ask for more. "Thank you for sparing him, *onmyouji-sama.*"

His face twisted. He suppressed the expression quickly, but she had seen his quick disgust. She bowed her head, ashamed of her request and of the affinity she felt for the *kitsune.*

The *onmyouji* reached out a hand and grasped the fox at the shoulders, pulling it upright by a handful of skin. It yelped — like kittens, they were meant to be carried thus only when very young — and pawed the air briefly, but then it went silent as Tsurugu lifted it. He turned and went to his horse.

Murame crawled to the door, watching him. He deposited the fox on the horse's croup, where it sat acquiescently. Then the *onmyouji* mounted and glanced back at her. Murame bowed low.

"I will come for you," he said unexpectedly. "Can you promise me to work hard? And to keep silence?"

She had no choice, she had nowhere else to go, and how could she refuse the man who had helped her once already? "Of course, *onmyouji-sama.*"

"Then look for me this midday." He turned the horse and rode away through the forest.

CHAPTER THIRTEEN

KAWORU crouched low, balancing on the horse's croup, and eyed Tsurugu's back. His withers hurt with the stretch of being carried like a kit. Now he felt he was braced as much for the *onmyouji*'s coming words as for the horse's movement.

Moments passed, and Kaworu licked his lips nervously. Why did Tsurugu wait? Delay only made it worse — or did he know that? Was this deliberate? Or was he merely ensuring Murame would hear nothing?

At last Tsurugu took a deep breath, and Kaworu flinched in anticipation.

"What," Tsurugu began, "were you doing?"

His voice was calm, steady. Kaworu looked up optimistically.

"You have endangered us all: Kaede-dono, Hanae-san, myself, your brother — and that girl herself, too. You risked the lives of each of us, so that you could toy with her."

I wasn't toying with her! Kaworu thought, but he could not have spoken it aloud even if he had dared.

"You have ignored my mandate, and while abusing her disadvantage. It was a loathsome thing you did."

Now Kaworu did respond, a short bark of protest.

"You know what fate you would bring on a helpless girl, trapped by her circumstances. It is despicable."

Determined now to speak for himself, Kaworu changed form, shifting from fox to human youth. The horse, startled by the sudden appearance and weight of a second rider, jerked and skittered to one side, dislodging Kaworu, and he tumbled to the ground.

Tsurugu turned the prancing horse and regarded Kaworu flatly. "What now?"

Kaworu rose, shaking away leaf litter. "I did not bed her."

"You were certainly in her bed."

Kaworu shook his head, hot embarrassment coloring his treacherous human skin. "I slept beside her, but that is all. She was cold last night. Dangerously cold." That was why he had gone to her; winter had come suddenly and he didn't think she was prepared.

Tsurugu eyed him doubtfully. "You did nothing else?"

"I've been bringing her food," Kaworu said. "I came to see that she didn't freeze. I want to help her!"

Tsurugu sighed and held out a hand. Kaworu took it and pulled himself up, hearing Tsurugu's soft catch of breath as the action strained his healing wound. Kaworu settled behind the saddle, his eyes away from the *onmyouji*.

"If you truly want to help her," Tsurugu said, "you won't bed her."

"I know, Tsurugu-sama."

"It would be poor charity to bring her vegetables and steal her life."

"I know, Tsurugu-sama," ground Kaworu. It was a

primary reason Tsurugu admonished them so strongly to refuse the household's many invitations. A *kitsune* in the bed could be a dangerous disease.

"I will bring her to Kaede-dono," Tsurugu said. "What you did was well-intentioned, but now you may leave her entirely to her *okugata-sama*."

Kaworu nodded, watching the fallen leaves pass beneath them. "*Hai*, Tsurugu-sama."

狐

Murame followed the *onmyouji* into the *daimyou*'s house, not daring to speak but full of questions. She did not wish to return to work here, where she had been driven out, but she had promised obedience to Tsurugu-sama — and she had no choice, at any rate.

But he did not pause in the hall, or the kitchen, or at any of the outer rooms, but led her deep inside. What had she to do with the people of the *shinden*? Did he intend her for service here? It was impossible; she was not fit to serve even as a housemaid in this part of the house.

But he led her on to an inner room, with screens painted with scenes of fishing herons. He stopped and knelt, and Murame dropped to the floor. If Tsurugu knelt here, she could do no less.

A pretty maid came to summon them inside, and Tsurugu rose to enter. Murame remained on her knees, shuffling inside.

A beautiful woman awaited, reclining and observing them. Tsurugu knelt and bowed. "Good afternoon, Kaede-dono."

Kaede-dono! The great lady, the *okugata-sama*! Murame flung herself to the floor and pressed her face to a *tatami* sitting mat, fearing the lady would hear her pounding heart. Why had she come here?

"Rise, Tsurugu-sama. So, this is she?"

"It is."

"Sit up, girl, and let me see you."

Murame obeyed, trying to swallow against the pressure in her throat. She was a village girl, a farmer's daughter, a nothing — she should not even see the *daimyou's* wife, much less sit before her....

Kaede-dono pursed her lips. "And you say she will be reliable? What of it, girl — are you a good worker?"

Murame gulped. "I — I do my best, *okugata-sama*."

"Are you discreet?"

"If you wish it, lady, I will bite out my tongue." Murame's words surprised her, but her voice was soft, directed to the *tatami* as much as the great lady.

Kaede laughed, a rich, musical laugh like Murame might have imagined all great ladies must have. "That will not be necessary, I hope. What is your name, girl?"

"Murame."

"Murame-san, would you like to be my maid? You might assist Hanae-san in her duties and attend me."

Murame gasped and bent low again. "*Okugata-sama*, I am only a farm girl. I am not one who might be maid to such as you."

"Sit up, Murame. I have been unconventional in my choice of servants before now, and it is not for you to decide whom I choose."

Murame sat up slowly, and Kaede laughed again. "You have the weave of the *tatami* pressed in your forehead; how silly you look. This comes of protesting my wishes." She gestured to the pretty maid. "Hanae, please take Murame to be cleaned and dressed, as befitting my maid, and then you may instruct her in her first duties."

狐

Ogasawara gritted his teeth and forced a smile for the young woman before him. "You are of water, your personality, with a tendency toward the *on*. Feminine water." He looked at the older couple beside the girl. "This leads her toward quiet introspection. You might see that she is sensitive and imaginative. Also, she is likely very attentive to details."

The mother nodded. "Her embroidery is the finest for miles around. It sells very well."

"But will she be a good match for Naosuke-san?" pressed the father.

Who cares? thought Ogasawara savagely. *You little people with your little problems. Marry the girl off, get plenty of little grandchildren, go on with your little lives. It has nothing to do with me.* But aloud he said, "He is wood, and *myo* wood, so he will be confident, and practical, and his temperamental resistance will be tempered by her indirect gentleness. They will complement one another."

The mother sighed with relief, and the young woman smiled, her eyes shyly down on Ogasawara's table. Her father paid, and Ogasawara took the coins too quickly. He and Hideo would eat tonight.

He was an *onmyouji* of the Ogasawara, he had served the *daimyou* himself. He should not be telling fortunes for farmers and tradesmen. He should be head of the family, not stupid Chikahiro. He should not be hungrily working toward a rival *daimyou's* lands, losing most of each day in hawking fortunes to peasants, carrying only a few tools of *onmyoudou* and a single memento of his dead Matsue.

Nor should he, he knew, allow himself to wallow in these furious thoughts, but the anger was easier — easy to cultivate, and easier to bear. If he thought of Sanjou-dono staring gape-mouthed at the salt-packed head of Naka no

Yoritomo's wife, he did not think of pale Matsue, cut and still. If he pictured Chikahiro groveling low before the man who had killed the mighty Naka-dono, he did not hear his cousin's mocking laughter.

Hideo was beside him, staring hungrily at the handful of coins. "Is it enough? Can we have rice? And vegetables?"

Ogasawara passed him the coins. "It should be enough. Go to the market, buy what you can."

Tomorrow they would go to the next town, and he would offer fortunes for a few days, earning just enough to buy barley or even rice, and shelter from the winter. And the next town, and the next, until they reached Naka no Yoritomo. And then he would change everything.

CHAPTER FOURTEEN

KAWORU kept carefully away from Murame in the *daimyou*'s house. He was not often called to Kaede-dono, and when he did attend her, he sat quietly beside Genji and kept his eyes from the new young maid assisting Hanae-san. He felt Tsurugu's watchful gaze on him at these times, but he heeded the injunction perfectly. Murame was safe and under the considerable protection of Kaede-dono. There was no reason to look after her now.

Tsurugu continued to heal well. "What of the *nozuchi*?" Genji had asked.

Tsurugu assumed a hurt expression. "Was I eaten? Did you find a blood trail?"

Genji grinned and snapped his teeth in mock savagery.

Tsurugu raised an eyebrow. "And I'll do the same to you if you don't get to your chores and behave yourself. Some are still complaining about the tear you made through the house."

"That was for your sake," Genji protested.

"Which is why I only told them you'd been suitably

chastised, without actually doing anything about it," Tsurugu rejoined. "Take a lesson from your brother and keep out of notice."

"He's only moping after that girl," Genji said with a smirk.

"I'm not moping," Kaworu protested. "I'm keeping my one tail out of trouble." He glanced at Tsurugu.

The *onmyouji* nodded. "Just as I warned, which is why I have trouble believing it. How is your practice coming?"

The twins exchanged glances. "Toyotsune-sensei won't be satisfied," Genji said resignedly, "but it's the best we can do with just ourselves."

"Do you want an outside eye?"

"I don't think it would help," Kaworu admitted. "We've been working, Kiyomori-sama. Even while you were ill. Every day."

"I believe you, but I'm not the one to be convinced. On another point, do either of you want to make the circuit with me tonight?"

Midorikawa-dono's travel had disrupted the *youkai*, as predicted, and reports of the supernatural abounded in the villages and among the travelers. Half were probably false, fabrications of story-seeded minds ready to see the worst, but against the rest, Tsurugu set a *kekkai* around the *daimyou's* house. Each evening he circumnavigated the walls, checking and reinforcing it. Naka no Yoritomo had not missed that while the village was apparently plagued with *youkai*, his home was immune. He had that very afternoon presented Tsurugu with a fine piece of jade from the continent.

Kaworu glanced at Genji and nodded. "We'll come with you."

Kaede woke with the first light, and she knew: This would be the day Midorikawa-dono arrived. All the subtle energy that had been building, a delicate cobweb few seemed to have noticed, would come to this.

"Okugata-sama." Murame entered on her knees, presenting a colored paper. "One of the twins brought this just now, from the *onmyouji-sama.*"

Of course they would have known, even before Kaede. Her subtle sense of the arcane, barely developed even after years with the *kitsune*, could not outpace theirs.

She took the paper and unfolded it, but Tsurugu had been discreet. It was only a simple painting of a half moon and a series of inhuman creatures descending a mountain trail, more inky lines and suggestions than detail, and perhaps nothing more than an idle sketch of the *youkai* night parade of stories. But Kaede understood; they would meet Midorikawa-dono and his retinue on the mountain.

She could not receive him here, no matter how she would like to honor him within the *daimyou's* household. It would be difficult and dangerous, and one did not ask Midorikawa-dono to conceal his station. At least it was another empty day in the household, with no guests, no events, nothing to distract Kaede from sitting and contemplating and being an icon of well-bred beauty and womanhood. It would be easy to plead fatigue or a headache and slip away in the evening.

"Thank you, Murame-chan." She would need an excuse for Murame. The girl was grateful and seemed trustworthy, but taking her to meet *youkai* and *ayakashi* was too great a leap of faith. Besides, a girl accused of both *kitsune-tsuki* and *kitsune-mochi* would want nothing to do with *youkai* if she could help it. She was eager and capable, once settled, and Kaede would begin training her in medicine when Midorikawa-dono's visit was done. But for tonight, she would leave Murame to her own devices, well away from Kaede's important guest.

She would need fine clothes this night. Unlike the *kitsune*, who could magic fresh clothing at will, she had to plan and dress for the occasion. She sat up. "Send Hanae-san to me, and go and set up the incense. I'll want a set of robes freshly perfumed."

十五

CHAPTER FIFTEEN

MURAME had been foolish, she knew. There was too much talk of *yuurei* and *mononoke* to risk leaving the walls, but she knew of no other way to reach the *kitsune*. She had not seen him since the *onmyouji* had taken him, and while it was likely he had been exorcised, there was a faint chance he was still in the woods around the hut. She had never properly thanked him, and though she had no appropriate gift, she did not want to appear ungrateful.

So when her mistress had dismissed her for the evening, she had gone to the hut, finding it untouched since she had left with the *onmyouji*. Still, she had left the rice she had saved from her dinner portions — *kitsune* were sacred to the goddess Inari, as was rice, so surely this gift would be appreciated for its intent — in the center of the door, where the *kitsune* had set the gifts of food it had brought. She hoped he was safe.

Now, descending the mountain, she was doubting her decision. The mountain felt... different this night. Even with the slanting evening sun, the shadows were deepening and she jumped at each noise. She glanced behind her and saw nothing, but that did nothing to ease her apprehensions. There was much she could not see.

Her footsteps in the litter and debris muffled the forest noises around her, and for a moment she considered humming to further drown the sounds that frightened her. But it would be foolish to handicap herself. She kept quiet, listening to her too-loud footsteps.

Twilight made the way difficult, and she hoped she was still going the right way. She slipped, half-losing her *zouri*. She paused, to refit it to her foot, and the footsteps did not.

She whirled, her heart racing, and saw nothing. But the footsteps continued. And then, something giggled.

Murame turned and bolted, fleeing down the mountainside and through the brush without care for ankle or cheek. She burst from the trees and sprinted across the wide, flat space lying between the woods and the *daimyou*'s house. There was someone there — a group in the meadow, walking toward the woods. The *onmyouji*! She ran toward them, gasping, unable even to call for help.

They saw her now — they were startled by her panic. The stream lay between her and safety, but she could swim. She flung herself into the water.

On her third stroke, something seized her and pulled her down.

狐

Kaworu saw Murame running at the stream and his stomach clenched. He started forward, one arm out as if to warn her away, but her panicked eyes did not seem to even see him. She reached the water and leapt.

He saw the *kappa* seize her and drag her under. Without thinking, he bolted for the water and dove after them.

The *kappa*'s shell was impenetrable, but its neck was exposed as it drew down the struggling Murame. Kaworu found it and seized it in a chokehold.

The *kappa* changed targets immediately, releasing Murame and clawing at Kaworu. The sharp beak slashed a furrow in his forearm, but he held on. Webbed fingers wrapped about his arms and dug tight — but they did not try to pry him off. They were holding him tight, drawing him closer. And Kaworu realized too late that trying to choke a water creature was probably futile.

He twisted, but the *kappa* held him firmly. He tried the escapes he had been taught, but it was difficult in the water without weight or traction, and the *kappa* only moved fluidly with him. He flailed, but the *kappa* merely twisted and let him strike uselessly into the yielding water.

The water roared in his ears and his vision darkened as they sank. He needed air. He kicked, he wrenched, he sobbed. His body acted without him and tried to breathe. He choked.

He was dying. There was nothing but water and his terror, and he was dying.

Then there was a great sound over the roaring in his ears, and something struck him hard. The impact made him gasp, and it was sweet, sweet air which entered him. He gagged and coughed and breathed, and through the coughing he realized his fingers were spasmodically clutching grass.

Hands took his shoulders — Genji, he knew. He coughed and reached with one hand to grasp his brother.

Then the hands withdrew, and Kaworu sensed something else. Someone else.

"Face me."

Still coughing and wheezing, Kaworu knelt and fell forward in a low bow. His arms were shaking. Beside him, the *kappa* bowed as well, water spilling from the natural depression in its head.

"*Kappa-san,*" intoned a velvety dark voice, "do you know me?"

Kappa and Kaworu raised their heads together. Before them sat a large fox, soft gold even in the fading twilight. His tail wrapped about his feet and only the barest tip moved in a steady twitch.

"Of course I know you, Midorikawa-dono," answered the *kappa*. "You are the present lord of this land."

The fox nodded once, a slow incline of his head. "And did you know, *kappa-san*, that this one is my own?"

It was not quite possible for a *kappa* to go pale, but this one managed, shrinking partly into its shell. "*Kyuubi-dono*, how could I have known?"

Kaworu knew he should be silent, but he could not suppress the coughing. Somewhere to his right, Genji knelt and watched. Where was Murame?

The water had drained wholly from the *kappa*'s skull depression, and he was beginning to tremble. "With respect, *tono*, it was he who attacked me."

Midorikawa's golden eyes shifted to Kaworu without his head moving. "True."

Heartened, the *kappa* continued. "And he had defaulted on a promise to me — three cucumbers he promised, and he brought only two. After this deceit and then his attack upon my person, how could I be blamed for defending myself?" He rubbed agitatedly at the empty basin in his skull. Already he was sagging with weakness.

Midorikawa's gaze returned to the *kappa*. "What was this earlier agreement?"

The *kappa* realized its error. "I — he came to my pool...."

Midorikawa's eyes narrowed, and the *kappa* bowed its

head in brave resignation. There was a crack like too-near lightning, and the gold fox was suddenly the size of an ox. Nine tails lashed about him as he leapt, and the *kappa* simply vanished.

The great gold fox turned to Kaworu. Kaworu swallowed, forcing a lull in the coughing, and pressed low in a deeply formal bow. *"Youkoso, chichi-ue."* Welcome, Father.

CHAPTER SIXTEEN

KAWORU, now in his fox form, walked alongside his brother as Midorikawa-dono's retinue wound its way through the woods. His coat was only damp, as he had gone into the water as a human, but the cold night air cut through it. He told himself this was why he shivered, and not the cold wet blackness of the water.

Beside him, Genji gave him a concerned look. "That was really stupid," he said quietly. "And brave. But really stupid."

Kaworu nodded.

"That's the girl? What were you thinking?"

"I didn't think at all. I just — where is she? I know he let go of her."

"She came up first," Genji reported. "*Chichi-ue* ordered Takeda-sama to carry her back to the house. Kaede-dono believes she will be discreet."

Of course Murame would say nothing of the *kitsune* in the field. Murame would not speak the word if she could help it. She was probably already wrapped tightly in her robes, rocking, just as she had been when he had first found her in the hut.

Kaede-dono rode before them in a palanquin, carried by four small *hitosu-me-nyuudou* bearing her up the mountainside. They wound through the woods, a miniature night parade, until they came to Inari's shrine. Tsurugu-sama must have thought it a safe meeting place.

But it was the simple shrine no more; powerful illusionary magic had made it a pavilion of luxury. Kaworu could hardly believe its transformation. He paused and bowed as Midorikawa-dono and Kaede-dono took their places in the center of the pavilion, then moved with the others to take their places about the arcane court, all in their truest shapes and forms. Midorikawa's golden fur gleamed in the torchlight, his nine tails shifting around him. Tsurugu stepped forward, not so large as Midorikawa but with seven tails held gently aloft. Kaworu resisted the urge to press down his single tail in embarrassment.

Tsurugu spoke words of welcome to all, but Kaworu paid little attention. He was scanning the gathering for other familiar faces. There was Toyotsune-sensei, and there Koremitsu, and there was Takeda — he must have caught up after returning Murame to the house.

"I would be pleased if we might have entertainment," Midorikawa was saying, and Kaworu came to attention with a little jerk of realization. Eyes shifted toward him and Genji. "Ichirou, Mataichirou — are you able?"

Even if Kaworu had wished to be excused after his near-drowning, he would not have said so before such an assembly. Genji looked at him, but he only bowed. "It would be our honor."

They rose and took human form; their man-dances were

more appreciated for the extra skill required. Their matching dancers' robes made them nearly indistinguishable as they moved to the center of the pavilion and took their positions.

A *tanuki* began to beat a rhythm, and Kaworu's pulse quickened to match it.

They leapt as one, springing apart and then together, whirling and dipping and reaching. This was a strong dance, borrowing leaps from the continent's aerial dancers and sequences from the fighting arts. It required strength and concentration and never failed to exhilarate the brothers as well as their audience.

But as they danced, Kaworu's chest grew tight, and a moment later his breath began to wheeze. He took a stutter-step before his next leap, failing to match Genji exactly. He recovered and made the next movement, a slow, powerful sweep of the arms, in perfect time. He tried to deepen his breathing, control it, but it was the fuller breaths that caught at him.

They swept together and Genji rushed the next movement a little, letting Kaworu see he was changing the sequence. Kaworu hesitated and fell into mimicry, so that the movements rippled smoothly from one to the other until he discerned Genji's intent, and then he cut short a spin so that they moved together again into the final sequence of the dance. They ended with two great leaps which brought them crouching together and froze in perfect control.

Kaworu fought it, but in the moment of precise stillness, he coughed.

Immediately beside him Genji gave a dry little cough as well. Then they rose in unison, bowed, and retreated.

Someone rose to speak praise, but Kaworu was intent on reaching the trees outside the pavilion, where he dropped low with great hacking coughs that shook him, trying to direct the sound into the ground so that it would not carry. Genji knelt beside him. *"Ani-ue?"*

He nodded, he would be all right.

"That dance is too long, anyway."

Kaworu nodded again. In the firelit pavilion, Midorikawa's court was proceeding. No one seemed to be looking for them. Kaworu coughed and shifted into his fox shape, wrapping his tail about him for warmth.

Genji shifted and settled beside him, tail wrapped to the opposite shoulder, shoulders and hips touching. Around them the night cooled as they sat quietly together.

狐

The deep dark of the forest was fading when the pavilion began to empty of guests. Kaede-dono's palanquin set off down the mountain, and *ayakashi* dispersed through the trees, Midorikawa-dono's first audience finished. He had not come this way for some time, and there was much to say and do.

"Ichirou, Mataichirou," called Midorikawa, "come here."

They approached, knelt, bowed. Tsurugu watched them, in wonderment of seeing the twins so wholly correct. Even when their comportment was perfect in the human world, there was always an intangible sense of play and playacting, a game they were enjoying, but here they were correct for form's sake.

"Rise; there is no need to be so formal now that we are among ourselves," Midorikawa-dono said, his voice soft and dark. He had a voice to match Kaede's, Tsurugu realized. Both were resonant, musical, powerful without effort or menace.

The brothers sat upright, their faces composed in twin expressions of attentive interest. *"Konbanwa, chichi-ue,"* Genji offered. "Your journey was uneventful?"

There were a few who might make the *kyuubi*'s journey

unpleasant, but most of those would have no reason. "Very pleasant, thank you."

"I trust *haha-ue* is well?" Kaworu asked.

"Your mother sends her love," Midorikawa answered. "Perhaps you will see her soon."

This interested the brothers. "She will come here? Or we will accompany you home?"

"We will speak on that later," Midorikawa said with easy dismissal. "Now tell me how you have been progressing under Kaede-dono. Are you prepared to give me a demonstration?"

There was the slightest of tensions as the brothers caught their breaths and passed into a practiced recovery almost at once. "At your pleasure, *chichi-ue*."

It was late, but *kitsune* were not bound to day and night as humans were. Midorikawa turned to catch another's eye. "I leave them to you, Toyotsune-sama."

Toyotsune bowed to the *kyuubi* and then faced the brothers. "Let us start with your *kata*."

Genji and Kaworu performed their practiced movements for Toyotsune's critical eye, but it was Midorikawa's approval they hoped to win, Tsurugu knew. They stepped, reached, bent, twisted, punched, kicked, leapt through their *taijutsu*, moving together and then in complementary motions, their defenses and attacks overlapping as a single multi-limbed unit. They were almost entrancing to watch.

Toyotsune, however, did not look impressed. When the twins had finished and bowed, chests heaving, the *taijutsu* master nodded and frowned. "You have been practicing regularly?"

"As often as we could get away," Kaworu answered breathlessly. He coughed. "We could not draw attention, but it has been pretty regular, and nearly daily in the last weeks."

Toyotsune's mouth twitched to one side. "Then one

might think you would be in better condition, Akitane-kun."

"*Ani-ue* is recovering from the water in his lungs," Genji offered in protest. "If he had not trained so well before, he wouldn't be so able even after nearly drowning."

"Is that so, Taneaki-kun?" Toyotsune smiled in slow anticipation. "Then you with your hale and hearty lungs will be able to show us the next exercises yourself?"

Genji, still panting, stiffened a little and then bowed. "Of course, Toyotsune-sensei."

Tsurugu sighed to himself. Genji had a valid point and had only spoken in defense of his brother, but he could have chosen his words more carefully. It was unlikely this extra *kata* would do much good as discipline, but neither would it harm him.

His brother — Mataichirou to family and intimates, Akitane to the *youkai* court, and Kaworu to the humans who needed a name to amuse and misdirect them — took a seat between Tsurugu and Midorikawa. Midorikawa's heirs were too valuable to risk letting their names fall into human hands, so while they were with Kaede-dono, they used neither their *zokumyou*, their number names, nor their *nanori*, their adult names. It was yet another game for them.

Akitane — it was difficult for Tsurugu to think of him as anything but Kaworu after so long — was still breathing hard and occasionally coughing. Tsurugu reflected that it might be good to send him to Kaede-dono for something to help clear his lungs. Kaede-dono was the wife of a powerful *daimyou*, but she had been a medicine-seller when Tsurugu first met her.

Midorikawa no Kurou Akimasa, the nine-tailed golden lord, looked unhappy as Genji moved through his routine, glancing from one of his sons to the other. Tsurugu, watching, nodded slowly. It did seem wrong to see them apart, instead of performing together as always. Genji — Ichirou — did well and finished strong, but somehow he looked only half himself as he stood alone.

Midorikawa sighed, and Genji moved his head as if he wanted to twitch the ear he didn't have. But Midorikawa wasn't disappointed in his son's performance, Tsurugu guessed; he was wondering how he would eventually face the question of inheritance. Already it felt wrong to see one brother standing alone.

CHAPTER SEVENTEEN

MIDDAY sunlight dappled the wooden decking where the *kyuubi* waited. "Come and sit, Tsurugu-sama," invited Midorikawa-dono amiably. "I am anxious to hear from you, now that we have some time of our own."

Tsurugu seated himself beside the *kyuubi*. "Thank you, *tono*. It is good to sit with you again."

"And you, my friend. These few days have been too full of business. You have been well here?"

It was not the polite inquiry it seemed. "Mostly, *tono*."

Midorikawa's eyes dropped significantly to Tsurugu's shoulder. The *kyuubi* missed little. "So I noticed. What was that?"

"Things have been unquiet, and I have been maintaining a *kekkai* about the house. I went out to meet a few *youkai* I did not want coming any nearer. That was one of them."

"I hope you came out the better."

"I came out, as you say. That was better." Tsurugu

smiled grimly.

Midorikawa shifted into his handsome human form as a smaller creature brought refreshment. *Sake* was better sipped than lapped. Tsurugu followed.

"And that is the worst you've had here?" Midorikawa gave him a penetrating gaze.

Tsurugu took a slow breath. "I killed a man. A friend."

Midorikawa looked across the illusion-draped shrine and sipped his liquor. "You would not do such a thing lightly."

"He knew."

Midorikawa raised an eyebrow. "About you?"

"About me, and about Kaede-dono, Hanae-san, Ichirou and Mataichirou.... He knew all of us, and he would not be dissuaded." He looked at Midorikawa and saw the unspoken question. "He told no one. And the twins were invaluable in their help."

Midorikawa looked across the shrine again. "I am glad to hear it — that they were useful, I mean. Not that you were brought to killing a man." He sipped. "I am sorry."

Tsurugu nodded.

"I trust whatever decisions you make here," said Midorikawa, his eyes finding Tsurugu's. "That is why you are here with them."

Tsurugu nodded again. "I am... very aware of the trust you have placed in me, *tono.*"

It pleased Midorikawa to aid Kaede-dono here, but it was not wholly in obligation for the favor she had once done him. The *kyuubi* worked for his own ends. When the medicine-seller's daughter had wanted to come to Naka-dono, Midorikawa had seen an opportunity to both repay her favor and to conceal his sons, with Tsurugu set to watch them all.

"I'm very glad I have someone such as you to whom I can entrust them," the *kyuubi* said, "and on whom I can depend to guard and support our friend Kaede-dono."

Tsurugu resented the betraying warmth of his human form. His fox shape would have shown no traitor blush. "I know how you wish to preserve her."

"Her, and her position. Her place with the *daimyou* is as convenient for my purposes as for hers — though not, perhaps, for all others."

Now Tsurugu knew his flesh was burning. "She is devoted to him."

Midorikawa-dono had mercy and changed the subject. "And my sons were safely away from other eyes. You wanted to speak with me before they joined us?"

"Yes, *tono*, though I'm afraid I'll have little time for it. I saw them talking with Takeda-san only a moment ago. They're very prompt for you." Tsurugu frowned to himself, trying to condense all he'd carefully prepared into a few hurried phrases. "And that is just it — I mean, your good opinion is very important to them."

Midorikawa raised an eyebrow. "Isn't that as it should be?"

"Of course they respect their father and lord. But — they are very aware of your every opinion, every disappointment or frustration."

Midorikawa frowned in confusion and then looked startled. "Are you saying — you think they are afraid of me?"

"Not afraid. They respect you, certainly — but they are not wholly themselves around you. Not that this is necessarily bad," he added with a wry smile. "But I fear my lord does not see them as they truly are. It will make your task more difficult."

"My task is already difficult enough," he grumbled.

"What is it?" asked Kaworu, entering and bowing as he spoke. "What's wrong?"

"Your manners." Midorikawa gave him a significant

look.

Kaworu bowed again, more properly this time. "I'm sorry, *chichi-ue*. I only heard that you were disturbed."

Midorikawa sighed. "Mataichiro's great heart leads him to overstep," he commented to Tsurugu, and Kaworu looked as if he were trying to decide whether he should apologize for this trait. "Where is your brother?"

"Just here; he comes."

True to his word, Genji entered and bowed. "Good afternoon, *chichi-ue*, Tsurugu-sama."

"Come, our meal is prepared."

A few small *youkai* served the food and then left them to eat and talk alone. Tsurugu could see the twins' agitation growing, as they wondered why they had been brought to this private meal, but they held themselves in check and behaved with impeccable manners.

Midorikawa-dono finally ended the waiting. "Mataichiro," he said over a piece of fish, "who is the girl and why did you fight the *kappa* for her?"

Kaworu coughed in surprise and adjusted his eating sticks. "She is a servant in the *daimyou*'s house," he answered, his voice light. "She serves Kaede-dono now."

Midorikawa lifted his eyes and looked at his son. "And?"

"And?"

"And why did you fight the *kappa* for her?"

Kaworu's eyes shifted. "I'm not entirely certain," he answered, considering. "I'd helped her after she found trouble with the other servants — they thought she was *kitsune-tsuki* or *kitsune-mochi*, and they beat and chased her into the woods. I took food to her. I — I suppose it seemed natural to help her again."

Midorikawa looked to Tsurugu. "They still look for a *kitsune-mochi*?"

Tsurugu shook his head. "Many of the servants are superstitious, but they are suspicious of nothing in particular," he answered. "The only danger was that we've already discussed, and it is done."

Midorikawa nodded and looked back to Kaworu. "And why did you help her?"

Kaworu was visibly challenged by the question. "Why shouldn't I? She suffered because of us — not directly, we hadn't done the things she was blamed for, and of course she's neither *kitsune-tsuki* nor *kitsune-mochi*, but people thought of us as they hurt her. And it was in my power to help her. So I did. Was that wrong?"

Midorikawa smiled crookedly. "That remains to be seen. Are you fond of this girl?"

Kaworu looked accusingly at Tsurugu. "I have done nothing to endanger—"

"Never mind," Midorikawa interrupted, gesturing dismissively. "Of course you are, or you wouldn't have risked fighting a *kappa* in water." He looked intently at Kaworu. "That, by the way, was a very stupid, but very bold, thing."

Kaworu wasn't certain how to respond. "I didn't think, I only—"

"It's obvious you didn't think." Midorikawa sighed and looked at Genji, who was watching intently, a bit worried. "As I said before, you have great heart, but it can rule your mind. This is a splendid trait for many roles — a priest, perhaps, or a warrior. It is not, however, the best trait for a ruler."

The twins went very still. Genji opened his mouth slightly, as if he wanted to speak but couldn't quite bring himself to do so.

"And so, I think it will have to be Ichirou." Midorikawa glanced from one to the other. "Ichirou will return with me and begin learning statecraft."

Genji's eyes widened, and he looked as if he couldn't say anything at all.

Kaworu found his voice more quickly. "And I?" he asked, his voice nearly steady. "I will come with you and—"

"No," Midorikawa said softly, "you will stay here and train to support your brother. You will study with Tsurugu-sama and continue to assist Kaede-dono."

Kaworu's expression slid from worry to near-panic. "Here?" he repeated. "But I—"

"You will have much to learn to aid him."

"But I should come with—"

"I have made my decision," snapped Midorikawa, teeth flashing in his human face. "Do you require me to repeat myself?"

Kaworu flinched. Genji shook his head and managed, "No, *chichi-ue.*"

"Good." Midorikawa looked at Kaworu. "You'll have your human girl, at least."

Tsurugu frowned to himself. Midorikawa-dono had meant well, but that was poorly played. Now Kaworu would be conflicted over Murame as well.

"We leave tonight," Midorikawa said to Genji, "so prepare as you need." He rose from the table, and the others followed. "I will see you both later this evening."

Tsurugu considered it was better to follow Midorikawa-dono out and leave the brothers to themselves. They had farewells to say, and it would not be easy.

CHAPTER EIGHTEEN

TSURUGU no Kiyomori sat still, looking out over the vivid green of the hills. Wind tugged at his bound hair, but he ignored it, remaining motionless. Below him, he could see the village and the ribbon of road that snaked through empty fields and on to the *daimyou*'s great house.

Kaworu had gone missing that morning. Tsurugu had thought to collect Kaworu early and occupy him for the first days of his brother's absence, but shortly after dawn he was already too late. He had heard Jirou complaining as he neared their quarters. "Stupid boy! Shirking again!"

"He did lose his twin yesterday," someone put in reasonably. "He might be off grieving."

"Grieve he may, but when his chores are done," grumbled Jirou. "I don't care if he sobs while he scrubs." But then he fell quiet, which was as good as an apology from him.

For a moment Tsurugu worried — had Kaworu tried to follow Midorikawa-dono's retinue? But he had called upon his natural and supernatural senses, and he had tracked Kaworu to the hills. He had not bothered to conceal his path.

Tsurugu climbed the mountain slope behind the village, where wood was frequently cut and there were wide patches of open ground among the sheltering growth. He did not call; if Kaworu were capable of answering, he would not have fled here. Instead, he sat, and he waited.

Gradually he became aware of a slow movement behind him. He kept still, his eyes on the horizon. A moment later, a pale young fox crept beside him, belly to the ground, chin pressed low as if it cowered or groveled. Tsurugu did not move.

The pale fox flattened into the waving grass and stayed. Tsurugu exhaled slowly, as if the fox could be frightened with a sudden breath, and carefully extended an arm to rest his hand lightly upon its quivering withers.

The fox flinched but remained where it crouched. Tsurugu left his hand there, waiting. After what seemed a long, long time, there was a subtle movement and then Kaworu bent shivering beneath Tsurugu's hand. "Kiyomori-sama," he wept. "He's gone."

"I know," answered Tsurugu softly. "I know."

"I couldn't — all night — I've never been without him." Kaworu rocked back and drew his knees to his chest. "And it's foolish to feel that way — I'm not a kit, to crawl behind my mother and litter — but I miss him already."

Tsurugu nodded. "Of course."

"I should have gone. I don't mind that he was — we've always known only one of us could succeed *chichi-ue*. But I should have gone with them." Kaworu rubbed at his face. "I hate human tears. They are inconvenient and shameful." He sniffed. "But...."

But it does feel better to weep as a human than to hold one's sorrow as a fox, Tsurugu completed silently. He wrapped his arm about Kaworu's shoulders and sat still.

狐

Murame slid the door open and, still on her knees, saw Tsurugu-sama in counsel with Kaede-dono. Kaede was not behind her screen, but conversed openly with the *onmyouji*.

So it had been the first day she had come to the *okugata-sama*, only she had been too overwhelmed to notice it at the time. While Kaede-dono was shielded from all other men in the house but the *daimyou*, she occasionally met face to face with the *onmyouji*. Why was that? Did his art require him to see her truly?

They couldn't be lovers, Murame had dismissed after a brief speculation, or they would use masks and more romantic subterfuge. This was more... business-like.

"I have brought tea, Kaede-dono. I will bring another cup for the *onmyouji-sama*."

"No, I'm just going," he said.

Kaede nodded and spoke to Tsurugu-sama. "He'll be all right, then?"

"With time, and something to occupy him."

They spoke around the edge of something, and Murame couldn't help but look at them curiously as she placed the tea table.

Kaede kindly obliged her. "One of the servants," she said gently, "was taken yesterday by the *kappa*."

Murame gasped, in surprise and remembered terror. She looked at Tsurugu-sama and pressed herself forward to the floor. "I have not spoken of it, as my lady bade me, but I must thank you for saving me that night." She rose and swallowed. "Did you rescue him as you did me?"

Tsurugu shook his head slowly. "No, he was lost."

Her stomach clenched. "But — but you said just now he would recover!"

"That was his brother," Kaede corrected, not

unsympathetically. "It was one of the twins."

"Oh," Murame breathed. "How sad — even more so, I mean. To lose a brother, and a twin."

"Do you know them?" Tsurugu asked.

"No, not at all, only that they were in the house." She swallowed. "I — I was only thinking of the *kappa*, and — me. I'm sorry."

"Don't apologize for your fear, Murame," said Kaede gently. "It is after all well-founded, and we are grateful you are still with us. Now let us finish here, and then we will have our lesson after."

"Yes, Kaede-dono. I'll bring the medicine box." It was unbelievable that the *okugata-sama* would know and teach medicine, but so much that was unbelievable had come to Murame lately, she no longer lost time wondering at it.

She retreated from the room — at least she had won Kaede-dono's trust, to be permitted to see her meeting freely with the *onmyouji* — and went to fetch the medicine box.

CHAPTER NINETEEN

"KIYOMORI-SAMA," said Kaworu, "teach me illusions."

Tsurugu did not pause in his measured placement of the colored *tama*. "Illusions?"

"I am no *onmyouji*," Kaworu said, "but I am *kitsune*. I should be able to make illusions before I can work *onmyoudou*. Teach me, please."

Tsurugu smiled. "I can teach you *onmyoudou*—"

"You can try," interrupted Kaworu. He sighed.

"You're making progress." Tsurugu straightened the Water *tama*. "As I was saying, I can teach you *onmyoudou*, but I cannot teach you to be a *kitsune*. That comes with practice and growth."

"You mean age." Kaworu tipped onto his back, staring into the sky. "So there's nothing I can do."

"That is not quite true." Tsurugu sat back and eyed the young man opposite him. "If you wait to gain skill before you practice, you will die unpracticed and unskilled."

"You speak like a sage," grumbled Kaworu, but he sat

upright. "All right, then. How do I practice?"

Tsurugu closed his eyes and reminded himself Kaworu was in a kind of grief and required patient handling. "You use illusion every day," he said. "Every human in the *daimyou*'s house sees not a fox, but a young man in servant's clothing."

Kaworu rolled his eyes. "Hanae-san can do that, and she isn't the *kyuubi*'s young."

"Enough of that. Brooding will not bring skill any faster, but it may risk your welfare when I tire of it."

Kaworu hesitated and took a breath. "Yes, but — you understand what I mean. I can make myself human, but I cannot make myself *any* human. No one has ever mistaken me for someone else, and it is our signature, what we are most known to do." He paused and frowned. "Can you take someone's form, Kiyomori-sama? I've never seen it."

"Yes, of course," said Tsurugu, "but I do not need to."

"Still, I would like to be able to do it. It is humiliating to hear stories of foxes met on the road, pretending to be people the travelers knew, and to know I can't even do such a thing."

"Very well," Tsurugu said with a sigh, "one try."

Kaworu brightened. "You'll help me?"

"Yes. Now, sit properly."

Kaworu straightened on his knees, balancing himself, and set his hands on his thighs. He took several slow, focused breaths, and as Tsurugu watched he grew still.

"Now, close your eyes, and draw your breath to the base of your ribcage. Feel the energy there. Still the rest of your body, and focus your *ki* entirely on that point."

Kaworu was absolutely quiet outside of the gentle movement of his abdomen as he breathed.

"When your focus is complete, hold that balance stable and we will add the new illusion. Are you ready?"

Kaworu breathed four more times, perfectly cadenced,

and then nodded once, as if he could not spare the concentration for more.

"Excellent," said Tsurugu. "Now, take all of that energy, and carefully bring it from your ribs to the top of your head. Concentrate on reshaping your form. Think of transforming yourself, of becoming another, of looking exactly like your twin brother."

Kaworu's concentration cracked like frail ice and he snorted even as he clasped a hand to his abdomen, as if hoping to stem the spill of *ki*. He opened his eyes and gave Tsurugu an amused and irritated glare. "That was hardly fair."

"We are *kitsune*. We do not hold to fair." Tsurugu began tracing lines around the *tama*. "And you should not complain. Look how well you did in your first attempt? Why, I'd wager Jirou wouldn't even know you apart."

Kaworu sighed and rolled back to sit cross-legged. "Is any of that accurate?"

"It is one way of doing it, yes. You will want to practice. But don't expect to accomplish a full change soon, so be sure to practice well out of sight." He finished sketching lines and straightened. "And now, the insulting cycle. Wood controls Metal, Metal controls Fire, Fire controls Water, Water controls Earth, and Earth controls Wood."

狐

The months passed far more quickly and more comfortably in Naka no Yoritomo's warm household than they would have in the dilapidated hut. Murame kept within Kaede-dono's chambers as much as possible, reluctant to return to the common areas where she could be accosted by the other servants. They knew her again now, but they largely ignored her, which contented Murame. The *okugata-sama* was teaching her medicine, and one day, she would have the power to help those who had once tormented her — or to refuse them. She hadn't quite decided which would be more appropriate.

The sun broke early and bright this day, signaling the imminence of spring. Blossoms would come soon, and blossom-viewing events, and spring cleaning. Still, the promise of warmer weather was welcome.

"Murame-san," someone hailed her.

She turned and bowed toward the polished boards. "*Onmyouji-sama*." He often greeted her, and he was more kind than he should have been.

"Will you come down with me? A storyteller has come today, and we should have entertainment tonight."

"Stories?" She hesitated. "I have had enough of the fantastic, *onmyouji-sama*."

He laughed. "If it comes to that, I have enough experience with *ayakashi* and *mononoke* to put any storyteller to shame, but why not listen, anyway? Come, it will be a good evening."

And so she went with him, staying close to his side as they entered the servants' area. A few glanced in their direction but somehow did not seem to note her. She breathed more easily. She was old fun, nearly forgotten, and the *onmyouji* was a cloak of protection in himself. She seated herself comfortably beside him and tucked her legs close, surprised to find herself anxious for the stories.

The storyteller set his hands on his knees and looked around him. "What would you hear?"

"No *youkai*," growled a man up front. "Too much of that already."

"Oh?" The storyteller sat forward, anxious for news or a new tale. "What of *youkai*?"

"Nothing now," another said, rolling his eyes at the first. "The *onmyouji* killed the *kappa*, and it's been quiet since."

"Your *onmyouji* killed a *kappa*?" The storyteller looked around the crowded room. Oddly, no one pointed out Tsurugu in the rear corner, even when glancing toward their corner. "That is very interesting. *Kappa* are skilled healers and bone-setters, if won to one's aid."

"Yes, but more often they're devourers," answered a woman sharply. "It had eaten a servant boy. One of the *oyakata-sama*'s favorites, too. He was attending the *onmyouji*, and then, snap! He was gone. And the *onmyouji* worked a great spell over the water and he broke the *kappa* into a hundred pieces."

Murame felt cold, and beside her Tsurugu made a low sound of amusement. "This storyteller had best be careful, or he will lose his trade to her."

The storyteller seemed to sense this as well. He straightened and, without preamble, began a tale of romance and battle on the mainland. It was a heady story, more suited for the *daimyou*'s party than a room of servants, but it was wholly different from the argument over the *kappa*. The teller kept the tale short, holding his audience, and his voice rose and fell in sweeping drama as he described the tragic and noble death of a hero and the achingly beautiful woman who died for grief and his love.

The tale ended, and the listeners stirred and nodded their approval. The storyteller began another tale that at first seemed to be about another noble warrior but soon included a vengeful *yuurei*. Murame shivered and shifted closer to Tsurugu for unconscious protection. The story ended well, with the successful exorcism of the *yuurei*, and the storyteller paused for a drink.

"Would you like to hear of a *kitsune*?" he asked, wiping his lips. "And what comes of lying with one?"

Murame stiffened as the audience cheered approval. She had spent the night beside a *kitsune* in man-form. He had not touched her, and she still did not quite understand it.

"Once, there was a scholar," the storyteller began, "a brilliant man who loved his books and scrolls. He lived alone and spent all his time in his research. Then one day a student came to him, a handsome young man, and they began to study together.

"And as they studied, the scholar began to regard the young man with a closer and keener eye" — the storyteller's ribald expression made his audience laugh — "and he took the young man to his bed.

"Now, this went on each night, as the scholar was very fond of the handsome young man and he had spent all of his time until now with only his books. But very soon the scholar fell ill, and he ceased studying as he lay in his bed, and his only joy was when the young man came to him.

"The young man begged to be released, but the scholar refused, claiming their bed-play was all that remained to him, and as he was clearly declining, he wished the young man to stay until his death."

The storyteller took an air of gleeful anticipation. "And then, the young man came to the scholar, and he said, My lord, I am bound as your student to tell you, I am the reason you are ill. It is your relations with me which are sickening you, for I am a *kitsune*, and by our acts I am stealing your life."

Murame's stomach caught and twisted.

"I will go now, said the student, and you will recover. And he did, and within days the scholar's health began to return. And he regained all that he had been — only he did not take a handsome student ever again."

Was it true? If the fox-man had taken her, would he have sickened her as well as broken her? Murame's fists clenched and her nails bit into her skin.

Randy jokes were being traded by the laughing crowd,

but the *onmyouji*'s voice rose above all. "Tell us the tale of the fox-wife, now, if you please."

The storyteller looked about to find Tsurugu. "Ah! I hadn't seen you there. But certainly, for it's a lovely story." The room quieted once more.

"There was once a man who met a beautiful young woman on the road. She had no family, but she was lovely and well-mannered, and so he married her and brought her to his home. They lived together for many years, and she bore him three sons and three daughters.

"One day, as they sat down to eat, a dog ran in from the village and began barking at his wife. She screamed and then, as the dog rushed at her, she changed suddenly into a fox and fled. The man realized that his wife had always been a fox-woman and that he had been deceived.

"The man drove away the dog and then walked in the direction she had fled. He did not see her, but he called out to the forest, 'You are a fox, and you have deceived me. But you are my wife, and the mother of my children, and I love you. Please return to me, and you will always be welcome.'

"That evening, a fox came into his room, and while he watched, it rose and became his wife. He welcomed her, and she slept in his arms. The next morning, she rose and departed as a fox again. And every night thereafter, she came to him, and their love continued ever."

Murame hugged herself and looked at her knees. So *kitsune* did not always kill their partners. What made the difference? And — how had the *onmyouji* known her thoughts?

He glanced down at her, again seemingly aware of her unspoken question. "Are you finished here?"

She nodded, sensing he might speak to her if they left. They rose, and she followed him out of the storytelling room as the assembly called for another story.

In the dark, on the wooden *sunoko* that ran the length of the house, Tsurugu paused to look at the moon. There was no one else near, and Murame guessed this was the opportunity he offered her. *"Onmyouji-sama...."*

"Yes?"

"Late last autumn — when you came to where I was hiding, and you took the *kitsune*...."

"Yes?"

"I — I had not — he had not touched me."

He looked at her and raised an eyebrow. "Did you wish to? They can be very attractive."

"No!" Murame answered, and she saw from his quick regret that he had only meant to tease her, forgetting. Ashamed, she quickly continued, "No, he only brought me some food and things, that's all. But — the stories — what makes a *kitsune* dangerous? If he had.... Is it the males which take the life?"

Tsurugu sighed. "No, not that. Think on those two stories — aside from their sexes, what else was different in them?"

Murame frowned and clenched her fists, afraid of giving the wrong answer. "The fox-woman bore him children. And — and he loved her."

Tsurugu nodded. "Love is the balm which soothes pairing with a spirit creature. Most *youkai* have no great love for humans, nor humans for them, but a few do form lasting attachments — and if they love one another, then neither is harmed."

She thought. "They say Abe no Seimei was the son of a man and his *kitsune* wife."

"So they say. And look what a mighty *onmyouji* he was, with such a blend of blood."

Murame drew a fingernail along the railing. "And if they do not love?"

"Then it is dangerous to bed a *youkai*. Sometimes very dangerous." Tsurugu looked at her. "Do you understand?"

She nodded. "If he had.... He might have hurt me, isolated in that hut." She frowned. "But he didn't — the one time he took a human form, he assured me he wouldn't touch me. Does that mean... was he being careful of me?"

Tsurugu laughed. "Do not try too hard to guess the minds of *kitsune*, Murame-chan. They are mischievous tricksters at best."

She forced a little laugh. "I suppose so. Thank you for answering my questions, *onmyouji-sama*."

But in her bed that night, she remembered again the fox-man's whispered reassurances while she recoiled in fear. No tale had ever featured the *kitsune* soothing its victim in place of seduction or trickery. Why had her *kitsune* been different?

And why did she think of him as her *kitsune*?

CHAPTER TWENTY

"ITADAKIMASU."

"Itadakimasu."

With the ritual phrase, they began eating. The *yamabushi*, or mountain priest, beamed as he lifted the cup of tea to his lips and sipped loudly. Across the table, his tall companion scowled and slurped a mouthful of *sake* from his own dish. "You ought to change your guise," the taller man suggested. "Monks aren't usually seen eating meat." He lifted a lump of rare meat and swallowed it without chewing.

The *yamabushi* placed a protective hand on the staff beside him. "But how will I carry my *shakujou?*"

"Hide it."

The inn's landlord came to kneel beside their table and, with a dubious glance at the monk, inquired if the meal pleased them.

"Your meal more than your town." The taller traveler frowned. "I was hoping to find work here, but it's unseemly quiet."

"It is a very quiet town, yes."

"Seems there'd at least be some brats running through the streets, making noise. Or are all your kids too well-bred for games?"

"No! That is, there aren't many children in the streets, you're right." He looked at the *yamabushi*. "Would you like more tea?"

"Yes, thank you." The *yamabushi* watched him pour. "Tell me, what troubles the children? If they're ill, I might help. I have some experience treating the ailments of the young."

The owner glanced between the two men, and then looked around the empty restaurant. "You cannot help them once they are gone." He took a breath. "In the last year, seven children have disappeared. Grown men and women, too. There are some who say a monster in the forest spirits them away. *Kamikakushii.* Of course," he added with an emphatic thump of the teapot, "I don't believe in such nonsense."

The tall man and the *yamabushi* exchanged a tired glance. "Well, we'll look elsewhere for work, then." He downed the last mouthful of *sake* and nodded vaguely to the proprietor. *"Gochisousamadeshita."*

He rose to leave, and as the monk began to count out coins onto the table, the tall man slipped a wooden staff through his *himo*.

The proprietor frowned from the weapon to his customer. "You have been in the mountains a long time?"

The tall man smiled a guileless smile. "Many years now." He turned to his companion. "Are you ready?"

The proprietor watched the two men as they went, and only after they began walking toward the dense forest at the edge of the village did he turn back to collect his money. Among the coins scattered on the smooth wood lay a single black feather.

狐

"For an ascetic, you carry much gold."

The monk harrumphed and shrugged his shoulders several times, as if adjusting a cloak. "One of us should pay for what we take."

The tall man shrugged. "I repay my debts in another way." He glanced at the monk. "But you didn't give only money. You left him a charm, didn't you?"

"He gave us information." He watched his tall companion snatch a clumsy handful of blossoms from a tree and begin dropping the petals, one by one, as they walked. "And besides, you have terrible manners."

The tall man was no longer listening, and the monk followed his companion's gaze to a richly-decorated palanquin advancing down the narrow road. As the tall man watched its approach, he drew the staff from his *himo* and leaned upon it as if it were a walking-stick.

The monk stepped out of the way; such a vehicle would not brook interference. His tall companion waited a moment longer before he also moved to the side, letting the staff drag a line through the dust in front of him.

As the palanquin rolled past, a loud crack splintered the quiet. The near wheel sagged and crunched into the dirt. The curtains pitched as the vehicle pitched forward, and the two men caught a tantalizing glimpse of the veiled figure inside as she clutched at the side.

"What has happened?" The lady's voice was silk and summer rain, captivating and demure. She caught one corner of the curtain with a painted fan, peering out without revealing herself.

A servant bowed deeply. "The wheel has collapsed, Fujiko-hime."

"Fix it at once."

"Yes, Fujiko-hime — only, we will need materials and tools, and it will take some time...."

The tall man stepped forward and, ignoring the servant's disdainful glare, bowed low. "Please, *hime-sama*, allow this humble one to assist. I can repair the wheel in less time than it would take my lady to describe this plum blossom." His fingers dwarfed the pale flower he proffered.

The lady's servant cursed and moved to strike the big man for his insolence, but he froze at the sound of a delighted laugh from within the palanquin.

"Such cleverness must not be punished! I will accept his offer. If he can repair the wheel before I compose a poem on this flower, he will be my guest this evening." The servant sputtered a protest, but she spoke over him without pause. "However, if he cannot do as he brags, then he will be flogged. Present the blossom to me."

The servant lifted the flower on a fan to her. The tall man bent and braced his shoulder against the frame. His muscles bulged, and a moment later he heaved the palanquin upright. His broad shoulders obscured what he did — yet when he straightened a moment later, the wheel was whole again.

When informed, Fujiko-hime only laughed in her musical voice. "Of course he has done what he said — for how could I capture in poetry such a perfect bloom, had I all the time I could desire?"

狐

They followed the palanquin to the lady's home, which lay deep into the thick wood surrounding the village. The tall man looked about them as they approached, eying the walls and long *rou* extending into the darkness. "Was such a structure here before?"

The monk answered with an emphatic negative rather

unsuited for a holy man. "Nothing such as this, not in the entire mountain. Can you not feel the *you-ki* saturating this place?"

The tall man licked his jagged teeth, tasting the dark current flowing through the shadows. "How can they not know what lives here?"

"They are ignorant in the way of things which matter." The monk sniffed. "After all, it is nonsense, as you heard."

"Come, my bold speaker and wheel-mender, and his friend," called the voice from the palanquin. "Go with my servants into the *tai no ya*, where you will be given clothing more suitable for dining."

Deferential servants tried to dress them, but the men pushed their hands away and grumbled. In the end, the tall man wore new clothing but kept his staff, conveniently short, tucked into his *himo*. The *yamabushi* was washed and given a new *happi* over his monk's garb.

They were led to another room, where they knelt on luxurious *tatami*. Fish and pickled vegetables were already placed for them on low *zen*.

"*Itadakimasu,*" the *yamabushi* said, taking his eating sticks.

The lady was behind a painted screen. "Go ahead, enjoy yourselves," she said. "Such brave talk must be rewarded."

The *yamabushi* wrinkled his nose; the *daikon* were pickled a little too strongly. "We thank you for your hospitality," he said. "Have you always lived here?"

"Not always," she said. "But I have made it my home."

"And you are here alone?" asked the tall man. "No husband?"

She laughed, and it was half-purr. "No husband. Does my brave speaker mean to speak more bravely? You would need a fine poem indeed to win your way toward this dais."

The tall man swallowed half a fish. "I only mean it is a

pity you have no one to share your meals, when they are so delicious."

"I am glad you find it pleasing."

"Very." The other half of the fish disappeared.

The *yamabushi* forced himself to swallow another piece of vegetable. The tall man glanced at him, and he sighed and teased a bit of fish free with his eating sticks.

"Some *sake*, I think?" suggested the voice. A servant poured for him.

The *yamabushi* shook his head. "No, I am a monk, as you can see." He touched the *shakujou* lying beside him. "And I do not think I should risk it. I am already too sleepy from this fine meal." He yawned, hastily covering the indiscretion with his fan, and fanned himself briskly.

"Was yours such a long road today?"

"Long enough." The tall man slurped the bowl of *sake* all at once. "That's good."

"What brings you down the road, brave speaker?"

"My friend asked me to travel with him, and I needed fresh work to occupy me."

"And have you found what you sought?"

"I found good *sake* and good company, and that's all a man need ask." He belched. "Looks like I'll be having his share, though."

The *yamabushi* had settled over his *zen* and was snoring softly. The lady, rather than being offended, only laughed. "It seems your journey has been long indeed. Yes, do take another bowl."

But the tall man did not finish the second bowl, as he leaned upon one elbow and then, gradually, slid to the *tatami*.

The servants bolted from the room, closing the *shouji* behind them.

The great lady came from behind the screen, her

movements languid and graceful. Her glossy dark hair dragged across the room, stretching half again her height. She rustled in layered silken robes to where the *yamabushi* lay and looked down on him with a smug little smile. Then she glanced to the tall man opposite him, her smile never changing. She folded her hands and purred.

Neither man shifted. The *yamabushi*'s quiet breathing made a faint counterpart to the purr.

"Itadakimasu." The woman closed her eyes and dipped her torso, almost a bow, and uncoiled into a great cat nearly as large as the woman had been. Lips twitched, showing teeth brightly white against the glossy dark fur, and she made a pleased, arcing pounce at the *yamabushi*.

With a little sound the *yamabushi* twisted away and the cat struck the *zen*, scattering dishes and uneaten food. The cat hissed and sprang away, facing the monk with hair raised and tail erect.

The *yamabushi* backed away, one hand reaching for the *shakujou* as the other held up his fan like some improbable shield. *"Bakeneko."*

The cat's ears flattened further, and then it was a woman again — or half-woman, the shape of a woman with the malevolent gaze of an angry cat. Claws tipped her splayed fingers, and when she spoke her teeth were too sharp. "Not a bold speaker, but clever." She smiled. "But not clever enough to avoid following me into my home."

"This is not your home," said the *yamabushi*. "You have come here but lately. Did you think of who might have a prior claim?"

She did not answer, as she was springing over the tall man's rush. His grasping hands missed her, and they all turned to face one another once more.

"Bakeneko," the tall man repeated. He lurched forward,

his shadow growing unnaturally long. His outline rippled and warped, until it was no longer the figure of a man but of a hulking beast. The fabric of his clothing sagged and became ragged fur. He drew the slim staff, and it bulged and became a bulky club.

"*Oni!*" The woman-cat hissed, and her head swiveled toward the *yamabushi*. "And what are you?"

"If you'd had more care, you might have known before now. As you might have known this is my mountain."

She bounded toward the monk, gleaming claws extended. Mid-air she left the woman form and landed again a great cat. She sprang for the *yamabushi* and he leapt directly into the air. Her claws tore the *tatami*.

With a hiss, the creature swung its head, looking for the monk it should have crushed.

"*Bakeneko!*" The voice was a screech.

The cat looked up and leapt aside just as the dark shape of the *tengu* dove, slashing at her eyes. The cat dodged again and again, spitting rage, but the *tengu* was faster. Beneath a blinding sweep of feathers, the cat screamed and stumbled, rolling across the floor and leaving red.

A low, rumbling chuckle rattled the *shouji*. The *oni* stepped near the writhing cat. With a rustle of feathers, the *tengu* landed opposite him.

"*Itadakimasu,*" said the *oni*.

CHAPTER TWENTY ONE

NAKA no Yoritomo frowned down at the *chokuban*. "An unlucky date."

Tsurugu took his hands from the divining board. "Yes, *tono*. And I am watching the danger from the west, which still has not yet become clear. In short, it appears you should take great care."

The *daimyou* blew out his breath sharply. "I'll be hunting that day, with a fine band of *samurai*. Most of them would not hesitate to heed an *onmyouji*'s warning, but Ayumu-dono will be among them, and...." Naka-dono sighed.

"He is the one who thinks to ally himself to both you and Sanjou no Takeo?" asked Tsurugu.

"The same. And he has been speaking to some of my other men. I can prove nothing yet, and I don't wish to appear arbitrary to those who have been hearing his poison, but when I find a way.... For now, however, I dare not show any weakness before them, even in something so sensible as heeding an *onmyouji*'s caution." He looked again at Tsurugu. "Is the day unlucky for me, or for my house? For Kaede-dono?"

Tsurugu turned the *chokuban* to occupy his hands. "I wish I could say with certainty, *tono*. But I will look again."

"Tell me what you learn. And I will watch Ayumu-dono with particular care."

狐

The road was still empty, but they were coming. In the concealing brush, Ogasawara sat very still, listening intently. Beside him, Hideo shifted his weight, and Ogasawara threw him a warning glance that made the servant freeze in place.

Now two figures came up the road, talking amiably. One, a *yamabushi*, walked with a staff but didn't appear to need it. The other was a big, broad-shouldered man with a shorter staff through the *himo* tied at his waist. Ogasawara smiled silently; this would be difficult, but the benefit could be very rewarding indeed.

It had been the merest luck that he had sensed them coming, a chance spell he had idly worked while waiting for the tea water to heat. Now, though, he had within his grasp the chance to make his first strike toward winning back his honor and position.

"It's just a mad itch," grumbled the big man, pulling one thick arm across his body and reaching futilely behind his shoulder with the other. "It's healing fine."

"Let me see it," said the one with the staff, angling his head to look at the exposed shoulder. He tipped his head oddly, as if his eyes focused differently than normal. "Those were some deep scratches—"

Both of them went rigid at once and then tried to recoil, but their feet did not leave the ground. The big one bellowed a wordless sound of rage, and the other jerked his staff to readiness and scanned for an opponent.

Ogasawara stepped from the forest, smiling cautiously. "Good morning," he said with breezy politeness. "Whom do I have the pleasure of addressing?"

The big man looked down on him and bared his teeth. "We are not so easily caught as that, human."

"To the contrary, it seems you are easily caught after all." Ogasawara gave a little laugh. He couldn't let them see his concern; he had to convince them he was too powerful to withstand. "Now I need only ask."

"Not likely," said the shorter one with the staff, watching him warily.

Ogasawara made a wide pass about them, staying well away from the circle he'd etched in the road dust. Even the smallest disturbance could bring disaster. "There is always a way," he said, "and this is a very remote road. We are not likely to be disturbed."

"We won't give you our names," snarled the big one.

The one which looked like a *yamabushi*, Ogasawara thought, would be the cleverer, and also the weaker. That was the one to keep off-balance and unable to concentrate. Use him as leverage against his stronger friend. "What of fire? Not terribly original, but often terribly effective."

He worked a spell, carefully setting it in place, and checked the restraining circle — still good. He looped a long string of fire in the air and dropped it about the shorter man's neck. "Decide quickly."

The fire jerked inward and wrapped about the man's throat and jaw, licking at face, ears, hair. He screamed and slapped at it, but the arcane flames did not go out. The big man roared and clawed at his companion's neck, but there was nothing to be seized, only incorporeal flame.

The shorter man tried to drop to the ground, but his legs were fixed in position by the circle's spell, and he could only sway above the waist, flailing and screaming.

Panic took the big one — not a panic he would ever feel in battle, facing a threat, but a panic of helplessness before an opponent he could not touch or reach. He turned to Ogasawara. "Stop! Stop this!"

"Your names." Ogasawara was sweating with the strain of holding the two spells, hoping desperately the creatures could not see how dangerously close he was to losing them.

They could not; one was feeling terror for perhaps the first time in his long life, and the other was on fire. "Stop this!"

"Your names!"

"Atsuhide!" the big man bellowed, clutching his burning friend. "I am Atsuhide!"

The flames flickered and faded, and Atsuhide pulled close his stricken friend, moaning in sympathy and fury. Ogasawara panted, his blood pounding in his ears. That had been close; another few seconds and he would have lost the fire or the circle. He swallowed and reinforced the circle. It had nearly failed, and that he could not risk. He had only one name.

"Atsuhide-kun," he said, and the creature turned to look at him, head rotating slowly as if against its will. The name hummed with energy in his mind; it was real. "Good," Ogasawara said. "Now, his name."

The big creature snarled. "You—"

Ogasawara cast the fire again. The smaller man howled in renewed pain and jerked free of his big friend, wrenching from side to side in the imprisoning circle.

"His name," prompted Ogasawara.

"It won't bind him unless he gives it himself!" shouted the big man. "And he cannot while you do this!"

Indeed, he was only screaming incoherently, likely not even hearing Ogasawara's demands. But Ogasawara did not work blindly. "His name!"

"Shigetake!" cried the big man, and Ogasawara let the fire die again. His knees were trembling, but his loose clothes would hide this. Beyond the circle, Hideo was staring white-faced, jaw hanging. So long as he didn't move from his place and distract Ogasawara or disturb the traced circle, all would be well. Ogasawara was nearly done.

This next part was tricky, but it required finesse rather than brute strength like the circle and fire. Ogasawara concentrated and then relaxed the circle for just a heartbeat. The burnt creature, clutching its head and trapped by its own rigid legs, collapsed backward and froze again as the circle's hold flickered.

Ogasawara stepped close to the circle, carefully avoiding the thin drawn line keeping him alive, and looked down at the stricken *youkai*, arched backward and shaking with the strain. Posture mattered in these things. "Your companion is right," he said. "Your name is not binding unless you give it yourself. But having it at all gives me some measure of power, as you know." He stretched out his hand over the burnt man. "Enough to burn all of you now."

The panting creature's eyes widened. The big man roared in rage, but he could not move from the restraining circle. Ogasawara cupped his fingers. "Give me your name, Shigetake-kun. Give it to me from your own lips."

The injured man moaned, and then his cracked and blistered lips opened. "Shigetake *desu*," he whispered.

"Shigetake," repeated Ogasawara, and it rang true in his mind. He smiled, exhausted and relieved and incredibly pleased.

He waved aside the circle, scratching the outermost line with his foot. Hideo gasped and jerked back, but the smaller creature only fell to the ground. Ogasawara felt himself begin to grin. "On your feet, Shigetake-kun," he ordered.

The big man lifted the other, who moved gingerly. His skin was raw and seeping about the neck.

"Now, show me your true forms," Ogasawara ordered.

The big man bared his teeth, and they were jagged and uneven. His shoulders swelled even further until he looked like a human bull on two legs, even to the horns jutting from his skull. He growled his resentment, and the sound was that of a tiger.

"An *oni*," breathed Ogasawara. He had wondered, but he had not guessed it would be such a powerful one. He was glad he had caught the two together, for he would never have held this one if it had not panicked for its friend.

He looked at the friend, whose new long, beak-like nose was scorched raw. He wore a mountain priest's robes, burned away at the top, and his staff was now a priest's *shakujou*. "And a *tengu*. How wonderful."

They glared at him with baleful expressions, and he felt a curiously exhilarating mixture of fear and triumph. They would turn on him if they could — but they could not.

"Go now, and heal," he said imperiously, "so that you will be ready when I call."

The *oni* grunted a snarling assent and took a step.

"Acknowledge me!" Ogasawara demanded shrilly. "Own me as your master."

The *oni*'s eyes flared with dangerous rage.

"Atsuhide-kun," commanded Ogasawara, "acknowledge me."

Atsuhide twitched and then got slowly to the ground, his wide shoulders tight with restrained resentment. His massive teeth ground the words, "You are my master."

Ogasawara's blood ran hot through him, burning with triumph. He reached out and touched a horn, wrapping his fingers about the coarse grain. Atsuhide's breath caught at this fresh indignity, but he knelt beneath it as he must. "And you, Shigetake-kun?"

The *tengu* knelt and bowed, inhibited by his injuries. "I own you as my master, *onmyouji-dono.*"

"Good." Ogasawara gestured. "Now go."

They stepped out of the circle, gave him one final hateful glare, and then vanished as *youkai* could. Ogasawara turned to face Hideo, watching slack-jawed from the ground. "Now you see," he said, exhausted and pleased, "I will recover my place. And the next time you betray me, I'll have that one do the flogging." He jerked his head. "Up, you lazy beast. We have much ground to cover."

Hideo glanced around him and rolled stiffly to his feet. "Where are we going?"

"Now that we are no longer alone, we will go east to Aoida, to the lands of Naka no Yoritomo-dono." Ogasawara turned toward the rising sun, shading his eyes. "I owe his bride a visit."

CHAPTER TWENTY TWO

IT could be observed that Naka no Yoritomo did not like to leave his wife, but given the *onmyouji*'s warning, she might be safer than he would be. He bade Kaede-dono farewell and then, on his way to his horse, he paused beside the *onmyouji*. "I trust my wife's safety to your care, Tsurugu-sama."

"It is an honor I accept with grave consideration, *tono*."

The *daimyou* lowered his voice, looking over Tsurugu's shoulder. "And, nothing more... to know?"

Tsurugu shook his head. "Only the same, the unlucky date."

"That is little help; it could equally mean that I meet my death on this outing or that I will hunt poorly and embarrass myself before these fine *samurai*." He shook his head. "I'll be careful. I'll let the others take the game that day, and I'll stay well behind the archers — and Ayumu-dono." He smiled and made to go.

"Only one thing more, *tono*." Tsurugu swallowed as the *daimyou* turned back. "I saw that you should — be prepared to accept help from an unlikely source."

Naka no Yoritomo raised an eyebrow. "Are you saying it is Sanjou no Takeo-dono who may come to my aid on my unlucky day?"

Tsurugu shook his head. "No, *tono*, not quite so unlikely as that. But be… open-minded."

The *daimyou* laughed. "I will keep that in mind. Watch things here." He went to his horse, spoke with the other *samurai*, and then mounted and rode out the gate.

Tsurugu looked after him, wondering. He had not told all he knew. Even confident in his secret, it would need a strong mind to dare speaking all, and he did not understand it himself. With Tsurugu, Hanae, and Kaworu here, what *kitsune* would aid the *daimyou*?

狐

The shouting woke Kaworu, shocking him out of sleep and nearly into his fox form. It was still fully dark in the servants' quarters, so he simply formed clothes about him as he ran, bolting through the night toward the center house. He had heard Tsurugu's voice among the others, and he could sense an inhuman presence.

Guards crowded the *wataridono* uncertainly, looking up and down, but Kaworu was lean and quick and he slid among them like quicksilver. He could feel it now, a thrumming of energy from near Kaede-dono's chamber. What had happened?

Here the guards were standing close, too crowded to weave through, and Kaworu slipped off the *sunoko*, taking his fox form to race beneath the floor and to the rear of the *wataridono*. He took human form once more and climbed inside the endmost chamber.

Tsurugu did not turn his head, keeping his eyes on the young man with sandy-brown hair before him. "Be still,

Kaworu-kun," he said. "I am much occupied here."

The sandy young man glanced at Kaworu, his dark eyes gleaming. "So, I am not the first to come, I see."

Someday, Kaworu would be strong enough to conceal himself wholly, so that anyone beyond a stupid human wouldn't immediately see him for what he was. Someday. He could think of no retort sharp enough, so he kept quiet and went to sit behind Tsurugu, as if it were respect that held his tongue instead of inadequacy.

The stranger turned back to Tsurugu. His nose was a bit too flat, but he was otherwise pleasant-looking. "I have told you all I know, *onmyouji-sama.*"

"Not all, I think," Tsurugu answered evenly. "What is the name of this man, your master?"

The man shook his head. "I do not know his name, I don't. But he is too thin for his height, gaunt. He sleeps poorly and calls his man-servant Hideo. And he had some lovely prayer beads."

"Had?"

The sandy young man tipped his head to one side and smiled, withdrawing a gleaming set of beads. "They were a trinket for a fortune told. Aren't they pretty?"

"Very. And, why have you told me this? I am quite skilled, I know, but you might not have been caught so easily."

The man bobbed his head. "We have heard that this house uses *kekkai* but does not pursue the *youkai* here. I can see now—" his head and shoulders wove toward Kaworu and then back to Tsurugu, almost snakelike — "that the word among the *youkai* is true, that you will deal fairly with us." His lip curled, baring teeth slightly too long for his human face. "The other, my master, is unlike you."

"And he sent you to thieve and spy here."

"He would have me kill the *okugata-sama* here, if I

could reach her." The man's flat face seemed to stretch, and his teeth sharpened. "He presses us beyond our nature, *onmyouji-sama*. I have no wish to kill a woman who has never done me harm, and the arrogant fool had not thought to specify that I should not be questioned."

Tsurugu nodded. "You are clever and noble, *kawauso-san*."

"And I am unfortunately bound to serve him. But you know his intent, *onmyouji-sama*. Please remember his unwilling servants when you act."

"Of course." Tsurugu raised his hand. "If your master asks, be truthful and say you were intercepted, but say when you were interrogated you told me an attack was planned here for the next new moon."

The sandy young man nodded.

"Now, take your leave." Tsurugu moved his hands, and an indefinable sensation of pressure, notable only in its sudden absence, eased. The young man bowed to Tsurugu and then dropped to the floor, folding into a long, brown shape, and then the river otter ran rippling across the floor and slid outside just as Kaworu had entered.

Tsurugu rose, dusting his knees. "Come, Kaworu-kun. There's little time."

狐

"An attack upon my lord?" Kaede's voice, usually so rich and self-assured, now held a note of sharp worry. A rustle of fabric from behind the screen indicated she had shifted forward.

Miyake Hidetoshi, Naka no Yoritomo's captain, fumed where he sat. "And we can do nothing?"

"Far from nothing," Tsurugu answered. "You can take armed men to join the *tono* and escort him safely home. Two days' hard ride should carry you to him."

"But you said the attack was to be tomorrow," Kaede pressed. "The day you warned him was unlucky."

Kaworu, listening unseen in the corridor, clenched his fists. All they had here — all that Midorikawa-dono had directed them in — was predicated on Kaede-dono being the wife of Naka no Yoritomo.

"We cannot arrive in time," Miyake-san muttered fiercely. "Even my best, at their best, could not cross that terrain so quickly. We would have to ride around the mountain and arrive too late. And this enemy will be watching, certainly, with more agents to withstand us."

"Can you send a *shikigami*, Tsurugu-sama?" asked Kaede tightly.

Tsurugu shook his head with obvious frustration. "Not so far, Kaede-dono. I am sorry."

Someone stirred beside Kaworu, startling him. He had been listening too closely to the conference and had not noticed the figure sliding on her knees beside him. Murame, the maid, only glanced at him with wary eyes and then leaned toward the *shouji* herself, listening.

"What about messengers?" Kaede asked, her voice edged with frustration and worry. "Could men without arms and armor scale the slopes more quickly than warriors? Perhaps evade the watchers? With warning, Yoritomo-dono might protect himself."

"It is very dense growth and difficult terrain," Miyake answered tersely. "We will send men, but it will be nearly impossible."

"Choose your fastest," she said. "If any one saves the *daimyou*'s life, he shall have considerable reward." Her voice caught. "Even if the chance is small — we must try."

Murame turned her head to look at Kaworu, and then she glanced at the floor. She started to speak, but her voice caught. Kaworu felt suddenly too close to her.

She tried again. "Four legs are faster than two."

For a moment he could not respond. He stared, uncertain, as if he did not understand her.

She lifted her head and looked at him. "I'm right, aren't I? It is you? And you can speak, when you like?" She glanced toward the *shouji*. "They need someone quick and unseen. You can save him."

Kaworu blew out his breath and looked at the floor between his knees. If he did not speak, if he did not answer, she might believe herself wrong....

The *shouji* opened, and Tsurugu nearly stumbled over them. Kaworu scrabbled backward, but already the *onmyouji* was glaring. "What are you—"

But Murame flung herself past him in wholly inappropriate fashion, pressing her face to the floor before her mistress. "Forgive me for speaking out of turn," she rushed, stumbling over the words, "but it may be possible to save the *tono.*"

Miyake had gone out the far side of the room, already fetching the fastest *ashiguru* to carry the critical message. Kaede-dono leaned around the screen cautiously. "Yes?"

Murame gulped and kept her face to the floor. "Send the *kitsune.* He will be swift and undetected."

Kaede-dono blinked once, and then she said evenly, "You have kept your eyes well open."

"I did not see at first, not for a long time," Murame said, as if pleading forgiveness. "But you and the *onmyouji* — you must know something together. And there is a *kitsune*, I know. Surely you must know of it, too."

Tsurugu knelt beside her. "You knew I knew of the *kitsune.*"

She nodded to the floor. "And you agreed not to kill him

— which, I see now, if he were known to you, if he serves you, was natural." She gulped again. "But — I am very sorry to speak, but — if you send the *kitsune*, he might reach the *oyakata-sama* before anyone else, and without detection."

"True," said Tsurugu, "except that we know our opponent is taking *youkai* and watching. Kaworu-kun!" He turned. "Can you be swift?"

Kaworu squared his shoulders. "Like the mountain wind."

"And cautious?"

He looked at Kaede-dono's face, streaked with silent tears and, for the first time in his memory, unhappy and desperate. "Not until my warning is safely delivered."

"That will do. You'll have to speak your message; you won't be able to carry anything." Tsurugu took a measured breath. "The *daimyou* is hunting over the northeastern ridge. Riders will be taking the road, but you'll go over the mountain. Be a little cautious — you heard what our enemy is sending?"

Kaworu nodded solemnly. "An *oni*."

"Right. Stay out of sight and move quickly."

"Hai, Tsurugu-sama." Suddenly the room felt very tight and formal, despite the strange and unexpected openness.

Tsurugu nodded. "Then go."

Kaworu turned and started down the stairs at a run. Outside men were assembling, gathering gear and supplies, but he darted through them and made for the far side, where he scaled the tree and leapt the wall. He settled into a rhythmic lope and started for the forest.

CHAPTER TWENTY THREE

THE mountain was not one Kaworu had visited in his leisurely explorations, but all mountains were similar just as all were different. It was a matter of observation to find the streams which made a path through the densest growth, to follow the curve of the immense shoulders into more accessible climbs. Game was plentiful in this remote area, and he paused to breathe while he waited for a small rodent to grow unwary and venture out from beneath a fallen branch. Then he was on his way again, Kaede-dono's urgency ringing through his mind.

The girl Murame had been right — four legs were faster than two, and a compact and agile fox could cover this dense territory far faster than a human. Kaworu slid along the ground, pressed through tightly woven branches, and once squeezed through a rotting log when it was the safest path through a wide thicket of thorny bushes.

The sun rose and slid across the sky, obscured by mountain and trees. Kaworu sometimes slowed to a walk, as he climbed or caught his breath, but he tried to keep a ground-eating jog where he could.

Where would he find Naka no Yoritomo? The far side of the ridge, yes, but that left a great deal of ground to search. If he made good time across the mountain but then failed to find the *daimyou*.....

Twilight came early on the slope, and the sky was darkening by the time Kaworu crested the ridge and began to pick his way downhill. He wanted to stop and rest, to be cautious in the dark, but Kaede's urgency drove him on. He scented for any clue to the *daimyou*'s party — surely so great a gathering of men should stink even to this height — but found nothing.

He considered. Spring hadn't yet greened the upper slopes. Deer would be feeding on the nutritious fresh shoots at the lower elevations, and a hunting party would go where the game would be most concentrated, the low basin to the east. He started downward, putting the last of the light behind him.

He struck a game path after a few hours, following it downward, grateful for the easier passage. Shortly before dawn he paused, drank, and then snatched a groggy squirrel which forgot to scan thoroughly before coming out onto a low branch. He finished the meal and then climbed onto a jutting rock to scan the basin in the first weakly-grey light.

Below and to the east, sheets of brightly-colored fabric fluttered, marking the hunting camps. With an odd rush of simultaneous relief and renewed urgency, Kaworu bounded off the rock and started downhill at a lope.

The grasses grew high as he neared them, and he had to bound into the air occasionally to see his goal. He hoped no one would notice the quick fox leaps, but they were likely tired from the night watch and expecting little trouble at dawn. Finally he paused, crouching, and took his human form, shaping servant's garb around him. Then he pushed toward the *jinmaku* bearing

Naka no Yoritomo's *mon*, or crest.

"Stop there!" barked a man bearing a bow, half-reaching for an arrow. "Who are you?"

Kaworu had not realized how deeply the habit of not speaking to humans had taken him. "I — I bear an urgent message," he panted. "From the *okugata-sama* and Miyake-sama."

The archer scratched his chin with his thumb. "So you say."

"Please let me pass. It is a matter of life and death."

The man looked skeptical. "I don't remember you."

"Does that matter?" burst Kaworu, frustrated with the man's density and being stalled so near to his goal. "I don't know you, either, but I don't question your presence to protect the *oyakata-sama*. Why delay me? The *daimyou* must hear me at once!"

It was the wrong response. The man's face darkened and he whirled his bow down and forward in a vicious strike.

Kaworu didn't wait for it, but dropped to the side and bolted. There were only a few enclosures; he would find Naka no Yoritomo in one of them, if he could stay ahead of the furious archer bellowing after him.

Others were looking now, alerted by the archer's shouts, and they turned suspiciously on him. He angled away from them and then darted back, sprinting with exhausted muscles as they cut to intercept him before he reached the *jinmaku*. Kaworu dove, skimming beneath a pair of outstretched hands, and slid on his chest beneath the cloth walls, immediately rolling to the side as the men poured after him.

There was no evading them now. Hands seized him and jerked him to his feet, pulling at his arms, his hair. He growled before he caught himself and executed a move that dislodged several hands, but there were too many to shake himself free.

"What is this?!"

One of the men drew away and bowed low. "Our most sincere apologies, *tono* — we shall have him removed and—"

"Naka-dono!" Kaworu tore his head away from the man pushing it down. "Kaede-dono sent me!"

"Wait." The *daimyou* held up a hand to freeze the armed men. "I know this one; he serves my wife. If he brings a message from the *okugata-sama*, why was he not brought immediately to me?"

"He said the *daimyou* must hear him," said the archer scornfully. "The *daimyou* must do nothing — if it pleases the *daimyou* to listen, he may honor this wretch with—"

"It is life and death!" cried Kaworu. "Your life is targeted this day! Kaede-dono and Tsurugu-sama have sent me to warn you!"

There was silence for a moment. The archer spoke first, disdain heavy in his voice. "If your wife believed you in danger, she would send Miyake-sama, not some houseboy."

Naka no Yoritomo said quietly, "This is the unlucky date of which Tsurugu-sama warned me, and he instructed me to look for help from an unexpected source — such as a houseboy who does not speak." He turned heavy eyes on Kaworu. "This day, of all days, I will hear this."

He gestured, and Kaworu was released. He stepped forward and knelt, bowing forward. "Tsurugu-sama captured and questioned a *youkai* sent against your wife. She is safe — it never reached her. It told of an attack planned during your hunting trip, this day, when an *oni* will be sent against your camp. Miyake-sama is coming by the road with a company of warriors to escort you safely home, but I was sent ahead to warn you."

Naka no Yoritomo eyed him critically. "You look as if you'd run ahead of a company of soldiers all night. If this is so, what am I to do now? Run ahead of the *oni*?"

"Leave this place. It is an *onmyouji* who sends this against you, and he knows you are here. Go somewhere where he does not easily know to find you. Meet Miyake-sama and return to your home where Tsurugu-sama may defend you."

The *daimyou* nodded. "My men are without equal, but I will not ask them to face an *oni*. Let us fall back for now and wait until our *onmyouji* can identify the one who sent this threat, and then our action shall be swift and effective."

They could never simply do the most sensible thing without specifying they would redeem or avenge or aggrandize themselves in the future, but at least he was doing the sensible thing. Kaworu nodded with pleased relief.

Naka no Yoritomo began issuing orders, and Kaworu was forgotten. Guards had to be organized, explanations had to be made to the hunting *samurai*, camp had to be broken. Kaworu retreated quietly to one side, still catching his breath. He took some water from a pitcher and hoped no one would notice him for a few moments. He was exhausted, now that his urgency was spent, and he didn't want to be pressed into service to take down the *jinmaku*.

He would return with the *daimyou*'s party, and they would all be proud of him. Bold and stupid, perhaps, but he had just saved the life of the *daimyou* and thereby Kaede-dono's position. He grinned to himself. It had been a long night, and he was hungry and fatigued and bruised, but it was worth it.

By some minor miracle he was left alone until they began moving out of the site, and he rose to join the servants following the *samurai*'s horses. The sun was well up now, but it was still early. Dew lay thick around them and birds were singing as the *daimyou*'s party started down to meet Miyake's company. They moved out of the lush site where they had camped and followed a wide path along a shelf, wooded slopes above and steeps below, winding ever downward.

Then the birds went silent.

A great dark shape plunged down the slope above them, bursting from the trees with a roar that seemed to shake the air. Men scrambled, a few screamed in shock or fear, and then the shape landed among them, whipping a great club about it. Men crumpled and were flung to the side as others bolted, leaving their equipment and packs behind. The *oni* lifted its horned head and roared a challenge, scanning the broken line, and then it started toward the horses.

Kaworu ducked and fled to the side, sheltering beneath a bush and shifting in its concealment to his native form — no one would be watching him now. He flattened close to the earth as *ashiguru* rushed to form a wall before the riders, but they didn't have enough time to present a plausible defense before the *oni* smashed though, knocking men and weapons aside. It did not pause to fight or finish them; its target was Naka no Yoritomo, who raised his sword and faced the creature squarely.

The *daimyou*'s horse, however, wanted no part of this fight, and it plunged and shied away and unseated the *daimyou* before bolting with the other horses, some with riders, some without. The *oni* roared and rushed forward.

A *samurai* drove from the side and struck hard with a *naginata*, the weapon's head sliding deep into the *oni*'s flank. The pole whipped from his hands as the *oni* whirled and the man scrambled away. The pole caught against an *ashiguru* and tore the wound, and the creature bellowed again. It swung its club at the *ashiguru* and missed, and then it spun for a moment trying to claw the *naginata* free. After a moment it succeeded, and then it turned back, scanning for the *daimyou*.

Even a skilled warrior and *daimyou* such as Naka no Yoritomo could not fight such a thing. This *oni* was large and powerful, and a surprised hunting party did not have the strength of arms necessary to overcome it. Treachery was needed. Kaworu took several quick breaths, bracing himself and forcing down the terror that shook him as the *oni*'s roar shook the ground.

The *oni* slammed his club into the ground and turned, looking for the *daimyou*. Then it saw Naka no Yoritomo, struggling with one leg twisted from his fall from the horse, scrabbling away from the melee. It snorted and charged, heaving its club overhead. Someone rushed to help Yoritomo, but he shoved the man fiercely away, drawing a short blade as he stumbled. He came to the edge of the shelf and, trapped, spun back to face the *oni*, putting his back to a thick tree and lifting his inadequate weapon in a half-hearted stand as his face betrayed mortal fear. The *oni* dropped its horned head and rushed him, ready to crush him against the tree.

And then *daimyou* and tree vanished, and the power that was to have destroyed both carried the *oni* charging off the shelf in bewildered fury. It scrabbled for a moment but could not halt its massive bulk's momentum, and it slid out into empty space. Trees cracked below with the impact of muscle.

Kaworu pressed flat to the ground against a concealing rock, tail tight against his body, shaking. The stick he had illusioned into a tree was jabbing into his ribs, but he could not move. He had never done such an illusion, and never with so much at stake, and he had not feigned the terror on Yoritomo's face.

Men were shouting all around — some had seen Yoritomo swept off the cliff, and some had found him to one side, shouting for a sword as his had been broken in his fall. Eventually they would probably decide that an unknown soldier had seized a garment from a pack, emblazoned with Naka no Yoritomo's *mon*, and bravely drawn away the *oni* to save his lord. Now, however, it was important to gather the wounded and transport the *daimyou* safely to Miyake and his men.

Kaworu would meet them later. They would not move quickly, not with men injured and the scattered horses to be caught. He would rest here, catch his breath. The desperate illusion had taken the last of his strength; surely his legs would not support him now. He shivered and closed his eyes. Only for a few moments.

CHAPTER TWENTY FOUR

OGASAWARA no Manabu kicked at a discarded support pole for *jinmaku*. "He certainly found them," he commented, looking around at the trampled area littered with abandoned gear. "You don't suppose they managed to kill him before he reached Naka no Yoritomo, do you? But we could hardly miss a corpse of that size."

"Maybe he just didn't come back to you."

"I had—" Ogasawara stretched out a hand to block Hideo's progress. "Quiet. Do you see that? Near the edge, alongside that rock?"

Hideo squinted. "A fox?"

"Indeed. And fresh coin in our purses."

Hideo rubbed at his chin. "How's that?"

"I'll explain later, just be quiet now. Go around the far side, and if he somehow gets away, grab him."

The fox was lean and leggy, probably an adolescent. That was good; fewer would pay to see a captive child, and yet an older fox might present a challenge to keep. He was careless, exposed but for a rock on one side, and utterly asleep. He was not old enough to have the kind of power that might justify such neglect.

Ogasawara took up a stick from beside the sleeping fox and began to sketch a circle about him. It wouldn't be as secure as a properly prepared circle, but that was why he had set Hideo to snatch the fox if it bolted. That would be nearly impossible, of course, but even Hideo was better than nothing.

He closed the circle and began to work his spell. The fox woke and jerked upright, but his paws could not leave the ground and he fell forward, striking his muzzle. Immediately he pulled himself upright and snarled, all teeth flashing ferociously.

Hideo came closer, eying the teeth warily. "You want to keep that?"

"Quit fussing and get some cord to muzzle and bind it."

"What?"

"He can't speak as a fox, so I cannot ask him for his name. Without a spiritual binding we'll have to do it physically. And I cannot release the circle to do it myself, so get to work."

The fox was afraid, its ears flattened and body as crouched as it could manage with its feet glued in place, and the whites of its eyes showed as it glanced from Ogasawara to Hideo.

Hideo took a strip of fabric and reached gingerly for its head. The fox slashed with a snarl, drawing blood as Hideo leapt back. The fox thrashed but could not run.

"Fool!" snapped Ogasawara, keeping his eyes on the fox. "He can't turn to reach you. Place your hands on his ribs and work your way forward, holding him still until you can scruff him and tie his mouth. Hurry!"

Hideo approached again, even more gingerly, and grabbed for the fox's torso. It whipped its head but, with feet firmly affixed to the ground, it couldn't twist far enough, and its teeth snapped on air, whiskers brushing Hideo's skin. Emboldened, Hideo shifted his hands forward, bracing the fox as it writhed, and took a handful of scruff. The fox wrenched sideways and fell awkwardly to the ground, legs still pinned in place, and its spitting snarl was interrupted by a pained yelp as Hideo shoved down, twisting the trapped joints. He slid the fabric about the snapping jaws, wrapped twice, and pulled the ends tight, closing the mouth sharply. Then he tied the ends at the base of the fox's skull, fixing the muzzle firmly in place.

"Good," said Ogasawara, relaxing. "Now tie his legs — tightly, so that he doesn't have room to shift forms. I don't know if he has the power yet, but you don't want him getting loose while you're sleeping, that's certain."

They did not find the *oni*, but when they started back, Hideo carried a young *kitsune* on his back.

狐

Naka no Yoritomo swept into his wife's chamber without ceremony, not taking the time to shed even his armor. "Kaede! Are you well?"

She flung herself about him with equal lack of ceremony. "Yoritomo-dono! You are here!"

"Yes, safely home, thanks to your warning. But you? The boy said you were unharmed?"

"Yes, yes, of course. The *youkai* never reached me — Tsurugu-sama intercepted it as soon as it arrived. You were not attacked?"

"We were. Call the *onmyouji* and we will discuss it all."

Tsurugu came, tea was brought, and they sat with Miyake to review the harrowing events. "For a moment I thought you were with us after all," the *daimyou* confided to Tsurugu. "I felt sure we had a *shikigami* in our midst."

"The *oni*?" Tsurugu was clearly perplexed.

"No! No, that was quite real. But some were certain they saw me pushed off the cliff by the *oni*. And indeed, there seems no other reason for it to leap to its presumed death. But of course, I was not carried off in such a fashion, so it must have been someone in my *hitatare*."

"A brave and noble man." Miyake's voice was sober with respect.

"Tsurugu-sama's warning was very apt," said Naka no Yoritomo. "I would not have expected an assassination warning from a houseboy — but his alert meant we were armed when the attack came."

"But where is he now?" asked Kaede. Her hand, just visible beyond the screen, twitched toward the *fusuma* as if she expected to see someone there. "I wish to thank him myself."

Yoritomo shook his head. "I'm afraid I never saw him again after I first spoke to him. I had other concerns than the whereabouts of a servant boy."

Behind her sheltering screen, Kaede went still. "Then he didn't return with you?"

"I cannot say. We left no dead or wounded behind, so he is here, however he may be. But I have not seen him."

"No dead or wounded were left," said Kaede slowly, "save the one carried over the cliff by the *oni*."

"That is true. But it could not have been your servant," answered the *daimyou* with a gentle smile. "However handsome some find him, he could not have been mistaken for my stature." He gestured to a waiting servant. "Go and find the *okugata*'s servant who brought me the warning."

But an hour later, each corpse and each wounded man had been checked, along with the kitchen and the sleeping quarters and all the places a servant might be found, and none had seen him.

狐

Hideo looked uncertainly at the cage where the fox lay on its side, tearing frantically at its face with its forepaws. "You sure that's all right?"

Ogasawara groaned, tired of the fox's noise and Hideo's questions. He wanted sleep. "He's trying to trick you into letting him loose."

Hideo frowned. "He doesn't look tricky, he looks crazy." He crawled from his makeshift bed toward the cage. "He — ew! He's mad!"

"What?" Ogasawara rolled over and was hit with the odor; the fox had urinated over himself and the ground. "See, he's trying to manipulate you into opening the cage. Let him stew in his own filth. Serves him right."

The fox went still for a moment, wheezing through the tight muzzle, and then began clawing at it again. "He's going to hurt himself," said Hideo.

"Then he'll learn to be still, won't he?" snapped Ogasawara. He sat up and threw his shoe at the cage. "Shut up!"

The fox flinched away, pausing in its clawing. "See?" And Ogasawara turned away again.

Hideo rubbed at his chin. "What if it's just a fox? If we're doing all this for nothing?"

"All foxes are *youkai*," Ogasawara answered tiredly. "Some are just too young to realize it. This one may be weak, but it's a *kitsune* as certainly as it's got a tail."

He had bartered with a tradesman, the cage for a share of their first festival's profits. As he closed his eyes and heard the fox begin clawing at its muzzle again, he hoped it would be strong enough. The stupid creature wasn't giving up.

But that would change.

Murame slid the door and entered her mistress's room. "I've brought your supper, *okugata-sama*."

Kaede-dono sat still, her hands tightly folded in her lap, staring at the polished floor before her. To the side, Hanae-san was rigid, and she wiped quickly at her eyes.

Murame set aside the dinner *zen*. "What is it? What's happened? I heard the *oyakata-sama* had returned safely!"

"He did." Kaede's voice was short, quivering. "But the messenger we sent did not."

The *kitsune* — the *kitsune* who had fed and kept her, whom she'd pushed forward into his task as messenger.

"It seems," Kaede said, her voice fracturing, "he died saving the *tono*, drawing the *oni* over a cliff."

Murame's breath caught in her chest, squeezed tight. Hanae whimpered, a suppressed sob.

"Tsurugu-sama has gone to look, to be sure. But…." Kaede gestured as she began to cry. "Leave the supper, and come."

Murame sat between them, holding herself close, and wept into her knees with them for a fox-boy she had hardly known.

二十五

CHAPTER TWENTY FIVE

BY the third week, the *kitsune* seemed to have adjusted to the routine.

Hideo kept the creature constantly muzzled, as was only prudent even in its cage. The tight muzzle and narrow cage, just the length of its body, kept the creature from changing forms if it were capable. It would have been a battle between bonds and wood and flesh, and a *kitsune* was too wise to break itself in such a fashion.

Each evening Hideo looped a cord about its neck and held it at the back of the skull while he gave the fox food and water, grasping tightly enough that sometimes the fox had difficulty swallowing and he had to loosen the cord. Hideo took few chances. He did not like the fox's teeth, and he knew his master would be most displeased if the creature escaped.

By day, they took the cage and set up a trestle display behind Ogasawara's fortune-telling table. On market and festival days they erected a cheap sort of *jinmaku* around the cage to conceal it and charged admission, and at smaller gatherings they simply collected from those gawking about the cage. The *kitsune* rarely resisted now, aside from occasionally clawing at its muzzle. Generally it lay in its cage, and on demand it would produce a small flame, just enough to impress the onlookers without presenting a danger. *Kitsune-bi,* foxfire, provided light without heat, making it was the perfect demonstration for awing villagers.

Ogasawara had wanted to display the *kitsune* in both its shapes, but that didn't seem likely. He couldn't wring its name from it as a speechless fox, and he couldn't force it to take a human form, as pain or distress naturally drove them to fox shape. And the thing was intractable enough that he couldn't risk loosening its confinement enough to allow it the space to shift, as it would be like grasping quicksilver to hold it once it was free to change shape at will.

So it stayed in the cage, clawing intermittently at its bloodied muzzle, and Ogasawara displayed it for bits of coin. It wasn't ideal, but they were eating regularly with the thing supplementing his fortune-telling.

Today's festival was a small one, starting late because of a rain shower, and they didn't bother with the *jinmaku*. Sometimes giving people the choice to look was less effective; better to show them and leave them with a sense of obligation. They erected a small vertical banner with a crudely-painted *kitsune* — Ogasawara had generously added a few extra tails for effect — and then they set the trestle and cage between a vendor selling rice balls and a display of brightly-colored carp brought from the mainland. The fish were seven of a brilliant gold color, one orange, and two of a bright yellow. Ogasawara had never seen anything like them.

The fox was resting, as it did mostly now. Its coat was dulling and shedding more, and while it struggled conveniently less, it also seemed to require more prompting for a proper display of *kitsune-bi*. Ogasawara would have to speak to Hideo about feeding it more. It didn't look too thin, but something was wrong, and people paid more for a better show.

Ogasawara walked back to look at the carp again. They were very pretty, almost mesmerizing as they swam and slid over one another. Matsue would have been fascinated by them.

He wanted to walk, and Hideo could keep the booth. Ogasawara bought a handful of rice balls and began to wander the little festival.

狐

Tsurugu kept downwind, lest Kaworu catch his scent and somehow betray him, but he needn't have worried. The fox showed no interest in the festival crowd nor, indeed, in anything. He lay still, glassy-eyed and breathing harder than he should.

A muzzle, Tsurugu saw; there was a strip of dark cloth bound tightly about his muzzle, keeping his mouth tightly closed. His fox body could not sweat, and without the ability to pant, he was overheated and fevered. It would be removed at times, to feed and water him, but it would not be enough.

There were two men near the cage, a stocky fellow with a hangdog expression and a lean man eying the crowd. Even without the *kawauso*'s description, Tsurugu would have known the *onmyouji* as the dangerous one. He would prefer to avoid a direct confrontation with him; better to wait until he was distracted or away.

Wait a little longer, Kaworu-kun. I will come.

It had been a chance moment at the *chokuban* that brought him here. Tsurugu had sat down with paper and brush, grinding ink to write the awful letter to Midorikawa-dono. *Lost his life in saving the* daimyou.... *Bravely drew away an* oni *and sacrificed himself....* Tsurugu tested phrases, all sour and wrong. There was no palatable way to break the news of a son's death. And Genji…. He glanced down at the inkstone, too wet and now muddy and wasted beneath his distracted fingers.

He should read for Midorikawa-dono. Perhaps there might be a better time to send such devastating news. He went to the *chokuban*, knowing it was useless puttering to forestall the inevitable. There was no good moment, either, to tell of a son's death. But he had to occupy himself somehow until the inkstone had dried….

Tsurugu had read for Midorikawa-dono, and then Kaede-dono, and Naka-dono, and then for Hanae-san. And then, in a moment of wishful grief as much as anything else, he had thought of Kaworu as he manipulated the board, and it had responded.

He stared at the star-pocked board a moment, absorbing the implication. If Kaworu had a fortune, had a future, then Kaworu was alive.

Tsurugu read for himself, and for the first time in months, the west was an auspicious direction. Merciful goddess.

Tsurugu had made an excuse to the *daimyou* about going to purchase materials that a servant could not be trusted to evaluate properly and ridden out. He had stopped only at the shrine, to ask Inari-sama to aid his search and to preserve Kaworu if he indeed lived, and then he had started west. He had hardly known what he sought, but one day he overheard farmers talking of a captive *kitsune* at a festival, and then it was only a matter of finding them.

He did not know who had taken Kaworu or how he had survived the *oni*, but that could wait. Now, all that mattered was retrieving him.

The chance came that afternoon, when the *onmyouji* left the booth. Tsurugu straightened at his uphill vantage point, scanning the area. There were far too many people still about the booth, and more were arriving as the festival swelled. The other man, sensing profit, began calling them toward the cage. "Come and see the captive *kitsune*!"

Tsurugu snarled softly to himself.

A knot clustered about the cage, murmuring to themselves or calling to one another. "That's no *kitsune* worth notice," someone protested. "He's got just one tail. Probably just a field fox." He snorted. "Don't take much to tie up a dog, either. I won't pay for this."

"Can a dog work illusion?" The man rapped the cage. "Give us some fire."

The figure in the cage lay limp and still. Tsurugu's chest squeezed tight.

"Oi!" The man produced a bamboo wand, cut to a point, and jabbed it through the bars. "Get at it!"

The fox flinched, and a small tongue of white-green flame appeared beyond the end of the cage, hanging mid-air and consuming nothing. The spectators gasped, gestured, muttered, and the showman beamed as he started about collecting coins.

This would serve. Tsurugu's multi-colored circle was already set. He laced his fingers together and began to chant.

The small *kitsune-bi* bobbed and shifted, making one nervous woman call out in alarm. All turned their eyes on it, and it elongated to a thin pillar of fire.

"What's that rot?" demanded the showman angrily. He struck the cage with the flat of his hand. "Lay off!"

The flame bent sharply toward him, and he retreated a step despite himself. Then the foxfire whirled into the air and spun outward, shaping fiery characters in the air above the cage.

Release this one.

Most of the spectators could not read, but they feared the message itself, gasping and shrinking back. The fox jerked in his cage, his cramped limbs working. The *onmyouji's* servant seemed to have a handful of education, for he stared hard at the words, his mouth working as he tried to decipher. Or perhaps it didn't matter what it said. "Quit that!" He started for the bamboo rod. "I'll settle you—"

It is not his doing, wrote the foxfire. *He is mine. Release him.*

Most of the festival folk were stumbling away now, calling to one another in fear. The showman shouted after them. "Wait! It is only illusion! The *kitsune* is working its mischief, and it is only illusion!"

Tsurugu eyed the booths on either side of the *onmyouji's* display, emptying as the fiery letters drifted higher over the cage. Not the innocent carp, he decided, and concentrated. The rice-ball stand burst into bright orange flame. People screamed and fled.

"Illusion!" howled the showman defiantly. He seized the bamboo rod and started for the cage. "It is only—"

Burning fabric twisted and fell from the food stand, blowing in its hot draft against the man. He screamed and recoiled, beating the burning sheet.

A man in temple garments rushed toward the cage with a bared knife. Tsurugu half-rose and reached for the fire, but the blade only sliced the cords binding the door. He tipped the cage and the fox tumbled free.

The showman, free of the burning cloth, shouted at the man, but he did not approach the cage. The temple servant fled, leaving the muzzled fox on the ground. The fox struggled to its feet, staggered and tripped.

Tsurugu touched the folded paper that lay before him. It rose and fluttered away, and then a crack of expanding wings was heard overhead.

The fox crouched and trembled, and then a pale naked

youth knelt in its place. He tore savagely at the cloth strips about his face and pushed unsteadily to his feet. Something great and dark dropped from the sky and seized the boy, beating enormous wings and rising on the hot wind of the burning stand. A few humans stared after it, while others ran or shouted for water or called anxiously for family.

The ground, soaked from the earlier rain, did not spread the flames, and the booths smoked heavily. The fire would not last. With the circle safely ended, Tsurugu retreated into the safety of the forest, seeking the small glade he had discovered.

The *shikigami* descended and released Kaworu before reverting to a scrap of fluttering paper as the boy dropped weakly. Tsurugu rushed to him. *"Kaworu! Daijoubu desu ka?"*

The youth stumbled against him, panting. Tsurugu took his shoulders and knelt with him to the ground. "Be still. Catch your breath. Are you hurt?"

He was filthy and thin; he'd been hungry. Thirsty, too, by the scent of his breath. And if the muzzle had kept him fevered, as Tsurugu suspected, he might be disoriented and weak for a time. Tsurugu listened for possible pursuit, but there was nothing but Kaworu's gasping. It seemed few were willing to dash into the forest after an unknown spirit.

Kaworu's breathing slowed. *"Sumimasen,"* he managed. "I knew you had come."

His hairless body showed bruising along his ribs and shoulders, and his face was covered in scabbed welts, but he seemed otherwise uninjured. Tsurugu shrugged off his *happi* and draped it over the bare shoulders, as Kaworu didn't have the strength to form clothing. "I have many questions for you," Tsurugu said, "but the most urgent is this — can you travel?"

"My head is… I'm not steady on my feet. The earth moves."

It was only the muzzle-fever, Tsurugu suspected, and he

would recover in time. "We'll find a stream soon, and that will help. Let's go now, before they gather enough men to shame themselves into coming after us."

Kaworu obediently, perhaps gratefully, shifted into his native form. Tsurugu did the same and lifted his head, listening once more for pursuit, and then started south, the smaller fox following at his shoulder.

狐

Ogasawara pulled his sleeves more closely about him and tried to summon the energy to swear. Beside him, Hideo shifted and groaned.

Ogasawara had been away from the booth when a fire had broken out in the festival, sending some stumbling away as others raced to fight the blaze before it could spread. Ogasawara started for the booth. He didn't know if Hideo would have the presence of mind to seize the *kitsune*'s cage before it burned, and they were making fair profit on the thing.

But Hideo was running from several men with cudgels, and Ogasawara slipped into the smoke of the burning booths before he could be seen. The cage was on the ground and empty. Clearly something had gone very wrong with the *kitsune*, and its owners were to be held responsible for the disaster.

He had faded away with the smoke and crowd, sliding behind the unharmed booths, and fled into the woods. There he waited until Hideo, bruised but not broken, had limped to meet him.

"What happened?" demanded Ogasawara.

"I outran all but two. They were good runners but slight of build and—"

"Not that," Ogasawara interrupted with a dismissive wave. "What happened with the *kitsune*?"

Hideo shook his head in slow wonder, his eyes wide. "It wasn't the *kitsune*, I don't think. I was making him show fire, same as usual, and then the fire became letters and then the booths began to burn."

"A *kitsune* could do that, maybe," Ogasawara mused, "but it seems unlikely he would have waited so long."

"A *kitsune* couldn't have summoned that thing what picked him up and carried him away," Hideo added pointedly. "A giant bird of paper, it seemed. Enormous."

Ogasawara frowned. "A *shikigami*, you mean?"

"I've never seen one so big. The fox turned to a boy, and the paper-bird carried him off."

This was very curious. "Tell me everything."

Hideo had, in his fragmented, stupid way, and Ogasawara was left to brood on the implications while his servant slept and rubbed at the cudgel marks. A *shikigami*, not a *tengu* or other winged *youkai*, implied an *onmyouji*'s work, and one powerful enough to manipulate a creation of such a size.

Ogasawara's attention was caught by a piece of paper fluttering as if caught in a fickle breeze — only it moved improbably against the faint wind. It was a bright blue, and folded in the shape of a tiny bird which flapped its way toward him. He put up a hand and caught the little bird, which immediately stilled.

There was a bit of writing visible on the surface of one wing. He unfolded the *origami* figure to reveal a poem and note.

> My lord's wife is well;
> No otter's pad mars her sleep.
> Carp remain untouched,
> *Oni* dreams at mountain foot.
> One worth less than fish, have care.

Ogasawara stared at the paper a moment. So, the one who had stolen the *kitsune* — leaving the pretty fish unharmed beside the fire — was also the one who had foiled his attacks upon Naka no Yoritomo. The warning was clear: further attempts would be met with lethal force.

It was a fair warning. An *onmyouji* strong enough to turn back the crow and defeat the *oni* would be a formidable opponent.

He folded the paper slowly, following the lines, trying to recreate the little bird. This was very interesting, given what else he had learned. He had gone into the woods where Hideo had pointed the *kitsune*'s flight, where the *onmyouji* had met it and they had started away together. He had found the paper that might once have been the *shikigami* which whisked away his captive. And in the drying earth, hardening after the rain, were the prints of two men which became the prints of two foxes.

CHAPTER TWENTY SIX

TSURUGU came awake, all senses questing. He heard a small sound to his left, a short distance away, and relaxed. It was only Kaworu again.

He had worried Tsurugu all the first day, fevered and slow. That began to change when Tsurugu found water and a nest of voles for them to share, but even then Kaworu remained far too quiet.

That night they had sheltered against a fallen tree and curled into sleep, fluffy tails warming their noses. Kaworu had slept early and hard, as Tsurugu had expected. But he had woken a few hours later, bolting from the tree. Tsurugu rolled upright, shedding dead leaves, to see the boy shivering and pacing.

Tsurugu rose to human form as well. "What is it?"

Kaworu didn't seem to hear him. He walked a few steps away and rubbed tersely at his face, scraping the scabbed welts and then hugged himself.

"Kaworu-kun?"

Kaworu jerked around, the whites of his eyes visible in the moonlight. "I—" Abruptly he looked away. "I'm fine."

Tsurugu's stomach tightened. "I hadn't asked."

Kaworu rubbed his hand over his face again. "I couldn't sleep."

"You might be more comfortable in another shape."

"No." Kaworu's answer was quiet but too quick. He began walking again.

He had not held a human shape in weeks. He might need to reassure himself he could take it, that he wasn't bound in a cage. Tsurugu watched as Kaworu turned after a few steps and, self-conscious, brushed his face again.

Tsurugu kept his voice unnaturally neutral. "I'll sit up and—"

"No." This time the tone was sharper, hotter; now Tsurugu had shamed him as well.

Tsurugu clenched his fist and struggled for words to apologize without making it worse. "I didn't mean—"

He whirled, mouth half-open as he listened and scanned. A dozen paces away a bit of paper fluttered in the night breeze, and just as Tsurugu saw it the scrap flitted to one side, as if it had caught a scent.

Tsurugu leapt and thrust out his hand, snatching the paper from the air. His hand could not quite close on it, and it fluttered within the cage of his fingers. Tsurugu set his jaw and concentrated, bringing his other hand to focus on the paper, and a little flicker of fire caught the *shikigami* and devoured it.

Kaworu stared at the ashes crumbling into Tsurugu's palm. "He — he's looking for us!"

"He was," agreed Tsurugu. "And he will be yet, for this one will not tattle to him."

Kaworu licked his lips. "Will he come?"

"If he were certain enough to find us, he would not have

sent something to scout us out. I suspect he sent a dozen or more of these to search, in the hope of coming across something useful."

Kaworu shivered and brushed at his face. Then, realizing what he'd done, he jerked his face to the side and hunched his shoulders further.

Tsurugu shifted his weight. "That trick of fire isn't easy. I need sleep if we're to cover any ground tomorrow." It was at least somewhat true. He started back toward the log, and then turned over his shoulder. "If you aren't tired, you might keep an eye open for any others, just in case."

Kaworu gave him a suspicious look. "If you thought there would be others, you would not sleep."

Tsurugu turned his ashy palm up and splayed his fingers. "Fire, Kaworu-bouzu. Consuming fire, without a circle or a *tama*. And I haven't your youth." He dropped to the ground in his fox shape and coiled himself against the chill.

He had humiliated the boy in his fear, and worse, Kaworu knew he knew it. But there was little to be done. There was no shame in it, but Kaworu did not see that.

Tsurugu lay still, his tail over his eyes as he listened, and Kaworu paced and occasionally made small sounds which might have been from the cold. He could not yet form many layers of clothing. At last he returned to his place and curled into the leaves again.

Neither of them mentioned it in the morning. They spoke little all day. And the next night, when Kaworu had left the low branch on which they were resting, Tsurugu pretended the shifting branch had not woken him, and he had feigned sleep for the hour Kaworu paced and shivered.

Tonight it seemed more of the same. Tsurugu's chest ached. He had seen strong warriors vomit after battle, knew that some denied themselves water and food before a fight lest they humiliate themselves in terror or death. Kaworu had not even had the privilege of a fight, only the slow fear of captivity and the hot shame of being prodded to cheap tricks.

Tsurugu drew a slow breath and half-opened his eyes. As Kaworu's pacing turned back, he shifted on the branch and stretched a foreleg.

Kaworu froze, nearly balancing mid-stride, eyes fixed on Tsurugu. For long heartbeats, he did not move.

Tsurugu exhaled with a sleepy little snort and turned his head, shifting it to a more comfortable position on the branch. Kaworu eased forward, by his soft footfalls, and then picked his way to the base of the tree and settled against it.

No, he was not ready to face anyone. He sighed, frustrated. Kaworu deserved better. He would never have been taken by the other *onmyouji* if he hadn't risked himself for Naka-dono. Tsurugu was more than glad to have found him, but he didn't want to bring home this quiet, obedient stranger in the place of the insouciant boy he should have been.

CHAPTER TWENTY SEVEN

MURAME was bringing tea when the *onmyouji* returned. Kaede-dono admitted him at once, of course, and Murame was directed to remove the screen as Tsurugu and the fox-boy Kaworu — he lived! — entered and knelt, still soiled with road dust and sweat.

"You've brought him," Kaede said with more relief than Murame had expected. Her mistress was kind and considerate of her servants, and she had wept for his death in saving her husband, but still, he was *kitsune*.

"He was at a festival in Aoiyama," answered Tsurugu. "An *onmyouji* had taken him — the same, I believe, who has worked against the *daimyou* and yourself."

Kaede's expression stiffened. "Who is it who pursues us so? And why?" She shook her head and turned to Kaworu, still bowed. "We are more than glad you've returned safe to us," she said. "And we have not forgotten the *daimyou* owes his life to you as well."

"I am sorry I was not free to return to you before, Kaede-dono." There was something wrong with his voice, Murame thought — with his whole demeanor, in fact. Even when silent, he and his brother had often seemed on the verge of laughter, somehow always sharing a private joke. After his brother had died by the *kappa*, Kaworu had lost the laughter, and now he seemed somehow flatter still.

Had his twin brother been a *kitsune*, too? Or had both twins died, and the fox had taken the place of one?

Kaede looked at Kaworu and spoke, her words distinct and laced with a meaning Murame could not grasp. "Do you know the man who kept you?"

"His name is Ogasawara no Manabu," answered Kaworu, his voice colder, and something stirred visibly within him. "His servant is Hideo. I do not know his purpose. He serves no house, from what I could see, but seems to move on his own."

"His name and face are enough to give my lord's shadows," said Kaede with a faint air of satisfaction. "Now we will know our enemy."

狐

"Stay a moment, Murame."

The *onmyouji* and servant had gone, leaving Kaede-dono to muse. Now Murame left the tea set and looked to her mistress. "Yes, *okugata-sama*?"

Kaede folded her hands in her lap. "I have something to ask you — a great favor to me."

"Anything, of course, *okugata-sama*."

Kaede shook her head. "It is — it is not so simple. And I have no right to ask it of you, except that I think you might want it of yourself, and…."

Murame's throat closed. "Is it — is it Kaworu-san?"

Kaede let out a slow breath. "I freed a captive *kitsune*

once," she said. "I did not know it then, but it was the catalyst which would later change my life — which would make a medicine-seller's daughter, the promised bride of an exorcist, into the wife of a *daimyou*."

Murame blinked. "Did you save a great *kitsune*, then, and did he reward you?"

Kaede smiled. "Not a great *kitsune*, no, but one who had great friends. My reward came much later, but it did come." She looked solemnly at Murame. "*Kitsune* are tricksters and *youkai* always, but they are not ungrateful, and they remember those who have helped them. If you can do one a good turn, don't hesitate."

Murame looked down. "I — I don't...."

Kaede adjusted a fold in her robe. "Do you know that many nights, when Yoritomo-dono comes to me, we talk? Men love the pleasures of the flesh, no doubt, but they also love being able to speak to a woman as they cannot speak to another man." She eyed Murame. "I would not press you if you did not want to go to him."

Murame bit her lip and looked away. "I — when I was alone and hungry, he brought me help."

"Did he?"

"I did not know him at the time. But he has, as you say, done me a good turn, and I should return it. But he is not alone and hungry now."

Kaede made a small, eloquent gesture. "One can be alone and hungry in a banquet of a thousand, Murame-chan."

Murame hesitated and then nodded. She rose and gathered the tea tray, then slid quietly from the room.

狐

The fox was near the hot pool, picking his way among the rocks that half-concealed it. The pool was small, able to accommodate perhaps two or three people, and filled by a narrow steaming stream that fell from a rocky tumble above. It was a magical place even without a *kitsune* wading into the smoky water.

She paused, unsure of how or whether to approach. The fox selected a stick broken in the rocks and, holding it in its jaws, began to back into the water, sinking an inch at a time. Murame came closer, and the fox slipped the last bit into the water, holding the stick above. The stick seemed to move in the steam, and Murame realized its surface was now crawling with parasites fleeing the water. The fox dropped the stick and slid away, leaving the infested stick slowly whirling in the circling current.

"That was very clever," she ventured, though privately she wondered how long the fleas would remain in the pool. The fox rotated an ear toward her but did not turn. Aware but aloof, he rose from the water and shook, spraying the rocks and spiking his fur.

He had not fled, though, and that was something. "I brought some salve," she offered. "I thought you might want it."

It was the wrong thing to say, she realized — it called out his injury, and shamed him. She did not know how a *kitsune* thought of himself, but she must try to think of him as a *samurai* rather than a servant.

The fox seemed to shiver and then unfolded, rising as a nude young man, his thin back to her. It was a deliberate statement; to be naked was to be ugly, common, low. There was no allure, no draw to the *kitsune* now.

She took a slow breath. "Kaede-dono has been kind enough to teach me some medicine. I came half-hoping you would give me some chance of practicing. Is there anything I might do?"

He sighed and drew from nowhere a light *juban* about

his shoulders. "I am well, thank you. In fact, I—"

"You helped me when I needed it!" She flung the words at him, letting her voice waver a bit too high. "I would have died but for you. Please, let me do something now for you!"

The weight of obligation struck him, and he hesitated. Murame moved before he could gather himself. "Sit," she pressed, gesturing to an upright boulder. "It is only a little salve. It won't take long."

He sat with his back to the rock, graceful and reluctant, and the *juban* gaped white on his white skin. The only color in him was his dark hair and the dull red scrapes on his cheeks. He was too pale for a servant. "The bruises are old," he said gruffly. "They don't require much attention."

She knelt beside him and opened the little box of salve. "It is such a little thing to allow this." He remained still. She glanced down to the box and noted his hands on his thighs. "Your — what happened to your thumbs?"

His jaw tightened, but he did not answer. His hands were unmarked but for his thumbs, raw and torn with nails chipped and cracked halfway into the bed. Murame lifted her own hand, matching her thumb to her cheek and tracing the scrape, and something old and latent and cold uncoiled in her stomach. "You were bound," she breathed.

His hand moved then, a quick flick down his cheek as if brushing away an imagined irritant.

Murame didn't move — couldn't move. Old terrors she had half-forgotten stirred and crawled about her. "I'm sorry," she said, her voice barely audible over the falling water. "I know — that is, I know what it is to be — unable to move. To want to run, and to be unable."

His head turned toward her, his breath brushing warm against her, and she turned her face away with a tight little jerk. "I'm sorry," she repeated, and she didn't know if it were for him or herself.

She didn't realize she was trembling until his arm slipped against her shoulders, drawing her against him and the solid boulder, bracing her. "To scream for help," she said, her voice breaking, "to cry and call and know that surely someone must hear, but no one is coming...."

His arms closed hard around her and pressed her forehead against his neck, cradling her as she sobbed with pain she thought she had forgotten, thought she had suppressed and buried.

"It is hard to be helpless," he said into her hair, his voice whole and real for the first time.

This was the power of women, she realized as she cried. This was their strength — the strength of tears and of fears, of daring to bare what a man dared not. She wept for them both, and if his cheeks were wet as he held her, he could not be faulted for that. And if he grew stronger as he supported her, well, was that not his own strength?

They sat for a time, bathed in steam, and as the tears slowed she remained on his shoulder. Despite their exchange, or because of it, it was easier to stay too near to meet his eyes. He made no move to pull away. The water streamed down and splashed into the pool, and the steam caressed and hid them.

The air at last began to cool even through the steam, and Murame's damp clothes chilled her. She shifted against his shoulder and found he had relaxed his head against the boulder, his jaw no longer clenched. He turned to look at her, meeting her eyes for the first time. "You never used the salve," he said with the faintest of accusations.

She started upright. "Oh! I can—"

He shook his head. "These are old wounds; now they only need time."

She tried to smile. "I had thought old wounds healed."

"They do heal," he said gently. "But with time, and even healed wounds can scar."

"I'm sorry," she said, meaning for everything, and he nodded once. Then he withdrew his arms slowly and got to his feet. The *juban* collar was folded where she had been, and he straightened it.

"You must be freezing," she said with sudden guilt as the cold plucked at her steam-dampened clothing.

"That's easily solved," he said with a smile, and he shrugged into a *hitatare* that seemed to form from the steam itself.

Murame stared. "That.... I know what you are, and yet...."

He smiled, and it almost held his old arrogance. "Another time, I will teach you a magic of your own," he said. "But tonight, let's return before you catch cold, which would be poor thanks for following me all this way."

The flea-laden stick had wound its way out of the narrow pool. "You had no soak," she remembered. "You meant to wash and soak."

"Another time," he said, slipping his feet into *zouri* which had not existed a moment before. "We could soak together."

She tensed before she realized there was no suggestion in his voice, only companionship. Perhaps some *kitsune* did not desire human lovers. "That might be nice," she allowed.

They returned to the house without speaking, but Murame sensed something different between them — allied, protected and protecting. She knew his fatal secret and he had seen her deepest hurt; they were masters of one another. Possessors of one another.

CHAPTER TWENTY EIGHT

TSURUGU knew, of course, what Kaede-dono had wrought between her two young servants. He watched as closely as he could, but he didn't think Kaworu visited Murame in the days after. He remained in the servant quarters, working beneath Jirou's alternating rants on shirking and loud exhortations to live up to his heroic nature — for it was known he had been the one to warn Naka no Yoritomo of the impending attack — with greater efforts toward his chores.

Tsurugu had surmised Kaworu would be unlikely to open himself to anyone but his brother. With Genji away, however, Tsurugu had hoped for the next best option, the girl Kaworu had helped when she was in need. And Kaede-dono had been a step ahead of him.

Murame had proved a diligent and discreet maid to Kaede-dono, though she had guessed both Kaworu's secret (not terribly hard, once one was certain there really was a *kitsune*) and that Kaede and Tsurugu knew it. Tsurugu wondered if she would discern Hanae's and his own identities as well. She was a clever girl, given a chance.

Her visit to Kaworu, however short, was a relief; Tsurugu had other things to occupy his mind. The attack upon the *daimyou* was dangerous, but hardly surprising. Naka-dono made powerful enemies as a matter of course, and he knew and welcomed the risk. Few of those, however, would specifically target his wife.

Who sought Kaede-dono?

Whatever Kaede might conceal from her husband, she was truly in love with him and would do anything to protect him and her marriage. That meant both using and hiding the foxes. And whatever unspoken wishes might steal upon Tsurugu during a perfect firefly-lit summer night, all soft and scented with flowers, Kaede was devoted to her husband, and Tsurugu was bound to protect him as he was bound to serve her.

He would protect both Kaede and her happiness, then, by protecting her husband. And somehow, he knew, this also furthered Midorikawa-dono's end, whatever it might be; supporting Naka no Yoritomo must benefit the golden *kitsune* lord. His fondness and obligation to Kaede-dono was not all that motivated him to place his *onmyouji* and twin sons in her household.

Tsurugu would find this *onmyouji*, and he would meet him, and if necessary, he would destroy him — for the sake of Kaede-dono, and Naka no Yoritomo-dono, and Midorikawa-dono, and Hanae-san, and Kaworu-kun and Genji-kun, and even for Murame-san who now depended on Kaede-dono and the *kitsune*. This man threatened them all. Let him be prepared.

狐

Gennosuke wanted to move, so very badly, but Juubei-sensei had raptor eyes and owl hearing, and they had been told to stay still.

"As you enter, you meet separately a woodcutter, a maid, and an *ashiguru*." Juubei-sensei paced slow, deliberate strides down the line of kneeling youths. "You make casual conversation with each."

Gennosuke could no longer feel his feet. But a shadow did not move, and so they must not move.

"The woodcutter complains of his work, for the *daimyou's* house has purchased another load. The maid is displeased with the bustle of the house, for it means extra chores for her. The *ashiguru* grumps that he will be away from his favorite whore if his commander goes to meet with the *daimyou*."

Beside Gennosuke, Takeshi had braced his hands and was stealthily sliding the top of one foot across the wooden planking, relieving the pressure in his ankles and wriggling his toes.

"The woodcutter warns you of the *tono's* brutal temper. The maid whispers that the soldiers will secretly depart with the *daimyou* soon, to close against the traitor. The *ashiguru* warns you to stay out of the way, lest you be caught up and pressed into service."

Takeshi's toe caught the bound edge of the *tatami* and Gennosuke heard the faintest of scrapes. Juubei-sensei turned unhurriedly and knuckle-rapped Takeshi's skull with an audible *throk*. Takeshi flinched, bowed, and resumed the assigned position.

"Gennosuke-kun," Juubei continued as if there had been no interruption, "which of the three knows what you are?"

Gennosuke was trying to ignore the burn creeping up his calves. He closed his eyes and thought. "The *ashiguru* has warned me away. He suspects."

The *throk* caught Gennosuke squarely in the center of

his skull, more penetrating than such a simple movement would have suggested. He flinched backward, and his numbing legs screamed in abrupt agony.

"What would a simple maid know of the *daimyou's* intentions?" Juubei regarded Gennosuke with a faintly disdainful resignation. "If one speaks with knowledge above his station...?"

"...Suspect him." Gennosuke's head hurt.

"The maid is a shadow set against a shadow, and you would have followed her trail like a foolish dog into a badger's den."

Gennosuke nodded.

Juubei-sensei looked over them, and all seemed to hold their breath. At last he nodded. "You are dismissed."

Boys and girls rose, staggering on numbed legs. The first to the door stumbled down the steps, and they all laughed.

"Gennosuke-kun." Harume-sama was outside, as if she had known they would be coming.

She probably had. Harume-sama knew everything. "Yes, Harume-sama?"

"Come with me. We have a task for the *okugata-sama*."

CHAPTER TWENTY NINE

"WHY have we come out here?" Murame was smiling, but there was an edge to her voice betraying that she knew how far they had gone outside the walls, far from others' sight and hearing.

"Your mistress and my master are meeting, and so we have some time." Kaworu faced her. "I told you I would teach you your own magic."

This did not seem to reassure her. "I have no magic."

"I am a trickster, and so I gave you a half-truth. You have no magic like mine, but you can work a sort of magic, enabling a slender, pliant girl to break an arm or throw a grown man to the ground."

Murame blinked. "You mean, to fight?"

"Not to fight, necessarily, but to defend. Even a kitten may scratch."

Her mouth tightened, but he could not tell whether she was worried or pleased. "And you think to teach me this?"

Had he offended somehow? "If you would learn it."

She took a breath and then nodded. "I do not know what I may learn, and I may not be a good pupil. But I would be glad to know how to scratch if the need arises."

He smiled. "I think you will learn as much as you please. Come, grasp my wrist."

It was an easy first lesson, showing how a simple twist, wrist over thumb, could break her strongest grip. Then he had her practice, breaking free of his grasp from either hand.

"Now let's add a little claw to your scratch," he said. "Flatten your fingers into a knife blade, like this. Yes, good. Now, as you twist free, bring your knife hand around and chop off his hand."

Murame jerked back. "What?"

"It won't, of course. Even magic cannot simply cut off a hand. But act as if it will, and that will give it strength. Take my wrist, and I'll show you, slowly."

With what seemed glacial slowness he twisted his arm, breaking her hold at the thumb, and brought his hand above hers. With a steady pressure he cut down on her wrist, snapping the last of her grasp and pressing the hand away. "You see? Now try it."

She did. It was a simpler exercise than she anticipated. "You let go!"

"No, I didn't."

"You did. I'm not strong enough to break that."

"You did not need strength. Try again."

"See, you're not really holding."

He grabbed her hard, and she flinched, eyes wide. For an instant he felt regret, as when once just as his jaws crunched he'd realized the bird had a nest. "I have you now," he said, ignoring her alarm. "I will not let go if I can help it. You must break free."

She looked from him to her wrist, and then she moved.

His fingers reddened her skin, and her wrist did not slip.

"With power," he said. "I will not release you. Break it!"

She gulped and twisted. With a little cry she made her fingers a blade and knifed into his wrist, snapping his grip and jolting his stinging arm toward the ground.

"Kuso!" Kaworu shook his numbed hand. "That was well done."

She stared at him. "You mock me."

"Not this time." He dropped his hand to his side, a bit embarrassed that it had stung him. "Think on it. Practice it in your mind, and on me if you like. But be ready to use it."

She glanced at his hand. "Did it really hurt you?"

"And never, ever apologize for it." He caught her eyes. "You cannot break free if no one is holding you. If you use this, it is because he has already offended. You do not apologize for his offense."

She hesitated and then nodded once. "I understand."

"Good."

Was someone with them? Watching them? He wanted to rotate an ear to listen, but his inept human shape could not oblige. He glanced over his shoulder and saw nothing.

"You said...."

He turned back to Murame, who was looking to one side with a forced expression of indifference. "You said I might break an arm."

He smiled. "Not with this. That requires a bit more of your magic."

"I don't want to break anyone's arm. But I don't want ever to wish, afterward, I had known the means." Her eyes flicked to his, cautious and hopeful and worried.

He understood. "I cannot let you practice breaking mine, you know. Even foxes have boundaries."

She laughed. "I can be gentle. I know animals are

skittish."

狐

Murame returned to the house first; she would have duties to her mistress. Kaworu sat in the grass, enjoying the sunshine and breeze and scents from the hills. It had been too long since he had shirked his chores, and it would not do to let Jirou grow complacent.

He had not performed his *kata* since Genji had gone, and it had felt good to practice for even such a short time. Perhaps it was wrong to teach an outsider the fighting movements, but Kaworu did not see the danger. Murame would be unlikely to teach any warriors, nor indeed any of the *samurai* class, what a village girl had learned from a servant boy. They would not see their own knowledge used against them. And Murame needed it.

Something shifted in the air, and Kaworu knew there were eyes upon him. Not Murame; she had gone. He wanted to dart, but he remained still, listening intently, hoping his observer would betray himself.

A quick blur of moment drew his eye — a mouse, skimming over the ground? No, a tiny *youkai*, galloping through the tangled grass, waving stubby arms and piping something in a shrill, unintelligible voice.

Kaworu bent toward him. "What?"

Metal split the air above his bent shoulder and struck the tree beyond. Kaworu did not waste time looking after it but made his lean a roll, dodging to one side and coming up in a crouch.

"Nice," a male voice acknowledged grudgingly. "Or lucky."

Kaworu couldn't see the speaker. He flattened himself in the grass, making less of a target for a second throw. "Show yourself, unless you have courage enough only to strike in the back."

"That has nothing to do with courage, and everything with practicality," came the answer. "But I am not hiding."

Kaworu scanned the little ridge and saw nothing. His heart pounded in his ears, nearly drowning the tiny voice beside him. "*Kitsune-sama!* There, by the pine! In the pale grass!"

Kaworu looked again, and this time he saw a figure in the grass, motionless, half-invisible in soft grey. Kaworu's heart sank. "What do you want?"

"I know what you are," said the shadow. He was near Kaworu's own age.

Kaworu's stomach clenched. If he lived through this, Tsurugu would kill him. "What of it?"

"Did you know a man called Shishio Hitoshi?"

Kuso. Tsurugu would never have the chance. "Who?"

"He went to the *daimyou's* house to seek a *kitsune*, and he never returned. You are a *kitsune* near the *daimyou's* house. It seems logical you might know something of him."

"I did not kill him." It was the leanest of truths; he had knelt on the man's arm while another drew a blade across his throat.

"So you know he is dead."

Kuso.

For the space of a breath there was silence, and when the boy spoke again, his voice was tighter. "That is more than I knew, though I feared it." He rose out of the grass. "Shishio Hitoshi-san was my uncle."

Kuso. Kuso. Kuso.

Kaworu got to his feet. "I am sorry to hear of your loss."

The boy's face was blotching red and white as he stepped forward, but he spoke levelly. "You say you were not responsible. But he went to hunt a *kitsune*."

"You know," Kaworu ventured, "he accused the *daimyou's* wife of being a fox-woman herself."

That shocked the boy. "No! He would not — not without perfect evidence."

Kaworu made his voice casual. "She is not. I would know."

"*Oji-san* was loyal to the *oyakata-sama* above all. If he accused the wife, then there must be a reason."

This was not going as Kaworu had hoped; instead of supposing *seppuku* or execution, the boy would adopt Shishio Hitoshi's own suspicion. "Maybe you put too much faith in your *ojii-san.*"

The insulting extra syllable did not escape the boy's angry notice. "*Oji-san* was more than you could ever dream to be." His throat worked as he swallowed. "You know more than you say — and that girl knows things, too. She will tell me what you won't."

Kaworu stiffened. The threat to Murame was a challenge, an intent from which neither could now retreat.

They started toward one another, slow, deliberate steps that tested the ground beneath them. Kaworu had trained in *taijutsu* nearly since his eyes first opened, certainly since he could walk. He was not of Toyotsune-sensei's caliber, but he could hold his own against the average roadside bandit. This, he saw, was no bandit. The boy carried himself well, balanced for quick movement in any direction, and his soft grey eyes watched everything at once without focusing and limiting his attention.

Kaworu struck first. He attacked directly, hoping the boy's agitation would slow his reflexes. He knew the boy was armed — he had thrown something — and he could not give him time to use a weapon.

The boy in grey fell backward in a perfect *ichimonji* and

struck aside Kaworu's punch. He rocked forward with a counter, but Kaworu had expected it and was not there to receive it.

They stepped and slid and dodged through the grass, knuckles skimming flesh or garments and fingertips grazing intended holds. Kaworu had missed his first chance, and now he knew this was the type of fight for which Toyotsune had trained them — not to win, but to survive. His opponent had also started *taijutsu* when he first could walk, and he had not diluted his training with *onmyoudou* and poetry and dance.

The boy in grey caught Kaworu's arm and wrenched it downward. Kaworu shifted and slid out of the boy's surprised grasp, leaving a fistful of pale fur.

Now the fight closed with new ferocity. Kaworu leapt through the boy's legs and spun, shifting to human size to sweep his feet. But the shadow-boy rolled and came up with a savage jab. Kaworu twisted and shifted, and the fist passed harmlessly over his head. He reached upward and slashed the exposed arm, skin splitting beneath his teeth. Then he leapt away and shifted to human again.

The boy in grey coped with Kaworu's rapid shifting far better than he had any right. Kaworu sprang into the air as a human, inviting a solid punch to his unprotected flank, and then slid into fox form to evade the blow. He landed on the boy's shoulder and raked teeth over cheek and ear before bounding free. But the boy whirled and kicked, catching Kaworu in the hip and sending him tumbling.

His tiny fox body would be crushed if trapped on the ground — Kaworu shifted to human as he rolled and tried to get his numbed leg under him. The boy dove at him and they rolled in the grass. The shadow-boy's bloodied forearm slid to Kaworu's throat.

Kaworu writhed beneath the arm that trapped him, but the boy was not dislodged. He reached for some weapon, struggling to keep his hold. Kaworu wrenched his head to the side, pressing his cheek along the bone of the forearm, and shifted. His curved canine caught the flesh and tore another gash, ripping further as the boy instinctively jerked away. Kaworu twisted free, got his hind legs beneath him and launched, shifting mid-leap and driving hard into him with human weight.

They rolled again, and this time the boy in grey succeeded in retrieving whatever he was reaching for, and fresh panic lanced through Kaworu as the blade slid toward him. He got his arm against the boy's, holding it back, but he could not gain traction.

Light flashed oddly between them and the blade slid as if across a hard surface. The boy in grey hesitated for just a heartbeat, startled and confused. The light flashed again, and something like warm ice slid between them, forcing them apart. Kaworu glimpsed a faint five-pointed star almost visible between them.

Then something struck the boy and he was flung to one side, rolling across the crushed grass and to his feet. A woman, her hair bound and grey, loomed over Kaworu with an expression of iron, but her eyes were on the shadow-boy. Kaworu had scrabbled halfway upright when Tsurugu caught him by the scruff and tossed him unceremoniously backward. Kaworu yelped before he caught himself and immediately felt ashamed before the strange boy.

But the boy did not note Kaworu's humiliation, as he had dropped to his knees before the woman. "Harume-sama, he is *kitsune!*"

"I am not blind."

"He knew of *oji-san*'s death."

"He is not the one responsible," Tsurugu said, stepping forward. "He is—"

"Who are you to say?" demanded the boy.

The woman's hand rapped his skull with a sound like snapping bone. "Gennosuke-kun! Be silent. Or is my own word worth your distrust?" She gestured. "This is Tsurugu-sama, the *oyakata-sama*'s *onmyouji*. If he says his bound fox is no danger, it is so."

Gennosuke struggled to speak. "He knew of my uncle's death."

"And so did I, and so did Harume-sama, and so did the *oyakata-sama*," answered Tsurugu. "Which of us will you say is guilty?"

Gennosuke's jaw worked visibly.

"Harume-san and I have just met one another at the *okugata-sama*'s direction," Tsurugu said. "She has charged us with locating the *onmyouji* seeking to kill the *oyakata-sama*." He beckoned Kaworu without looking. "Kaworu-kun, as he may be called, has a grievance against this *onmyouji* and is willing to aid us. And as he did the *oyakata-sama* the service of saving his life from an *oni* sent to murder him, I think we may safely trust that he means the *daimyou* no harm."

This, at last, worked a change in Gennosuke, and for the first time he looked again at Kaworu.

Kaworu had taken the opportunity to refresh his clothing, so that he was spotlessly clean while Gennosuke remained grass-stained and dirt-smeared. He came and stood just behind and to the side of Tsurugu, a faultless attendant.

"This is Harume-sama," Tsurugu said, nodding toward the woman, "and Gennosuke-kun. They will seek out the man who threatens the *oyakata-sama*, and they wish to hear what you have to say of him. But first, I wish you two to make amends. Apologize to one another."

Kaworu stiffened, but before he could protest Gennosuke spoke. "No, Tsurugu-sama, it is I alone who should apologize. I acted without provocation other than knowing he was *kitsune*." He bowed toward Kaworu.

"Indeed," relented Harume, "that is often enough." Her eyes shifted to Kaworu.

"I know there is little love lost between our peoples." Kaworu bowed toward Gennosuke. "But we are to be allies now." It was hardly a proper reply, but he was not inclined to be gracious to the boy who had only by accident not knifed him in the back.

Kaworu frowned. What had become of the little *youkai* who had warned him? Had they trampled him?

Gennosuke rose and nodded. "Yes, we are allies indeed, if you saved the *oyakata-sama*."

Kaworu looked around, scanning the flattened grass, and then he saw the tiny waving arms. The little *youkai* smiled broadly and scampered away into the growth.

Harume knelt and settled in the grass. "Then let us hear of this man you saw, and we will go into the east and find him."

Tsurugu and Kaworu knelt as well. "His name is Ogasawara no Manabu," said Kaworu, "and he is an *onmyouji*. He is a slight man, but his servant is large and strong."

CHAPTER THIRTY

GENNOSUKE'S great bundle of twigs caught against a passer-by, pulling at his clothing. The man turned and shouted, aiming a loose blow in the direction of Gennosuke's head without much effort. Gennosuke ducked beneath it easily, bowing repeated apologies and stumbling away.

He adjusted the slipping bundle of branches and continued down the street. It was easy to move as a low laborer. Few paid him attention, and none would remember him if he returned the next day with a different trade. He was just another dirty boy to be ignored or pushed aside.

But those most ignored heard most, and the appearance of an errand could carry him into most places. Today he had learned the inn hosted two men very like those the fox-boy had described, and he wished to find himself a place where he could listen to them converse privately.

It had been difficult to grasp, at first — that someone was using *youkai* as subtle weapons and secret warriors. Harume-san had been angry in her silent way, outraged at this assault upon the *oyakata-sama* and, Gennosuke thought, a bit pricked in her pride. The *daimyou* had their shadows; wasn't that enough?

Gennosuke was anxious to please her with his knowledge-gathering, after she had been shamed by his attack upon the *onmyouji*'s pet *kitsune*. Well, how was he to know? The *daimyou* had been concerned about a *kitsune*, concerned enough to call for Shishio Hitoshi. That this one had agreed to help the *onmyouji* after being captured by the *daimyou*'s enemy was a fortunate but unpredictable turn of events, and he couldn't have been expected to know. She didn't have to thump his head right in front of them.

He set down his bundle of kindling and feigned a stretch, glancing about the rear of the inn. No one had challenged him. Now to find this strange *onmyouji*.

狐

"Tsurugu-sama! Tsurugu-sama!"

Murame's anxious voice rang down the *sunoko*, and Tsurugu turned to meet her. Murame did not often raise her voice. "I'm here. What is it?"

Murame's words were punctuated with little gasps. "Kaede-dono sent me to warn you. A man has come to ask audience of the *daimyou*, and he says he is an *onmyouji*."

If Tsurugu had been in his native form, his hackles would have risen. As it was, a tremor grew low in his throat where his body wished to growl. "Thank you for bringing me word," he replied, his voice burring. "Where is Kaworu-kun?"

"In my lady's room," she answered, her eyes wide. She had hidden him first. "I have told him to stay until I come for him."

Tsurugu nodded. "Return to Kaede-dono and thank her for the warning. I will come."

Well come, onmyouji-san, he thought. All his skill was

bent on confronting this man, and now he had come to Tsurugu's very home — the very place where Kaede-dono and all her *kitsune* lived. And he had asked to speak with the *daimyou*.

Very well, then, onmyouji-san. Bring your best.

狐

Kaede gripped her pleated fan, crushing it until it shifted in her hand, forcing all her anxiety and anger into the painted paper so that none remained on her face or in her voice. Beyond the screen, Naka no Yoritomo settled himself, smoothing out a wrinkle in his sleeve before admitting the stranger who had asked to speak with him.

Kaede took a slow breath and told herself that Yoritomo-dono would be fine. He was in his own home, surrounded by his own trusted warriors, and he was formidable himself. If this *onmyouji* attempted any attack — for surely this was the same man who had arranged the *oni*'s ambush — her husband would not be taken easily.

Nonetheless, she worried. Even a great swordsman could be caught unaware when relaxing in his own home. And an *onmyouji*'s attack might not be so easily recognized....

But that was why she had sent for Tsurugu. He needed to be warned — the *onmyouji* had overcome a *kitsune* before, and he would bear no good will toward the one who had stolen him back — and he would also provide an arcane defense for Naka no Yoritomo, whom she could not warn because she was supposed to be ignorant of this man.

One day, she dreamed, it would be delightful to explain to her beloved all that she did know, and all she did for his sake. It would be wonderful to say she wished to see this new *onmyouji* so that she could assess and watch him, rather than feigning a feminine and ignorant wonder at *onmyoudou* and a jealous desire to compare him to their own *onmyouji*. But not this day.

Yoritomo-dono signaled, and the *onmyouji* was allowed to enter. Kaede peered at him through the obscuring screen as he approached and bowed. She was not sure what she had expected, but it had not been this slight man. He looked unimposing and almost harmless as he bent low before her husband.

"Rise, and tell us why you have come."

The man sat up and addressed the *daimyou* respectfully. "I am Ogasawara no Manabu, an *onmyouji*. I have come hoping to do you a service, *oyakata-sama*."

Yoritomo-dono smiled tolerantly. "As it happens, Ogasawara-san, we have already an *onmyouji* in our household."

"Exactly so," answered Ogasawara. "And it is of him I wish to speak." His eyes flicked significantly to the others in the chamber. "Perhaps we might speak more discreetly, Naka-dono?"

That had been the wrong path to take, and Kaede was pleased to see Yoritomo-dono stiffen. "I believe," he answered, his voice only faintly cooler, "you may convey to me here whatever it is you wish to suggest."

Ogasawara recognized the error as well. "Of course, Naka-dono. It is only that I wished to avoid any potential embarrassment—"

Murame slid silently to Kaede's side, taking her place beside Hanae. The fox-maid looked worried, separated by only a thin painted screen from the *onmyouji* who had enslaved an *oni* and kidnapped Kaworu. Murame took her hand reassuringly and nodded to Kaede; Tsurugu had been warned.

On the polished floor beyond the screen, Ogasawara was recovering ground. "And so, if I could just have a word with your own *onmyouji*...."

Kaede shifted, rustling her many-layered robes, and she composed a quiet giggle, quickly suppressed.

Yoritomo-dono turned his head toward the screen. "You seem to have caught the attention of my wife."

Kaede took a breath and then pitched her voice carefully. "Forgive me, *tono*. I was only surprised that this man — and perhaps I have misunderstood — this man implies the *onmyouji* you have found for me is not to be trusted, and this after he warned you of the *oni* and told you where to find help."

That was a good play. The success against the *oni* was hard to discount, and the allusion to his bringing an *onmyouji* for her sake would prick Yoritomo-dono's pride.

He straightened slightly. "Indeed, I owe my life to Tsurugu-sama. What charge would you bring against him?"

Ogasawara smiled, unoffended, and bowed. "If he is as honorable and loyal as you say, then there can be no harm in letting me speak with him."

Yoritomo-dono smiled, faintly smug. "Indeed. And as you are so confident, there can be no harm in a little wager?"

Ogasawara hesitated. "My lord?"

"If you succeed in demonstrating that my faithful *onmyouji* who has served me so well is somehow a risk to me, then I shall deal with him as necessary and take you into my service instead, with suitable reward. If, however, you cannot bring a valid charge against him, I shall have you beaten from this house and down the road. Is that fair?"

Ogasawara smiled. "That is very fair, Yoritomo-dono."

Kaede's stomach clenched. The strange *onmyouji* was far too confident. He had to be aware of Tsurugu's secret. And the shadow-warrior Shishio Hitoshi had once broken the fox illusions; surely an *onmyouji* could do the same.

"Call for Tsurugu-sama," ordered Yoritomo-dono, and

he turned toward the screen. "This should prove interesting, my dear."

"Most interesting," Kaede answered, her voice a little forced. "I can hardly contain my curiosity." Indeed, her heart was pounding nearly audibly.

"I am here, *tono*," came a voice from the *sunoko*, and then through the screen Kaede could make out Tsurugu entering the open *shouji*. He moved deliberately, almost stiffly, and without so much as glancing at Ogasawara. He knelt and bowed to the *daimyou*.

"Well, Ogasawara-san?" prompted Yoritomo-dono.

"I would first like to enact a defensive spell," answered Ogasawara, "to protect you as well as myself."

Yoritomo's eyebrow raised. He was enjoying this more and more. "Indeed? But surely you recognize that we cannot allow a strange *onmyouji* to come into our home and work spells?"

"This will be for defense only," Ogasawara gently protested. "Tsurugu-sama may approve it himself. If there is no danger, he can have no objection."

"Very well," replied Yoritomo. "Go ahead."

Ogasawara gestured, and a big man hurried forward with a small coffer. Ogasawara withdrew several articles Kaede recognized from Tsurugu's practice and waved the servant away before fussing with them, arranging colored stones and chalking lines and adjusting wooden pieces. At last he sat upright and indicated the array. "Tsurugu-sama, your approval? Is it not for defense only?"

Tsurugu moved his head slightly — he had not even bothered to watch Ogasawara's preparations — and glanced at the array, and then he nodded once, curtly.

Yoritomo-dono had grown bored during the delay. "Well?"

"Now, *tono*," agreed Ogasawara. He raised a hand to point fiercely at Tsurugu. "Yoritomo-dono, I submit to you that your *onmyouji* is no man, but a *kitsune* masquerading in your household. You unknowingly harbor a *youkai*!"

Yoritomo's chin jerked with surprise, and he turned to Tsurugu, clearly expecting protest. The *onmyouji* sat still, and he said, "Well, Tsurugu-sama? Will you answer this?"

There was an instant's hesitation, and then Tsurugu spoke, his words flat and clipped. "It needs no answer, *tono*. You yourself have known my character since you first charged me with protecting your bride, when you set me to work alongside a man called Shishio Hitoshi."

Kaede's heart seemed to convulse in her chest. How had he—?!

Ogasawara was staring openly at Tsurugu, and Yoritomo-dono chuckled aloud. "A very fair reply, Tsurugu-sama," he said, "and I thank you for your tolerant participation in this farce."

"But—" Ogasawara began.

But Yoritomo had already gestured, and armed men had taken each of Ogasawara's arms. "And now," Yoritomo continued, "we shall conclude our wager. Take this man and flog him here, and then down the road as you like."

"Wait, my lord — Yoritomo-dono, let me show you!" But the *ashiguru* did something to Ogasawara's arm and he cried out and was taken from the room.

Tsurugu bowed once more to the *daimyou* and then inclined his head slightly toward the courtyard. Kaede, watching, made a guess as to what he wanted. "Yoritomo-dono!" she called. "Will you dismiss these present and take me to a room where we might speak? I have questions about what has been done here."

"Of course," answered Yoritomo-dono quietly, waving

away the small assembly including Tsurugu. "We may go to the eastern pavilion and watch this buffoon's unceremonious departure as we talk."

Tsurugu retreated from the room, still stiff and deliberate, and Kaede began gathering her many layers to go with her husband. "Why did he believe Tsurugu-sama could be a *kitsune*?" she asked as he came to her.

Yoritomo-dono shook his head and laughed. "I cannot guess," he said, "but nothing is further from the truth. A fox even in human guise cannot say *shi*, and no *kitsune* could manage that name. It was the most elegant answer Tsurugu-sama could have offered, and I really ought to commend him again on it."

And I, thought Kaede. How had he done it? She grasped her robes and started toward the eastern pavilion.

CHAPTER THIRTY ONE

TSURUGU left the *daimyou*'s audience chamber and started away toward the *rou*, the roofed verandas and rooms stretching away from the central house. Outside, laughter and jeers were rising as the stranger was stripped. Tsurugu stepped into his chamber and to one side, completely hidden from the crowded *sunoko*, and then he collapsed and flattened into a strip of brightly-colored paper.

A second Tsurugu stepped into the room and retrieved the paper, tucking it safely within his *himo*. Then he went on to his *futon* and dropped wearily, closing his eyes without even shedding his outer garments.

"A *shikigami*," Murame said from the door, awe in her voice. "You used a *shikigami*."

"I didn't know they could be made to talk," Kaworu added.

"You could not have done it," Tsurugu answered without opening his eyes. "And even for me it was exhausting. Do you mind closing the door and shutting up?"

Murame's voice became tentative. "Would you like tea, Tsurugu-sama?"

"I'd like sleep, and perhaps then tea," he answered gruffly.

"Yes, Tsurugu-sama."

Tsurugu sighed. "Kaworu-kun," he asked, opening his eyes and looking at the wall instead of the boy, "did you see them?"

"Only from a distance." His voice was reserved.

"Was it they?"

Kaworu's voice darkened. "It was."

A howl and a fresh cheer went up from the courtyard. "What you are hearing now is the flogging of the *onmyouji* Ogasawara. I shouldn't be surprised if the servant is included, too."

There was a short pause, and then Kaworu said neutrally, "I think I might go to watch that."

"Murame-san," Tsurugu said, "will you bring me that tea? I think I'll have some after all."

"Hai, Tsurugu-sama."

He had fallen asleep before she returned with the tea, but the soft rattle of dishes on the *zen* woke him. He sat up, heedless of his disheveled state, and accepted the cup she offered.

Murame sat very still, her hands folded in her lap, her head bowed. It was an appropriate posture for a servant. "Murame-san?"

"I have a question I should like to ask, *onmyouji-sama.*"

He took a drink. "Speak."

Her fingers twitched in her lap. "You did not answer the accusation yourself. You used a *shikigami.*"

"That is neither a question, nor news to me."

She flinched, and he realized she was afraid. "You

needed something to speak for you."

"I also wanted to be able to act from another direction if necessary." But now he only prolonged the inevitable.

"*Onmyouji-sama*, are you *kitsune*, too?"

He breathed, drank tea, smiled at her. "You know the answer, Murame-san, or you would not have asked."

Her fingers tightened. "How — how many?"

"Kaworu and his brother — who is not dead, by the by, only gone away — and Hanae-san. And I am, yes."

"And — and Kaede-dono?"

"No. Kaede-dono is not."

"But she is *kitsune-mochi*."

Tsurugu set the tea on the *zen*. "Listen, Murame-san, and think carefully. Kaede-dono took you into her service because you would be discreet. Is that changed?"

Murame raised her head, and her lips made a firm line. "I offered her to bite out my tongue." She raised her chin further. "The villagers accused me, burned me, cast me out, called me a liar and a deceiver and a madwoman. You gave me shelter, Kaworu-kun brought me food, Kaede-dono took me into the house and gave me a safe place. What do you see in me so base that you could think I would betray all this to those who have never believed me, who might call me a liar again?"

Tsurugu made her a little bow, startling her. "I am very sorry, Murame-san. I should not have doubted you."

She shook her head. "Do not apologize to me, *onmyouji-sama*. I am only a servant — your servant, and Kaede-dono's." She swallowed. "Though, I am surprised to find myself in such company." She hesitated. "Only three?"

"What, is three not enough?" Tsurugu took his tea again.

A nervous little giggle broke from her, and she ducked her head again, though less tense. "Three *kitsune* are more than enough, one should agree."

He emptied the cup. "Thank you for the tea, and now I must sleep. But — keep close to Kaede-dono, and if it seems the *oyakata-sama* should want me...."

She nodded. "Of course, *onmyouji-sama.*" She blinked, and her eyes were full of questions, but she bit them firmly down. "Sleep well."

CHAPTER THIRTY TWO

OGASAWARA rolled one shoulder and probed at it experimentally, swearing. He hurt worse today.

Ogasawara had come to warn Naka-dono, and this was the *daimyou*'s gratitude. Well, true, Ogasawara had come to kill him, but Naka had not known that.

"I'm hungry," whined the boy. Ogasawara glared at him, but the boy wasn't looking and missed it. "When do we eat?"

"Shuddup," grumbled Hideo.

They had found the boy on the road outside the village, selling wood from his bundle of branches with no one to miss him, just in time to press him to carry the little remaining baggage after their beatings. He had protested and argued until Ogasawara had cuffed him sharply several times, but it was difficult to properly discipline an insolent peasant while so sore, and the boy had been growing mouthy again over the last day. "Look, you said if I carried this stuff you'd feed me, and I'm hungry now. When are we going to stop?"

"Enough!" Ogasawara rubbed his eyes, burning with

road dust and exhaustion and shame. "We'll stop soon."

They'd purchased a few handfuls of rice and barley, not quite enough for the three of them, and they made a little camp away from the road where they were not likely to be disturbed. It was near enough that Ogasawara could send borrowed eyes easily to Naka no Yoritomo's house.

They set the grain to cooking, and he took a sheet of paper from the pack. He glanced at the boy, poking desultorily at the fire with a twig and staring at the cooking pot, and moved into the trees. Once he was safely away from the boy's eyes, he knelt and concentrated.

A moment later, the *shikigami* rose, and Ogasawara watched it wing toward the *daimyou*'s house. The fox would be watching and the *shikigami* would likely never make it into the house, but it was worth trying. He had to discover a weakness he could exploit, some way he could make the *daimyou* understand that Tsurugu was *kitsune*. Then Naka-dono would invite Ogasawara into his service, and Ogasawara would have privileged access to both Naka-dono and his wife.

He drew the polished comb from his clothing and rubbed his thumb over it gently. He nearly lost it as they fled, but he had snatched it from the ground. *Matsue....*

He would find a weakness, and he would enter Naka-dono's house. And he would carry both Naka-dono's head and his wife's head to Sanjou-dono, and he would see Sanjou humiliated before all his men, and Chikahiro abased before all the family, and he would have such a memorial for Matsue as she deserved.

It should have been done. The security of the other *onmyouji*'s position had surprised him, and now Ogasawara had only rooted it more firmly. He had never guessed it could have gone so poorly.

There were other ways. Acquiring a position within

Naka no Yoritomo's household would have been the simplest and most elegant, but there were others.

Ogasawara returned to the fire. The conscripted boy rubbed a dirty hand over his face, leaving a smudge. "Why does rice take so long to cook? I'm hungry!"

If Ogasawara were not so sore, he would slap the boy just to quiet him. "It's nearly done." He returned to the tiny bundle of their belongings, ready to set a *kekkai* around their sleeping place. The box containing the *tama* and other materials was still at the bottom of the bundle, but the packet of paper he'd left atop it all was gone. "Where is my paper?"

"I was hungry," whined the boy. "It didn't cook any faster though."

Ogasawara turned on him. "You burned my paper?!"

The boy rubbed his nose on his hand. "It was heavy to carry."

Ogasawara lurched toward him, but the boy scrabbled away and held up his hands in defensive protest. "What? It's just paper!"

Hideo, who had been drowsing a little distance away, shrank back and watched wide-eyed. Ogasawara lunged, catching a handful of hair. The boy shrieked and whined as Ogasawara slapped him, but he was too sore to make a good job of it. He threw the boy to the ground and snapped, "Hideo! Come beat this brat."

Hideo was no more limber than Ogasawara, but he climbed obediently to his feet. The boy whimpered and fled into the dark, and Hideo hesitated and threw a despairing look at his master.

Ogasawara could have summoned *youkai* to pursue the boy, but he was only a conscripted servant, destined to be discarded anyway, and Ogasawara was pained and exhausted already. He waved a dismissal. "More for the two of us," he said, squatting beside the cooking fire.

Stupid boy, burning the paper. It was possible to use other material for *shikigami*, of course, but that would have been the simplest. And he would need paper for *ofuda* and *shime-kazari*, to counter the fox-magic the false *onmyouji* might present. Stupid Naka-dono, to confuse fox-magic with *onmyoudou*.

Though no fox should have been able to answer as Tsurugu had, saying "Shishio Hitoshi" so easily, and Hideo had said it was a *shikigami* that had come for their young fox. But Ogasawara himself had seen the pawprints they left....

No, Tsurugu was *kitsune*, and it had been some powerful illusion which had produced the *shikigami* and made them believe he had spoken the impossible words. Ogasawara had never heard of fox-magic so strong, but it must be. He smiled. It would be splendid to have such a creature bound as his servant, when he had finished with Naka and Sanjou. He would parade it before Chikahiro, proving to all his superior *onmyoudou*. Soon.

"I'm hungry."

Ogasawara jerked to look at the dirty boy, crouching at the edge of the firelight. "You dare to come back here?"

"You said that if I carried, you'd feed me. I'm hungry."

Ogasawara plucked a handful of rice from the pot and squeezed it into a lump, and then he threw it at the boy. He caught it deftly, but the rice exploded and fell into the dirt around him. The boy pushed what he held into his mouth and then began plucking grains from the ground. Hideo laughed.

"That's enough for you," Ogasawara warned. "There's not much here. But carry again tomorrow, and we'll have a proper feast, rice and vegetables and even a fish." He would set the boy to thieve them while he traded for paper. This remote place would not value the polished comb properly, but he would be able to get enough paper.

Soon.

狐

"You see?" Kaworu stepped back, letting Murame trace the motion herself. "You deflect his grip, to run or to seize him yourself if you wish to throw him down. It is your own barrier."

"It's very close, though. I might prefer a barrier such as Tsurugu-sama makes." She practiced the deflecting strike again, her arm carving a slow circle in the air. "Can you show me that? *Onmyoudou?*"

Kaworu laughed. "Hardly."

"But Tsurugu-sama is teaching you, I know."

He shook his head. "I am learning *onmyoudou* as you are learning *taijutsu* — only the barest elements, in case of great need. I am no more an *onmyouji* than you are a *daimyou's* warrior or a shadow."

Murame acknowledged this with a sympathetic nod. "But you can tell me, how does it work? I know of the five elements."

"Five elements, yes," Kaworu said, "but that is hardly the end of it. Each element may be *yin* or *yang, on* or *myou,* and that makes the ten foundational pieces. But consider each element may also be aligned with any of the twelve zodiac signs, and that gives us the sixty tendencies. And when those are considered with the twenty-eight guest stars, the eight directions, the five planets, and—"

"Stop!" Murame cried, laughing. "I have run out of fingers already."

Kaworu smiled. "I shouldn't tell you how long it took me to learn them all. I prefer you to think me clever."

"I think you very clever. You tricked an *oni.*"

"And was promptly captured by its master."

Murame sobered. "Being captured is not your fault, but his. You were clever enough to escape."

"When Tsurugu-sama came for me."

"Which he did because you are a fine, clever student." She smiled. It was an incomplete argument, but there was no purpose to pursuing it. "Let me practice the strike." She traced the movement again.

"Not so fiercely," Kaworu cautioned. "Use his own weight against him, rather than try to beat him with yours. See? You want to be a tiger!"

"No tiger," she laughed. "But I will know how to scratch."

狐

Gennosuke pressed his folded arms over his stomach as it gurgled. In all the tales, in all the lessons and cautionary stories, he never yet heard of a shadow betrayed by his growling stomach, and he did not want the shame of being the first.

A few paces away, Ogasawara lay sleeping, his head pillowed on his little coffer of *onmyoudou* supplies. Gennosuke had not had time to destroy more of them, and he wasn't certain how essential they were. His people used the *kuji-in* and other magics without physical aids, and it seemed likely an *onmyouji* could be similarly versatile.

Yet even an *onmyouji* was flesh and blood. Gennosuke had been sent to find and observe Ogasawara, not to assassinate him, but he had seen enough to know the man was dedicated and dangerous. They had gone to a market today where Ogasawara had stood a long moment before trading a woman's comb for paper, and then he had spent the day painting spells on rectangular strips and folding cut sheets into *shime-kazari*. When a bamboo-cutter had asked to buy one of the *ofuda*, Ogasawara had refused.

They needed the money. Ogasawara had nothing left, and he'd ordered Gennosuke to steal the meal he'd promised. Gennosuke could have slipped any number of items into his sleeves — hours of light-fingered practice under Juubei's sharp gaze had seen to that — but it seemed more prudent to keep the *oyakata-sama*'s enemy hungry and desperate, grasping rather than secure, and so he'd gotten too excited upon spotting a basket of vegetables so that the seller had gestured him away, he'd dropped the fish he'd slipped incompletely into his sleeve, he'd half-hidden the little bag of rice against his chest where it was easily spotted. His heart had been in his throat — if truly caught, the punishment would make Juubei's chastisements seem feather-light and might even leave him unfit to serve as a shadow — but only one vendor had managed to seize him, and Gennosuke had executed an escape which left his skin abraded but intact. Ears ringing with blows, he'd fled to wait for Ogasawara, who had cuffed him further and cursed his clumsiness.

But Ogasawara had not sold the *ofuda*, despite Hideo's anguished expression and Gennosuke's affected whining. He meant to attack Naka-dono, and soon. And while Gennosuke had not been told to kill him, he thought now it was in the *daimyou*'s service to do so.

And so now he crept toward the sleeping *onmyouji*, his hand on the thin blade hidden beneath his ragged clothes, pressing his arm against his abdomen in a vain attempt to silence the rumbling. The scant rice and dirt from the night before was an unsatisfying memory. He had long dreamed of his first task for the *daimyou*, but he had not thought it would include nights of hunger and so many cuffs to the head. Still, none had suspected him for anything but a scrounging worthless peasant, and he would be able to tell the story well for his fellow students.

He reached Ogasawara and eyed the colored stones arranged about him. The *onmyouji* had set some spell in place before lying down to sleep. Gennosuke frowned. *Onmyoudou* was a way of divination, of astronomy and numbers and purification — but not of assault. He eased forward over the invisible line connecting the stones.

The air thickened and solidified before him, becoming a wall as solid as any about the *daimyou's* house. Ogasawara shifted where he lay, moving his head on the coffer.

Gennosuke drew back. And defense — *onmyoudou* also was a way of defense. Had the arcane barrier disturbed the *onmyouji*, or was it chance that he moved?

His stomach growled again, and a little distance away Hideo moved and made a sound in his sleep. They were all sleeping lightly in their discomfort and hunger. Gennosuke released the blade and moved away to his own sleeping place.

He would watch in the morning and learn what he could, and then he would slip away and report to Harume-sama. He wrapped his arms about his hollow stomach and waited for dawn.

CHAPTER THIRTY THREE

TSURUGU glanced toward the house. No one was near; the garden and pond were empty. In the *tsuridono* projecting over the pond, a covered pavilion for enjoying the water and islands, Kaede-dono sat alone, screened from the *rou* and main house.

Tsurugu crumpled the scrap of paper which had been a *shikigami* — a pitiful attempt, for Naka-dono's house was well protected — and went to the *tsuridono*. He bowed to the screen. *"Konbanwa."*

"Good evening, Tsurugu-sama." Her fan beckoned. "Come and sit. Yoritomo-dono is busy with accounts and regrets he will not be joining us to watch the sunset."

Tsurugu came around the screen and settled beside her. "Will he come later?"

"Possibly, but there was quite a stack of books awaiting him." She gestured to a small vessel. *"Sake?"*

"Perhaps in a bit." He seated himself near her. "We should have excellent blossoms this year."

She nodded, looking out at the budding trees covering the little man-made islands in the created pond. "Oh, yes, they will be beautiful." She sighed. "One year here."

Tsurugu looked ahead to the artfully-wild garden. "You are pleased?"

"I am quite pleased. I am—" She paused and smiled, a bit embarrassed. "I am very much in love with him."

"And he with you, if I am not mistaken."

"I think so. And that pleases me, too." Kaede-dono examined her fan. "Tsurugu-sama...."

"Yes?"

"When you were injured, when the twins brought you back — in your oblivion, you called for me."

Tsurugu's stomach clenched, and heat scorched through his neck and ears. "Did I."

There was an awkward pause. A fish splashed in the pond. Kaede-dono picked at a scuff mark on her fan. "Tsurugu-sama, I know why it is you came."

His stomach spasmed, and he was grateful for the encroaching twilight that blurred his humiliated flush. "I was instructed to serve and protect you, Kaede-dono. It was Midorikawa-dono who sent me."

"That is true, strictly speaking." She rubbed at the mark with uncharacteristic intensity. "Tsurugu-sama, I—"

"There is no need to say anything."

"I wish to. Please. I came to Midorikawa-dono with nothing — barely even a name, as my family would have taken it from me if they could. When the wife promised to an exorcist chooses instead to become *kitsune-mochi*...."

Tsurugu smiled. "It must have been very embarrassing for them."

"It was probably cruel of me. But I could not have borne that life, either. And Midorikawa-dono was kind enough to take me under his protection."

"He was grateful to you. And for all that we are a mischievous race, we do hold our gratitude."

"There was little need. It was a small service I had done, and years before. He owed me such a small obligation, if that, and now I owe him everything I am and all that I have." She flicked her eyes toward Tsurugu. "Including my protectors. For whom I am very grateful, as protectors."

Tsurugu inclined in a polite little bow. "It is my honor and my duty and my pleasure, Kaede-dono."

They were quiet a moment. Across the garden, the deer-chaser, or *shishi-odoshi*, filled and dumped its water, striking its rock with a hollow bamboo thump to startle any encroaching grazers.

Kaede lifted her head. "What was that?"

Tsurugu sniffed. "You have a terrible sense for cruelty."

Kaede laughed behind her fan. "My wicked games have lost their savor, now that I know you might use a *shikigami* to speak for you. That was a most clever trick."

"I would not care to try it often. I paid dearly for it."

"And concealed us all. Our protector."

Tsurugu looked far across the pond. "I would not permit harm to come to my family. I have no wife, or son, or servants, but — but I will act as if I had."

Kaede's eyes shifted over her fan.

Tsurugu cleared his throat. "I think I will have the *sake* now."

The breeze shifted and curled about them, rustling and rattling the budding branches. The *shishi-odoshi* clacked again, spilling its water. *Sake* burned down Tsurugu's throat and warmed him.

As he held out the shallow bowl for Kaede to fill again, he sensed someone else. He wasn't entirely certain how he knew, if he had heard or smelled a third presence, but he was suddenly aware they were not alone.

Kaede, too, looked behind them to the small screen that shielded her from any servants who ventured this way. "Who's there?"

Naka no Yoritomo-dono stepped from behind the screen. "I am."

"You've finished?" Kaede began happily, but Naka interrupted her.

"Quiet. I have heard your talk."

"Our talk? What, our game? But we spoke in jest, for—"

"I heard enough to know this is not true," he snapped, "and to know you lie to me even now."

Kaede hesitated. "Yoritomo-dono...."

Tsurugu set down the *sake* cup. *"Oyakata-sama—"*

The *daimyou* drew and slashed downward in one fluid motion, and Tsurugu recoiled as he threw a hasty barrier between them, deflecting the blade. Naka-dono cursed, and Tsurugu scrabbled backward.

"Kitsune-me! And I have invited you into my household, have praised you, have given you gifts." Naka stepped forward, and Tsurugu backed against the rail at the edge of the *tsuridono.* "And all the while, you were the very thing you pretended to hunt."

Tsurugu raised his hands in helpless supplication. *"Tono,* you know the service I have done for you and your house."

"Do I? Or was it spun illusion as well — false problems you pretended to solve, to manufacture my gratitude?" He moved and the *katana* sliced across the *tsuridono.*

Tsurugu flung himself backward behind a hasty *kekkai,* twisting over the rail and shifting forms so that he splashed as a fox into the water below. The blade bit into the wood and shaved shards that fell around him. He kicked off the pond's floor and bounded to the bank, not even pausing to shake water before jumping to the landward entrance of the *tsuridono*.

Kaede threw herself after Naka. "Wait! Yoritomo-dono!"

He wheeled on her, *katana* gleaming, and she shrank back and fell. Tsurugu shifted to human shape and started forward. If Naka no Yoritomo struck at Kaede-dono, his blow would not land, that Tsurugu could promise.

But Naka-dono only stood over her, his *katana* across his body, looking down upon her. She stared, her face tight with fear and disbelief.

After a moment he spoke, and his voice was clipped and terse. "You are not one of the Fujitani."

"No." Her rich voice quavered. "I am the daughter of a medicine-seller, who broke her betrothal and fled. I was never a widow."

"What service did you perform for this fox who has assisted you?"

"When I was a child, I freed a fox trapped by the exorcist to whom I was promised. That fox was the first wife of a *kyuubi*, and he remembered my act."

"A *kyuubi*." Naka-dono drew in a sharp breath.

Tsurugu did not dare to move, lest he upset what fragile balance kept the *daimyou's katana* from his wife.

"You are a traitor. A — a whore-spider, betraying me with this *youkai*." Naka-dono fairly spat the words.

Kaede's voice trembled. "Never, *tono*."

"What else did you bring into my household besides this one? Your maid, the girl the village called *kitsune-tsuki* or *kitsune-mochi*?"

Tsurugu hadn't known the *daimyou* knew his wife's maid so well.

"No, *tono*. She was wholly innocent, until they accused

her." There was an edge to Kaede's voice, though it shook.

"The others?"

"My maid, and the boys. They are *kitsune*, too."

Naka-dono clenched his jaw. "Why did you deceive me?"

Kaede's eyes shone with tears, and her voice shook. "You see why."

He gripped the hilt until his fingers went white, and then he lifted the sword and drew it across the sheath, returning it. "For the love that I have borne you until now, I will not kill you where you sit. But you will not remain another night in my house. If I see any of your wretched servants, I will strike them down. You have until moonrise to be gone."

Kaede, pale in the twilight, stared up at him, her face crumpling. "Yoritomo-dono...."

He spun and moved jerkily away, not seeing or pretending not to see Tsurugu crouching low beside the *tsuridono.*

Tsurugu climbed again into the pavilion and rushed to Kaede. "Kaede-dono — I am so sorry...."

She wept, collapsing forward and shaking with sharp, fresh sobs. Tsurugu wanted to take her, to hold her, but he had been the one to betray her — and not just Kaede-dono, but Kaoru and Hanae. And no matter what Kaede had told Naka-dono, he would not leave Murame untouched as he purged his house of *youkai* and their influences.

"Kaede-dono, we have to go. We have to find the others."

She nodded, crying, and Tsurugu envied her womanly ability to express her despair. He had pledged Midorikawa-dono to protect Kaede-dono and the others, and he had allowed disaster to come upon them.

CHAPTER THIRTY FOUR

HANAE'S fingers fumbled as she wrapped her mistress's clothes, tying Kaede-dono within her own cocooning garments as great ladies did for travel. "Where will we go, *okugata-sama?*"

"I don't know!" snapped Kaede, her voice raw. "I don't know. But we must be out of this house by moonrise." She shook her head. "Murame, leave those things. We haven't the time or the hands. Bring the medicine box, certainly, and then go to find some bags of rice and vegetables. Wherever we're going, we won't starve on the way."

"Okugata-sama." A woman in soft grey to match her hair knelt beside Kaede.

Kaede jerked away, stumbling into Hanae. "I have until moonrise, he said!"

"I have no orders to that end, *okugata-sama.*" The shadow-woman lifted her head. "I bring you information."

"Thank you, but I do not think the *oyakata-sama* will hear me now."

"I have already told him that the other *onmyouji* comes

now."

Kaede's heart, already racing, seemed to shake within her. "He comes?"

"He is moving toward this house and he is gathering *youkai* to him. The boy was with him and reports he comes like a warlord, through the hills in the east."

Kaede clenched her fists. "You have told the *oyakata-sama*?"

"I have. But—" The woman paused, and for a moment she could not decide how to speak. Finally she determined she best served her master by betraying him. "But, *okugata-sama*, he has only your word that Ogasawara-san is the one who called the *oni*. He has sent for him, to replace Tsurugu-sama."

"Merciful goddess. He has invited the snake into his house." For a moment Kaede could hardly breathe, could hardly form a thought. Ogasawara had warned Naka-dono that Tsurugu was a *kitsune*; of course Naka-dono would trust him now.

Hanae broke the frozen moment. "We must tell Tsurugu-sama. Perhaps he can intervene."

"Tsurugu-sama cannot stop an army." Kaede blew out her breath sharply. "But he may give me an army to meet them." She unfolded her arms within the cocooning garments. "Take these off me, and find something in which I can move. Cut short my *hakama*, or use something of Murame's, I don't care, but I will need to run and move this night. And then go and fetch Tsurugu-sama. We have little time."

狐

They carried little baggage for five people. They had some food, Tsurugu brought only his *onmyoudou* devices and charts, and only Kaede and Murame needed extra clothing.

In the hills to the east, the shadow-woman had said.

They picked their way through the darkening twilight. "We will stay at the shrine," said Kaede. "He will have to wait until the morning, too. There will be little moon tonight."

"He's an *onmyouji* with *youkai* at his command," Tsurugu answered bitterly. "He may have all the light he wishes. Many *youkai* can manipulate balls of light or fire." He glanced at Kaede. "But it would be simpler for him to wait until morning, yes, and he will be in no hurry if he has received Naka-dono's invitation. His purpose is better served if he enters quietly and politely, and then releases his *youkai* with the house."

"Where he may kill Yoritomo-dono as they sit together, and everyone within the walls." Kaede closed her eyes. "What can you provide me?"

"I will call to the *youkai*. I cannot promise who will answer, but we should see some rise to help you. You are in Midorikawa-dono's care."

"Bring whom you can. Tomorrow morning we intercept him, and we must have more than the four of us."

"Four?" Murame circled to face them. "What of me?"

"This has nothing to do with you," Kaede said firmly. "You are neither *kitsune* nor *kitsune-mochi*, and you can start a life elsewhere."

"How can you say this has nothing to do with me?" Murame swept her arm to encompass them. "You are my mistress, Tsurugu-sama rescued me from the mob which tortured me, Kaworu-san saved me from—"

"Neither the *daimyou* nor this hateful *onmyouji* will trouble himself with you, if you take yourself away now." Kaede's voice had a honed edge. "You may stay the night with us, but in the morning you leave us."

"No!"

"Then we leave you. But I will not risk you in this,

which is not your fight." She turned her face from Murame, refusing further protest. "Tsurugu-sama, can you protect our shrine for this night?"

"You know I can, Kaede-dono."

"Then let us hurry and take shelter."

三十五

CHAPTER THIRTY FIVE

KAEDE-DONO stood tall, fierce, resolute. In the slanting morning light, she looked nothing at all like a woman who had lost everything, who had no home, no husband, no name. "Call them."

Somewhere behind them a drum began — one of the *tanuki*, no doubt. The beats rolled through the wood, a great drum like those which called the *daimyou*'s men to battle and directed them over the crash and din of chaos, rolling through the forest and shivering the leaves on the trees, rattling through the ground, shaking Tsurugu's heart in his chest. The *odaiko* resonated and called and demanded, and from all directions *youkai* appeared, small things creeping from beneath leaves and deadfall, and man-sized things with a single staring eye, and horned things hunching beneath tall branches.

A woman appeared, her long neck snaking upward and outward as she came, and another with a second mouth gaping ravenously from the back of her head. A third joined them, white and cold and drifting, tinging leaves with brown and frost as she passed.

"Yuki-sama," Tsurugu said to the last with a bow. "Thank you for coming."

The *yuki-onna* bowed in return. "It is a woman who stands in need," she answered. "Of course we shall stand with her."

The *youkai* gathered and arranged themselves — not in ordered ranks, not as human soldiers might do, but in loose rings and irregular lines, on the ground and in the trees, eyes centered on Kaede-dono, silent and still and beautiful.

The drum ceased, and there was a moment of weighted silence. Kaede took a breath, and Tsurugu could see her fingers work on her *kimono*. Then she made a single, deep bow toward the arranged *youkai*.

Someone gave a keening cry, and others joined. Yips, yelps, shrieks, howls, and shouts rose into the dawn, an acclaiming cry as humans rarely heard, feet drumming the earth to replace the great drum. Kaede rose and turned again, facing where Ogasawara would come.

And from the opposite hill, came a man, wrapped in beads and *ofuda*, bearing a stick hung with *shime-kazari* and shaking it as he came, chanting. Behind him drifted another army of *youkai*, but these were silent, and they moved stickily, as if their varied limbs were not in agreement. They were conscripted fighters, and their heart was not in the battle. Tsurugu's stomach twisted; he had no wish to kill slaves.

"*Kitsune-onna*," called Ogasawara, pausing. "This can be simple. You have nothing — nothing to defend. You are shamed and outcast, and death will be your only release. Choose that now, and no one else must die."

Kaede did not move, and for a terrible instant Tsurugu realized she was considering his words — had been considering it since she had left Naka no Yoritomo's house.

"No," she said at last, and the word clawed his ears. "No, you are wrong. I have no home, I have no name, I have no husband, I have no life — but I still have a lord who must be protected. I know once you have my death, you will seek his." She inhaled and seemed to grow stronger. "And I will not die to give you that."

Ogasawara's mouth twisted into a sneer. "So be it. And on your own head be all deaths here."

Tsurugu stepped nearer and dropped his voice to a whisper. "That is not so. He is the aggressor, and it is his fighters who are enslaved. You only defend, and your army comes of its own will."

"That will be cold comfort when they are dead," Kaede said without looking at him. "That they chose death for me? That pleases none of us."

Tsurugu had no answer. He looked across at Ogasawara, who began shaking the *shime-kazari* again and chanting. A shiver ran through the *youkai* around them, and some of the smaller creatures simply vanished.

"He will exorcise your army," Tsurugu said. "Then they will not die for you."

Kaede looked simultaneously angry and sadly relieved.

There was a little blur of movement from the side, and Tsurugu raised a hand as he turned, ready to ward against a flanking attack from Ogasawara's forces. But it was Kaworu and Hanae, running to join them in fox form. Tsurugu relaxed, and Kaworu rose to his human shape. "I left her at the fallen hut. No one has thought to look there."

Tsurugu nodded.

He should order Kaworu away; it was foolish to risk the *kyuubi*'s son in battle with an *onmyouji*. But it would shame Kaworu, and he might prefer danger to further humiliation. And they would be glad of his help. Tsurugu said nothing.

And then Ogasawara's *youkai* shrieked challenge, and the battle closed.

CHAPTER THIRTY SIX

TSURUGU struck aside a misshapen figure with a hasty barrier and pushed through the chaos. The first clash had separated his little group, and he had at last found Kaede flanked by *youkai* women. The long-necked woman wound serpent-like about an opponent's body, pinning him as her two-mouthed sister cut him. The *yuki-onna* seized another and put her mouth to his, sucking his life in a long draw and dropping an icy corpse to the ground.

Leaving Kaede-dono to their protection for the moment, Tsurugu went next in search of Kaoru.

There was a ring of *youkai* pressing inward about Kaoru. The fight had an eerie, grotesque sort of beauty, as if one of the twins' dances had turned deadly. He had no weapons, only his hands, but he punched and struck and kicked and twisted with vicious efficiency.

The *youkai* around him hesitated; his defense was, though not impenetrable, at least difficult. But Kaoru could not maintain his whirling forever.

Tsurugu shook out a *shime-kazari* and chanted, and with a howl the nearest creature vanished, banished. Others looked to the *onmyouji* and fled.

Kaworu slumped and scanned the area, wary and winded. "Tsurugu-sama."

Tsurugu started toward him. "I need you to look for *tama*."

Kaworu braced his hands on his knees and gulped air. "What?"

"Ogasawara is directing *youkai* against us, but that will only destroy his fighters and mine and exhaust us both. It is a ruse. He will try to entrap us in a great circle, I am certain. I can feel energies beginning to divide and align, and we cannot allow him to bind all of us."

Kaworu's lip twitched in an unconscious snarl. "You think he's placing *tama* about all of this?"

"Or something like enough. It would be difficult, but if he succeeded…. You must do this," Tsurugu said. "I will not have the attention to spare, and only you are both knowledgeable enough and quick enough to check around us. Watch for him, but he might well use *youkai* to place the *tama*. You must seek them out and remove or disrupt them."

Kaworu nodded, his eyes wide with responsibility. *"Hai, Tsurugu-sama."*

狐

Kaworu would normally have closed his eyes and centered himself to seek the energy of a circle, but that was an unwise choice for a battlefield. He darted forward and side to side, seeking the edge of the conflict and keeping a wary eye, trying to bring his thoughts into quiet while he threw attackers down or wrenched their arms out of joint.

He struggled to hold his mind in place. This would have

been an excellent time to chant to steady himself, but he could not bring the syllables to mind. Quiet of spirit, indeed.

There! A flicker of white energy danced through him. *Metal.* He could not sense where it was; he could barely grasp it at all.

He pressed himself backward against a tree, looking around him but wrapping his hands around the smooth bark. *Wood against Metal, Wood against Metal.... Where are you?*

The white energy flickered again and hummed in his mind, and he whirled toward it. Up a little slope, the arcane energy glimmered in his mind.

Kaworu raced for the little stone, a curved teardrop of silver against a dark stump. Something lunged from the side, and he slid into fox form and skimmed beneath its reach, feeling its bulk dark above him. He did not stop to fight, but ran for the *tama*, shifting again to human shape and snatching it up without stopping.

"Drop that!"

Kaworu ran.

The monster charged after him, and Kaworu knew he could not outrun it, not in either form. He wondered whether it was charged to pursue him or the *tama*.

A big hand clawed at his shoulder, catching him backward, but he twisted away. It stumbled behind him and crashed on.

Once out of the circle, the *tama* was only a stone, without energy to draw up to locate it. Kaworu cupped the little teardrop in his hand and threw it hard, driving it far, far into the forest.

The creature roared and stuck Kaworu in the back, slamming him to the ground. Soil and leaves filled his mouth and his vision flashed as it landed atop him. Pain knifed through him, and he could not breathe.

Then the weight shifted and the monster rose, dangling him easily by a leg, and its other great hand batted him into the woods after the *tama*. Kaworu flailed but there was nothing to check his fall, and he landed in a thicket that crunched and broke beneath him, stabbing and scratching and gouging him in all parts.

Wood cracked as the monster came after him, and he struggled in the branches. His clothing caught and tangled, and he shifted to fox shape and scrabbled downward, crawling under the interlocking branches and crouching low to the dirt, gasping for air and shaking. It hurt to breathe.

The monster smashed a few bushes in frustration, but it did not seem to know exactly where it had thrown him, and Kaworu held his breath as it passed near on its return. When the crunch of its passage had gone, the din of the battle seemed suddenly to reappear, muted after the deadly footsteps.

He eased from beneath the bushes, belly dragging in the dirt, breath shortened by fear and pain. He should return to Tsurugu, but staying alert for the other *tama*. He considered briefly and decided he would make better progress limping on four legs than two, and he started toward the *onmyouji*.

狐

Tsurugu snatched leaves from the trees as he ran, breathing energy and command into each before tossing it into the air. Above them, the leaves bobbed and caught an unnatural breeze, pitching and bobbing away in different directions.

He slowed and dropped to the ground, breathing hard, and glanced round to be certain he was away from the strife. It felt cowardice itself to be hiding, but he could not hope to work this magic in the midst of battle. He closed his eyes and concentrated.

Perhaps a minute had passed when a presence neared,

brushing against his focus, and his eyes snapped open. Kaworu was a little distance away, watching and wisely waiting until Tsurugu had acknowledged him before approaching.

Tsurugu nodded. "Come on, then. What did you find? Or — what happened? How are you hurt?"

Kaworu shook his head. "I met an *oni* or some relation, but I'm all right for now. I found the Metal *tama* and the Water, and I threw them deep into the trees. It will take all his *youkai* hours to find them."

"Good. Then he cannot close his circle." Tsurugu closed his eyes again. "Watch for me, and let me work."

He reached for each leaf as it returned, gently grasping it and what it reported. The fifth knew where Ogasawara stood, and the seventh knew he was nearly between the useless Earth and Fire *tama*.

Ogasawara, frustrated in his attempt, stood at the edge of his own incomplete circle. Tsurugu concentrated. Trees ringed behind Ogasawara, a thick perimeter of brush and trunks. Wood.

Ogasawara stood within an incomplete circle.

Tsurugu's *onmyoudou* items were in the abandoned hut, too far. But other foci could be used, if with greater difficulty.

Tsurugu opened his eyes. "Kaworu, find a sword."

CHAPTER THIRTY SEVEN

KAWORU clutched the sword — taken from the dead grasp of an ox-headed *ushi-oni* — close to his side, minimizing its catching on brush and supporting his aching ribs. The pain was crawling upward, and each breath stabbed through him. If this worked, though, he would not need to run much more.

Where had that Metal *tama* been? He was near, he was certain. He could hear fighting all around him, but no one had spied him yet. He hunched low and wished his natural shape could manage the sword....

There! He could see the broken stump beside which the *tama* had sat. He leapt a fallen branch and ran for the stump.

Something rose out of the ground, round and massive and pincered. Kaworu veered and ducked beneath the grasping limbs. The great spider heaved after him, far faster than something so large should have been able to move.

Kaworu stumbled and hit the ground, and the hurt in his side flared into sharp, biting pain lancing all through him. He got to his feet without quite knowing how. Behind him the spider hissed and slashed at him, and a pincer opened his shoulder like a knife. Kaworu wanted to turn, to fight, but he was injured and if he fell to the spider Tsurugu-sama would never have a chance to stop Ogasawara. If he placed the sword, at least Tsurugu could save Kaede and the others. He ran.

But the pincer struck him again, and he realized he wouldn't make the stump.

He tried to make a desperate sprint, but he had no more strength, and the spider had eight legs to his two. Kaworu changed his grip on the sword, prepared to defend himself as he went down.

A blur of grey fell from above, skimming over Kaworu and kicking two heels hard into the spider's head. The spider hissed and crumpled beneath the heavy blow, and Gennosuke slid over the carapace and turned as he landed, driving a short, sturdy sword into the plated body. "I have this! Go!"

Kaworu had no breath for thanks, so he nodded once and started again for the stump. It was only a few strides away now, but it seemed all he could do to stumble to it. He jabbed the sword into the ground, deep and secure.

Behind him, the spider screamed and thrashed, and Gennosuke cut away one leg and then another. He rolled and feinted and retreated, and the spider, half-blinded with his first crushing attack, swung viciously and shrieked in pain and rage. Kaworu knew he should help Gennosuke, but he had no weapon and his body could hardly support *taijutsu*.

He felt for a branch and limped toward the battle. He took a ragged, stabbing breath and concentrated, and then he shouted. *"Oi! Ougumo-me!"*

The spider whirled on the new threat, seeing a massive warrior in full armor and wielding a great spear, and Kaworu fell back into an *ichimonji* defense as he brought up the branch, hoping beyond desperation that Gennosuke would not miss the moment.

He didn't, darting in and cutting where segments joined, and the spider shrieked and thrashed and fell, kicking as it died. Kaworu retreated, dropping his illusion, and clutched his throbbing side.

Gennosuke looked across the spider at him. "What happened to you?"

"An *oni*." Kaworu made the sign of obligation. "Thank you."

Gennosuke nodded, a quick jerk of his head. "Balance. A debt owed. Harume-san says I need more Earth in my nature." He wiped and sheathed the sword.

Kaworu tried to smile and then turned back toward Tsurugu.

It took too long to reach the *onmyouji*. He had to avoid fighting, and it hurt to breathe. He tried to feel for the energies in the air as Tsurugu worked his spell, but either the fighting disrupted them beyond recognition, or Kaworu was too exhausted and distracted to focus properly. He suspected the latter.

When he limped to where Tsurugu stood, however, he saw he was wrong. The *onmyouji* was not working his magic, but staring at an empty cup of rigid paper. Kaworu looked down at the empty cup and then to Tsurugu. "What happened? Where is the water?"

"Spilled. The fighting — it was spilled." Tsurugu looked at Kaworu. "Can you fill it?"

Kaworu considered and then shook his head. "Not after the *oni*."

Tsurugu swore. "I couldn't, either. Some things can't be forced in battle."

"Is there a stream, or…." Kaworu trailed off. Tsurugu would have thought of such things already.

"We're atop a hill. There is nothing here, not even dew on the leaves." Tsurugu glanced about them, looking in each direction. "Wood, Metal, Fire, Earth. We must have Water. Or something of water. This is too great to work without a focus."

Harume-san says I need more Earth in my nature. Gennosuke was a metallic personality, at Kaworu's first guess, and a shadow's career would benefit from Earth's practical stability. *Myou* within *on*, balanced — though Kaworu might have supposed a shadow would be more watery, all fluid and black and a thing of night, *on* and —

He turned to Tsurugu, eager with inspiration. "We could use a person."

"What?"

"A person, to represent Water."

Tsurugu hesitated only a second. "Murame. She is watery, and she is *on*-watery, and she is female. *On* within *on* within *on*. Bring her."

Kaworu thought of the hut, far up the mountain, and wanted to drop to his knees. But he nodded. *"Hai, Tsurugu-sama."*

He turned and jogged forward, clutching his ribs. A cry from the left caught his attention, and he ducked and looked for the source.

Kaede-dono had found a *naginata* somewhere, and she had sometime been trained to use it. The wife of a *daimyou* was still of the warrior class, and Naka-dono had not left her ignorant. Her movements were quick, jerky with fear, but they were correct and accurate, and she was holding a tall horse-faced *youkai* at distance.

Murame stood beside her, a short rake in her hand, breathlessly watching her mistress.

There was a dagger on the ground beside a creature who did not need it anymore. Kaworu put the grip in his teeth and shifted to fox shape, and then he ran at them.

The horse-faced *youkai* did not see the pale fox streaking low to the ground behind him, and Kaworu stumbled only a little with the pain in his side and carved along the taut hamstring. The *youkai* went down with a shout, and Kaworu darted to the women, panting as he shifted to human. "We need Murame. Tsurugu-sama thinks he can end this. Please come."

Murame flung her arms about him. "Kaworu-kun!"

He flinched and tried not to pull away. "Come this way."

CHAPTER THIRTY EIGHT

KAWORU felt strangely comforted by Kaede-dono's *naginata* as they pushed through the brush. He had borrowed Murame's rake — he, at least, was trained to use a staff — but he doubted his body. If it came to a serious fight, he would be fatally slow.

Tsurugu was on one knee, fingers interlocked, chanting. He did not open his eyes, but his head jerked to the side where the water *tama* should be. He had other ways of observing them now.

Kaworu pointed. "Murame-san, stand there, and do not move." She took the position, turning back to face them. Kaworu gestured to Tsurugu and the greater circle. "You are a point in the array. He thinks he can bind and entrap Ogasawara-san. But if you move, you will unbalance and unleash all the energy he is working."

Murame nodded. "I will stand here."

"No matter what." Kaworu swallowed. "I will guard Tsurugu-sama and you."

"Not alone," Kaede-dono snapped. "If Ogasawara-san is to be broken, I will be a part of it however I can."

They took their weapons and positioned themselves on either side of the *onmyouji*, Kaworu between Tsurugu and Murame.

It was a terrible period of waiting. Tsurugu's voice was a low murmur, barely audible over the sounds of combat. His fingers worked in quick, practiced gestures, locking and shifting and working. Something shrieked in pain or terror, very near, but though Tsurugu flinched minutely, he did not hesitate or open his eyes.

He trusts us to keep him safe, Kaworu realized. It frightened him.

Energies built around them. Kaworu could sense them faintly even through the chaos, though Kaede-dono and Murame did not seem to note them. "What's happening?" Murame asked, her voice nearly as soft as Tsurugu's.

"He's making a *kekkai* to contain Ogasawara," Kaworu said. "It will entrap him."

"What happens then?"

A roar interrupted them, and Kaede leveled her *naginata* toward the source of the sound. It was Ogasawara, enraged. "*Onore!* You won't finish it!"

He was coming. He could feel the *kekkai* forming, and he was coming to stop it. Kaworu gripped the rake and took a step to test his footing and his aching side.

Ogasawara was within sight now, shoving through the last of the branches and coming into the clearing. His servant and a few *youkai* followed.

Kaede stepped into his path, *naginata* ready.

Ogasawara's eyes blazed at her. "I have done what I have sworn. I have taken Naka-dono's wife from him, just as he took mine." He drew an audible breath. "But I am not finished yet. I will kill you, Kaede-sama."

"If you must." Kaede's voice was cold, indifferent.

"And then I will kill Naka no Yoritomo. I will split him and string his intestines like ropes about his house, and I will—"

Kaede moved with the *naginata* — too soon, and he was able to fall back from its long reach. He grabbed for the shaft of the weapon, and she dropped low and twisted it free. He scuttled backward. "Is that your tender point, then? Not your own life, but his?" He laughed. "And that is exactly why I must do it, you see. I would not have been glad to give my own life, but.... Why Matsue-san? What had she done, who was she that her death mattered in the games of powerful men? And I lost her, for nothing. And so Naka no Yoritomo has lost you, and you will lose him."

Kaede barked a single, sharp sound that might have been a laugh. "You would have done better to keep your vain words to yourself. I would have fought for my life, yes — but I will fight a thousand times for his." She set the *naginata* and challenged Ogasawara with her glittering eyes. "Come then, if you dare."

Kaworu kept his eye on them, breathing slowly. If he slid to the side, came in on Ogasawara's flank....

Ogasawara laughed. "You think to fight by strength? Even as a woman? You fool. My strength is the strength of those I command. Hideo!"

The big man behind him shifted.

"That girl — she is a part of the circle. Remove her or break her."

Kaworu's heart twisted and his neck prickled with invisible hackles. *No! Tsurugu-sama, finish it!* But such a spell, so large and so precise and centered upon a moving subject, could not be hurried, and Ogasawara knew it. Tsurugu was working his best. Kaworu had to protect him and Murame and

Kaede-dono.

They could not both attack Tsurugu, where Kaede-dono and Kaworu could defend him together. But coming at Murame forced them apart, weakening their defense. Kaworu clenched his jaw and turned in place, facing Hideo as he circled them.

Kaede was already moving. Ogasawara gestured, and the *naginata* was deflected by unseen hands. She retracted and thrust again, and again it was deflected. Hideo came around Kaworu, his eyes on Murame.

Kaworu intercepted him, clutching the rake as if it were some mongrel staff. "No."

Hideo hardly looked at him. "Move."

"No." Kaworu's words slurred into a growl. "We have our own business."

Hideo blinked, uncomprehending. "What?"

Kaworu bared his teeth. "You don't remember me?"

Hideo looked at him blankly. "No."

Kaworu snarled and stepped forward, bringing the rake handle around in a sweeping attack. Hideo jerked an arm and deflected the handle upward, seizing the rake and coming forward. Kaworu could not force his torn and exhausted muscles to react quickly enough, and Hideo's big fist caught him at the side of his head.

Kaworu stumbled back, stunned, and the second blow knocked him to the ground. His stupid body did not respond as it should. He tried to get his limbs sorted, arms and legs beneath him as two legs or four, but Hideo kicked him and his injured side exploded in agony, dropping Kaworu crying again to the ground. The world swirled in a bright flash and he thought he might vomit, and the thought terrified him because he knew he would never live through the pain if he tried.

Hideo turned to Murame, still at her position, immobile

and helpless and frightened. He moved toward her, almost slowly in Kaworu's blurred vision, and she shrank back without quite leaving her place. He reached for her.

Murame crouched, centering her weight, and launched straight upward. The heel of her hand drove under Hideo's chin, snapping his head up and back. She wrapped her fingers over his lips and dropped, using her body weight instead of arm strength as Kaworu as taught her, and Hideo toppled and spilled across the ground.

Murame planted one foot and kicked him in the head. "Get away! Get away and leave us alone!"

Hideo rolled, covering his head, and got to his feet. Murame tensed, still on her place. "Leave us be!"

Kaede was swinging the *naginata* in wide arcs about her, not reaching for Ogasawara but beating off something that could not be seen. Ogasawara circled her and started toward Tsurugu. Kaworu screamed a warning but no sound came out.

And then Tsurugu's eyes opened. There was no other movement, but Ogasawara's stride faltered. He took another step, but it seemed as if he were walking uphill, leaning too far forward as he moved. His next step was as if through syrup. The next, as if bound to something heavy behind him.

Ogasawara's face went purple with strain and fury. "*Kisama!* I will—"

A bellow came from behind them, and Tsurugu's eyes went wide. He could not form a defensive spell while holding Ogasawara—

A huge *oni* crashed past Murame, who ducked and screamed, and leapt over Tsurugu. He ducked his horned head and bulled into Ogasawara with a roar.

The spell snapped under the impact and they burst through it, plowing past Kaede as she dove out of the way. The *oni* smashed Ogasawara to the ground and began to pummel him with over-sized fists, still roaring.

Tsurugu was on his feet, one hand raised as if he wanted to act but was not sure how. Kaede rushed to him, away from the rage of the *oni*. Kaworu dug his fingers into the ground, frozen by instinct and injury. He knew this *oni*, had seen it rush him in the same way.

The *oni* paused, looking down at its work, and Ogasawara moaned. Not dead, somehow, not yet.

Belatedly Kaworu thought of Hideo, but the big servant had not moved, staring like the rest of them. He did not seem to think of the *kitsune* near him as he gaped at his half-pulped master.

A *tengu* flew over them and settled near the *oni*, the rings in his staff rattling in the unnatural quiet. "Atsuhide-sama!"

The *oni* looked pleased. "Shigetake-sama. *Ohisashiburi de gozaimasu.*"

"You are alive!"

"Plainly." He looked at Ogasawara. "As is he, for a moment longer."

The *tengu* tilted his head, birdlike. "I had — he had thought you lost."

"It took me a long while to recover enough to travel, and then I fought the return as hard as I could. But he summoned me anew, with all these for his battle, and now I have come to him." The *oni* bared massive teeth in a hellish grin. *"Itadakimasu."*

Murame screamed and recoiled, hiding her eyes. Kaworu struggled to his feet, catching his breath as each movement stabbed at him, and staggered to her, wrapping his arms around her and flinching as she clutched him. "You don't have to hold here any longer. Come away."

She nodded, and then without speaking she subtly

slipped beneath his arms and took some of his weight. They turned away from Kaede-dono and Tsurugu and the crunching *oni*, leaving Hideo wide-eyed, and limped away. Kaworu closed his eyes, trying to block away the hurt and weariness. If he could only rest — only sit a moment....

Murame gave a little cry and dropped to the ground, folding herself forward. Kaworu swayed, reaching for his balance, and then saw the figure before them. He clutched his side and knelt before Naka no Yoritomo.

He should have run — the *daimyou* knew him for what he was. He could kill Kaworu in an instant. But Kaworu could never flee, not like this; better to grovel and be helpless than attempt to run and trigger a reflexive action.

On either side of the *daimyou* stood several figures in grey. Harume and Gennosuke were among them. Kaworu kept his eyes low, for the *daimyou's* sake and because he did not want to see them. If the *oyakata-sama* ordered it, Gennosuke or Harume would kill Kaworu without hesitation. Their loyalty was beyond taint.

"Where is Kaede-dono?"

His voice surprised Kaworu. It was low, dark, strained, the voice of a man who faces something unpleasant and wishes to have it done as quickly as possible.

Murame answered. "Just beyond, *tono.*"

She did not betray her mistress; it would be difficult to miss the nearby commotion and Kaede's presence. The fighting around them had ended with Ogasawara's death, as his hold on the enslaved army was shattered. The *daimyou* asked for form, entering the battlefield as a conquering warlord, as much as for information.

Naka no Yoritomo eyed Kaworu for a moment, frowning. Kaworu had not bowed as low as he should, but he was afraid he would cry aloud if he pushed further. The *daimyou* stepped past him and started with his shadows for Kaede-dono.

"Help me," panted Kaworu, reaching to Murame. "Help me up. Then run."

"If you think I will run," snapped Murame, "you insult even my little honor. Hold tight." They stumbled after the *daimyou*.

三十九

CHAPTER THIRTY NINE

"KAEDE-DONO!"

Kaede tore her eyes from the *oni*'s bloody feast and turned to her once-husband. She took a breath and gathered all her ragged dignity and self-possession, and then she knelt properly in the crushed and torn grass, smoothly arranging her borrowed and torn clothing as if it were her many-layered silks. *"Tono."*

Beside her Tsurugu knelt and bowed, but there was a tension in him. He would no longer be passive before the *oyakata-sama*. If Naka no Yoritomo ordered their deaths, the price would be dear.

"Kaede-dono." Yoritomo looked around the little field of battle. She did not know how many *youkai* he saw; many were not visible to her. With a little grimace he seemed to judge that, if the crunching *oni* were not disturbed, it would not bother with anything else.

"*Tono*, I am on my way as you commanded. We stopped here to meet—"

- 253 -

"Quiet." He took a breath. "I saw much of the fight here. Most of what mattered."

"What?"

"We were in the trees." He nodded upward, a jerk of his head. "I saw your confrontation with this Ogasawara." He crossed his arms. "I heard your declaration."

Kaede's mind began to grasp at fragile straws, but she did not trust her judgment and she did not dare to hope. "What declaration was that, *tono?*"

"'I would fight for my life, but I would fight a thousand times for his.'" Yoritomo-dono looked down at her. "You might have fled him. He wanted me more. You did not have to meet him here."

Kaede shook her head. "I am not one to flee while my husband is the object of treachery."

"Not even your husband — the man who cast you out. Who accused you and betrayed you." He stepped forward and went to one knee to reach to Kaede. "Kaede-dono, beloved, I erred. Greatly."

She lifted her head. "You called me a deceiver, a traitor, a whore-spider."

He closed his eyes and winced. "And in fact you are *samurai*, a warrior woman, with loyalty equal to any of my shadow-hands. You hid the truth from me because you feared my reaction, and then I justified that fear. And in the end, when I sat and considered, I could find no actual harm done to my house."

Kaede held his gaze a long moment. "I am still *kitsune-mochi*. I am not Fujitani no Kaede, the widow of a great house, but Yamakawa no Kaede, the runaway daughter of a medicine-seller."

"You are the woman who defended her unworthy lord with a stolen *naginata*. That is enough."

She could not hold back the smile that stretched her face.

Beside her Tsurugu stirred, and for an instant she felt a pang of sympathy. But then Yoritomo-dono took her hand, and she did not think on Tsurugu.

Yoritomo-dono helped her to her feet. "I have never seen you so inappropriately dressed."

She laughed. "For fighting, I think I am far more appropriately dressed than in my lovely *juuni-hitoe.*"

"Tsurugu-sama — you are bound to serve Kaede-dono and her good, and have acted only in that service. Rise."

Tsurugu did, bowing again. He said nothing.

Kaede wrapped both hands about Yoritomo-dono's arm and turned to his grey figures. Murame and Kaworu were there, too.

Kaworu looked terrible, now that she saw him clearly outside the press of battle. He sagged against Murame, his eyes sick and dull with hurt. As Naka no Yoritomo turned toward him, his face tightened and he eased to his knees.

"Stop." Yoritomo-dono held up a hand. "I can see, do not push yourself. A bow cannot express more than the risking of your own life."

Kaworu paused on his knees, relieved and exhausted. "Thank you, *oyakata-sama.*"

Yoritomo looked at Murame. "And you?"

She bowed. "A girl, *tono.* I am only a girl. Though I wish I were something other, if I could have been of greater use to my *okugata-sama* this night."

He almost laughed at that. "My Kaede-dono inspires the greatest loyalties. How then can I doubt her?"

Tsurugu-sama cleared his throat. "*Tono,* if I may…"

"I was just about to order it, Tsurugu-sama," said the *daimyou.* "Take this boy and treat his hurts. And hurry."

Kaworu looked at Tsurugu. "May I....?"

Tsurugu nodded, stepping close. "Everyone knows. Go ahead."

Kaworu closed his eyes and slid into his fox form. Beside Kaede, Yoritomo-dono tensed a little; it was one thing to know, and another to see. But he owed his life to the broken fox, twice, and it was hard to resent that.

Tsurugu knelt and gathered the slight form — foxes were so much smaller than they appeared — into his arms, and the fox slipped against him with a muted whimper. Kaede touched Yoritomo-dono's arm. "Let's go."

CHAPTER FORTY

NAKA no Yoritomo looked down at the cramped figure before him. Hideo was sweating despite the cool air, bared to his scant *fundoshi*. His arms were bound high behind his back and his neck roped to his crossed ankles, forcing him forward over his splayed knees.

"You will answer my questions," Naka no Yoritomo said.

Hideo moaned. He had been bound some hours already, and his body would be burning throughout. He was a servant and had little honor to preserve in stoic silence.

"Tell me everything — who he was, and why he came for me."

Hideo tried to shift in his ropes, but the hemp held firm. "He was Ogasawara no Manabu, an *onmyouji*."

Naka no Yoritomo dug his toe into Hideo's ribs — not a kick, only a reminder of how completely he was at the *daimyou*'s disposal. "I know as much already."

"He was *onmyouji* to Sanjou no Takeo-dono, who exiled him after you attempted to kill Sanjou-dono's wife."

This time Naka did kick him. "Tell no lies! And do not accuse me."

"Please! I do not lie!" Hideo whimpered as he moved against the unyielding ropes.

"I did no such thing! If I had wished the woman dead, she would be dead. More, if I moved against his house, Sanjou-dono himself would have died; I do not waste my strength killing wives." Naka turned to a man waiting to one side. "Make him less comfortable. I will come again in a few hours."

"No, *tono*! Listen, and I will tell you all! Ogasawara-sama's wife was killed in place of Sanjou-dono's, and he was exiled because he had not prevented the attack. Then he went to his family, as the Ogasawara are *onmyouji*, and begged help but was refused. And so he swore vengeance on you, *tono*. This is true, I swear it!"

Naka frowned down at the big man. "But I sent no one to Sanjou-dono's house."

Hideo strained to bow, though his body could hard bend more. "Sanjou-dono believes you did. Please, great lord, I tell you the truth. Ogasawara-sama wished vengeance upon you for the loss of his wife and his position, and he said he would become great by destroying you when Sanjou-dono could not."

Naka waited a moment, and then he gestured to the waiting man. "Unbind him, and keep him near in case of further questions." Then he turned and went into the house, where his wife awaited him.

狐

Tsurugu sat back from Kaworu's limp figure and rubbed at his face. "We need a *kappa*."

Kaede-dono looked up from the medicinal powders she was mixing. "Murame, hold that steady. A *kappa*?"

"They are bloodthirsty predators, but they are also the

most skilled bone-setters and healers. And...." He stopped and looked at Kaworu, who lay very still, his eyes closed. Tsurugu lowered his voice anyway. "And something is badly broken inside, and it's tearing at him. I don't know if it can be repaired, but I know we're not the ones to do it. We need a *kappa*, if anything is to be done."

Kaede looked at Kaworu. "Where might we find one?"

"Since the one in the stream below is gone? I don't know." Tsurugu clenched his fists and looked at the helpless fox, stretched loosely on the *tatami*. Sunlight splotched the floor beside him, but it did not warm him. "We should send word to Midorikawa-dono."

"How?"

"I'll ask someone to carry it." Tsurugu took a breath, forced his voice to steady. "The *itachi* are very fast."

Kaede did not answer; she understood the significance of needing a speedy messenger. Beside her, Murame made a little choking sound.

In the inner corridor of the *wataridono*, a shadow stirred. Gennosuke uncoiled, making no sound on the planked floor, and slipped away.

狐

Gennosuke looked down at the water, dark but for ripples of moonlight across its surface. The river bent here, forming a deep pool, and for as long as Gennosuke could remember, children had been warned to stay well away from it. If there were a *kappa* nearby, it would be found here.

No one worked near even in the day, and tonight there was no one to be found for miles. No one would hear him call for help, and even if someone did, little could be done once he was pulled beneath the surface. Gennosuke did not know if he even liked the *kitsune* boy, and he suspected, despite the denial, that he knew something of Shishio-*oji-san*'s death.

But the *daimyou* wanted the boy to live, and Kaworu-kun had saved Naka no Yoritomo's life. That would have to be enough.

Gennosuke shed his clothing until he was wearing only his *fundoshi*, He stared at the water another moment, and then he stripped the *fundoshi* as well, so that he stood naked in the dark. He shook out a rope and tied a fixed loop about his chest, leaving a long tail loose. He measured out the length and then tied many-layered knots at the junction of a tree and its largest branch. He tested the rope length once more, checking that the loop wouldn't quite touch the surface and it would be difficult to pull his head underneath. He wouldn't drown immediately.

That would hardly help if he were devoured from beneath.

He stepped into the water, shivering with the cold of it, and turned his buttocks to the river. *Kappa* enjoyed cucumbers and human flesh, but they particularly enjoyed the *shirikodama*, a concretion of pure life energy residing atop the rectum. Given a chance, they would reach into their victims and steal that first, ensuring the human would die while the *kappa* enjoyed its treat and leaving plenty of meat to enjoy at leisure. Baiting buttocks was effective, but dangerous.

Gennosuke shivered and clenched tightly, trying not to think of a blue-green fist darting from the water into him to steal his life—

It was a terrible wait, naked and cold and knowing exactly what he baited.

Water rippled against his legs, wetting him. Gennosuke's breath caught and he flexed his fingers on the surplus rope.

And then something lunged from the water, drenching him in cold and clutching at him with cold, rubbery skin. Gennosuke jerked and nearly panicked, but he dropped the rope tail low in either hand and pulled the wet body close, binding it to him too tightly to maneuver a hand between them. The *kappa* screeched and hissed, and Gennosuke was jerked backward, snapping against the anchoring rope. The *kappa* jerked up short as well, and it screeched again and began to rake at him with rigid fingers.

Gennosuke seized the rope and, ignoring the raking, began to draw them both forward and away from the water. *Kappa* were terribly strong for their size, and only its poor traction, barely able to reach the ground as it hung from Gennosuke's back, kept it from dragging them both back into the river. The *kappa* screamed and kicked and raged, but Gennosuke kept on. Bruises would heal; if he did not get away from the water, bruises would be the least of his trouble.

He reached the base of the tree and flipped the rope's slack about it, making it easier to hold them in place. The *kappa* snarled. "Let me go!"

"I will," Gennosuke said, "but I must have your help first."

The *kappa*'s beak bit deep into his side, and Gennosuke cried and twisted, battering at the creature with one hand. The *kappa* might be too close to draw out his *shirikodama*, but it could still do him considerable injury. He wriggled and got another loop of the rope about the *kappa*. "Stop!" He flung the rope about the tree and tied another knot. Then he took a knife from the ground and cut himself free, leaving the kappa bound to the tree. "Stop, I beg you. I swear I will release you again. But you must help me first."

The *kappa* wriggled an arm free and began pushing at the rope. "Must I?"

"Please." Gennosuke hesitated. "He's badly injured. Only a *kappa* of great skill might save him, and even that is doubtful."

The *kappa* gave him a flat, amphibious glare. "You would malign the skills of one whose assistance you seek?"

"I do not malign. It is a near thing, they say."

"And what is that to you? And more importantly, what is it to me?"

"It is not much to me," Gennosuke said. "I dislike him, mostly, and I think he knows something of how my uncle died."

"And so you wish to save him so you may kill him yourself?" The *kappa* sounded almost bored.

"No. He saved the life of my *oyakata-sama*." Gennosuke exhaled. "I owe him my help for that."

"That may be, but it seems it's my help you want for him." Water glistened in the shallow depression atop the *kappa's* skull.

Gennosuke moved away and began to dress again. "Only because you are said to be the best."

The *kappa* laughed. "Flattery is a low sport, *bouzu*. Or did you speak to the other one?"

Gennosuke tied his *himo* about his waist, safely cinching his clothing. "The other one?"

"Or maybe you didn't." The *kappa* chuckled and then clacked its beak in frustration. "Look, I am—"

Gennosuke looped the rope about the *kappa's* ankles and drew it tight, jerking a knot into place. The *kappa* went rigid. "Wait. Don't—"

Gennosuke sawed at the rope holding the *kappa* against the tree. It lunged at him, breaking the last strands, and he heaved at the rope about its ankles. The *kappa* flipped and water spilled from the depression in its skull. It cried and clutched at its head. "No! My *sara*!"

Gennosuke threw the rope over his shoulder and pulled the *kappa* up like a sack of rice, head downward. It flailed weakly against his back, its strength gone with the water. "Don't leave me like this. Please, generous boy, don't do this."

Gennosuke started walking. "We have a long road to go this night. You might want to save your breath; you'll be dry before we're there."

The *kappa* wailed. "No, no, don't leave me so! I will go with you!"

Gennosuke kept walking.

"I'll be no good to you like this! I'll be too weak to work the medicine you want!"

Gennosuke kept walking.

"Enough! Let me down, give me water, and I'll go to help your injured companion, I swear it."

Gennosuke paused. "You'll swear?"

"I so swear."

Gennosuke lowered the rope, letting the kappa gently to the ground. "Turn around and swear."

The *kappa* got to its feet and shuffled a turn in place. "I give you my oath, I will go with you and give your friend what medicine I can."

Gennosuke nodded; the oath of a *kappa* was sound. He slit the rope and freed the *youkai*. "Go and fetch some water, then, and we'll be off."

The *kappa* stumbled to the river and half-fell, ducking its head and filling the shallow basin in its skull, and then returned at a brisk jog. "Let's go."

CHAPTER FORTY ONE

TSURUGU stared at the *chokuban*.

All day and half this night he had sat beside Kaworu, watching and feeling more helpless than ever in his doubly-magical life. He had at last returned to his room to wash his face and stretch. He needed to move, needed to breathe air not thick with Murame's unshed tears.

He stared at the *chokuban*.

He had considered reading before, of course, but he wasn't sure he should. *Onmyoudou* told of auspices and probabilities, not strict predictions, and it could not say with certainty whether Kaworu would live or die.

And even if it could, Tsurugu wasn't sure he wanted to know. Knowing Kaworu-kun would live would of course bring great relief and joy. But knowing he would die…. Tsurugu could not abandon the slender hope left to them. Kaworu was young, strong, loved. He might live.

No one had asked Tsurugu; they had not thought to ask, or they did not want to know, either. Hope was a small, frail thing, but terribly hard to uproot by force of will.

Tsurugu turned his back on the *chokuban* and started back to the *wataridono* where Kaoru waited.

狐

Murame knelt beside the still fox, watching his misshapen rib cage rise and fall. A single light burned near the fox's body, but it was enough to show his breathing was irregular and uneven. Murame watched, her eyes burning but not shedding tears, not yet. There would be enough tears to come later.

Kaede-dono was in Naka no Yoritomo's room. That was only expected, given that she had been restored this day, but Murame had seen her cast one quick glance backward to the room where Kaoru lay. Hanae had gone to attend her, as Kaede would not ask Murame to leave Kaoru for the short time that was left. Tsurugu had told the *itachi*, the wind-weasel, to hurry.

The pale fox shuddered, and Murame sat forward, her heart quickening. And then it was not a fox, but the boy. He gasped and choked, struggling with the change, and his fingers flexed.

She took his hand. "What are you doing? Lie still."

"I wanted to speak with you." He lay on his side, his fingers loose about hers, and his eyes opened and closed. "I wanted to ask you."

"Ask what?"

He coughed, and the movement tore whatever was caught within him, and he cried with the pain of it. Tears welled in Murame's eyes as she held his hand, helpless. Always helpless.

"Don't," he whispered. "Not yet. Be strong for now."

"I'm not strong. I've never been strong."

"You were splendid." Foam flecked his lips. "That ox Hideo knocked me down. Again. And then he came for you, and you threw him to the ground."

Murame laughed, a little choking sob of a laugh. "That?"

"He could not move you." Kaworu smiled faintly. "I'm glad you struck him down for me."

"You were my instructor, and so the victory goes to you." Murame sniffed and wiped the spilling tears from her eyes.

"I wanted…." Kaworu squeezed his eyes shut and screwed up his face, and she realized he was trying to stifle another cough. "Murame-san, I will never have a chance to ask."

"What are you talking about?"

His faint smile was less convincing this time. "I have heard you all. We are only waiting. I know, I understand. I only wish…."

Murame's throat had nearly closed. "They're coming. Tsurugu-sama has sent a message."

"Good. I hope they are in time." He licked his split lips. "If — if we had time, Murame, I would have asked you if you would come with me, when we left this place. If you would…."

She was crying in earnest now.

"I would have gone to your father, in the village, and I would have made him such a price that he would weep for it, and when I had taken you far from his stupid dog-loving village, he would have awakened to find a coffer full not of gold but of leaves and acorns and it would serve him—" He coughed, and his fingers jerked from hers, going to his torso as if somehow he could still the hurt.

Murame sobbed. "I am so sorry."

"What are you sorry for?" demanded a voice behind them. She whirled to see a boy all in soft grey, standing in the doorway. "You did nothing." He pushed the door back, revealing a blue-green creature the size of a large child, with a turtle-like shell and a beaked face.

She jerked backward, afraid even before she consciously recognized the creature. *"Kappa!"*

The boy in grey looked around. "Where is the *onmyouji-sama?*"

"Here!" Tsurugu dashed down the corridor. "You — you've brought a *kappa*. Please, come."

They entered the room, and the *kappa* looked at Kaworu. "This is he?"

Tsurugu came to kneel beside the *tatami*. "Something is broken inside him, beyond our ability to help. Anything you might do would be to our greatest obligation."

The *kappa* nodded, looking at him. "But he is not a boy, is he?"

Kaworu closed his eyes. "One day," he breathed.

"He is *kitsune*, like myself," said Tsurugu. "Can you help him?"

"I have given my word I would try," answered the *kappa*. "Bring me medicines and materials."

"I'll fetch the chest," said Murame, and she slid across the floor.

狐

Tsurugu, intent on the *kappa's* work, did not notice when the *daimyou* entered the room. It was only when Naka-dono coughed to announce himself that they jerked their eyes from Kaworu.

"Tono." Tsurugu bowed low, Murame following.

The *kappa*, his hands inside Kaworu, made a half-bow. *"Yoroshiku de gozaimashita."*

Kaede stood behind the *daimyou*. Naka-dono pointed

with his fan to the *kappa*. "That one is unknown to me." He made no demands; he was cautious now.

"A *kappa*, *tono*, brought for his bone-setting skill." Tsurugu picked up a dipper of water, and as the *kappa* bowed again to the *daimyou*, spilling water from his *sara*, he passed the water and the *kappa* poured it over his head.

Naka-dono looked down at them. "The boy… I did not think he was hurt so badly."

Murame choked and looked away. Tsurugu made an effort to speak through the stone in his throat. "He — it is a very near thing, *tono*."

Kaede watched, pale and silent, as Naka-dono went down on one knee. Kaworu made no movement, his mouth hanging open and dry. He reeked of *sake*; pinning him had not been enough to keep him still as the *kappa* worked.

Naka-dono looked at the bloody clothes, the *kappa*'s reddened hands, the basins and bucket of water, the too-still figure on the *tatami*. "This is the boy who crossed the mountain alone to warn me of the *oni*, and who lured it after himself to save me."

Tsurugu nodded. "It is."

"And then I cast him out of my house. And then he took this injury in defense of my wife, and myself." He clenched his fists. "It is not for a *daimyou* to say he has been wrong about a servant, but it would be foolish to say I have not been so wrong."

Tsurugu, sharp with fear and weariness, could not resist. "He is not merely your servant. He is the son of the *kyuubi*. His brother did not die, only returned to his father's court to learn statecraft."

"The *kyuubi*." Humans did not often encounter the nine-tailed *kitsune*, but their tales never forgot when they did. Naka-dono's arm twitched. "Will this *kyuubi* seek retribution for what has happened here?"

That was not what Tsurugu wanted to think on. "I cannot say, *tono.*"

Naka seated himself, and Kaede settled beside him. She reached out to touch Kaworu's face, brushed back a strand of dark hair. He did not stir.

Kaede looked at Murame, but the girl avoided her eyes. She avoided everyone's eyes. Touching someone, physically or visually, might break the frail control she held.

Tsurugu cleared his closing throat. "Where is Hanae-san?"

"I asked her to bring tea and rice balls," Kaede-dono answered. "I knew anyone still awake would be... tired." She paused. "I am glad you found a *kappa.*"

"If I may speak, *okugata-sama*, this one is also glad of it." The *kappa* shook his head. "This boy would not have lasted the night."

"But you can help him now?"

"I can help him, yes. As to whether I can save him — it is difficult to make promises, *okugata-sama.*"

Hanae knelt at the door, bearing a *zen* with tea and rice balls. She was tired, too. Her hair and clothing were still neat, but her face was wan and dark beneath the eyes.

"Bring *sake*, too," Naka-dono said tersely.

Hanae looked up from the tea she was arranging. "*Sake* with rice?"

"Then I won't eat the rice!" He rose. "Send some to my room." He paused and looked at Kaede-dono. "Will you come with me?"

Kaede hesitated for only a moment, but the choice was clear. Naka-dono was repentant now, but she must be diligent in rebuilding his trust and love, for her own sake and that of all the *youkai* presently beneath the *daimyou*'s roof. And Kaworu would never know if she were present or not. "Yes, I will come."

"Water, please," said the *kappa*, and Tsurugu ladled some onto his inclined head.

CHAPTER FORTY TWO

TSURUGU was returning from his room again when the visitors came through the gate. An *ashiguru* tried to argue with them, demanding their business, but the tall man kept walking, answering curtly as he made his irresistible way toward the house. Behind him Genji matched his pace, looking more serious than Tsurugu could remember. More soldiers were coming toward them, hands moving toward their swords.

"Midorikawa-dono!" Tsurugu intercepted their path and waved away the *ashiguru*, who was pleased to leave this intruder to the *onmyouji.* Tsurugu bowed. "I—"

"Are we in time?" Midorikawa's voice was thick and strained.

"You are. And I am most pleased to say it looks better than when my message was dispatched. A *kappa* was found to attend to him, and while he is far from whole, we — we're not as troubled."

Midorikawa nodded, a quick jerk of the head, but a little of the tension left his voice. "Take us to him, if you would."

Tsurugu glanced at Genji as they turned, and the boy's face was open and raw, full of worry and sudden, frightening hope. Tsurugu gave him a thin smile. "He doesn't look well — but he looks much better than he did last night."

They went to the room in the *wataridono* where Kaworu was and found him sleeping, on his back as the *kappa* had left him, Murame of course still by his side. Across the room the *kappa* leaned snoring against a pillar, a basin beside him and a jar of water within reach to replenish his *sara*.

Murame jerked upright as they knelt. She had been sleeping, too. Tsurugu caught her eye. "You should take some rest," he said softly. "Go. He will not be alone, and you will be better for having had rested yourself."

She nodded, guessing there was more to his suggestion and knowing she lacked the position to protest. She rose and crossed to the door, kneeling to exit.

"Don't wake him," said Midorikawa, his eyes on Kaworu. "Not yet." He swallowed.

Genji moved around his father and knelt. He looked at Kaworu as if blinking might let him slip away.

"How did he come to this?" Midorikawa-dono reached one hand to touch his son's forehead.

"He said he met an *oni*. But he did not look so bad at first. I think he kept fighting through the injuries."

Midorkawa-dono smiled sadly. "Bold and stupid."

"He more than proved himself." Tsurugu would give Kaworu the best report possible, and truth made it easy. "He ran through the enemy to find and disrupt the *onmyouji*'s circle, and then again to place our own. And when we required a *tama*, he thought of using a human representative, and our circle slowed Ogasawara-san enough to save Kaede-dono's life. He was at the center of all of it."

"My son would be."

Kaworu's mouth moved, and his faint, dry voice croaked. "Don't forget — tricked the *oni*."

"Kaworu-kun!" But he only moved his lips once more, and then he was gone again.

Tsurugu reached for the water bucket. "We had to give him quite a lot of *sake*," he said. "He's going to be dry and ill this morning, even aside from his own hurts. But it was necessary."

Genji took the dipper and dribbled some into the open mouth, slow and controlled, until Kaworu swallowed. "What was that about the *oni*? Was that the one which crushed him?"

"No." Briefly Tsurugu told them of Kaworu's mad rush to warn the *okugata-sama* and his illusion to draw the *oni* away. "And after that, he was captured by Ogasawara-san — but we had him safely back, as you can see."

As he spoke, Genji circled to the far side of Kaworu and gave him more water. Then he stretched out on his stomach along the bloodstained *futon*, propped on his elbows to watch his brother, his body close alongside the swathed Kaworu to warm him.

Tsurugu exhaled, relieved that Midorikawa-dono had come. "You traveled quickly."

"We were not far, and the *itachi* found us last night. His mother…. She will not have heard yet. And I am most glad I will not have to carry such news home to her." The *kyuubi* looked over Kaworu. "He needs another covering. He must have lost much blood, and he'll be cold."

"Midorikawa-dono!" Kaede-dono knelt at the door. "May we enter?"

The *kyuubi* nodded. "I am glad to see you well, Kaede-dono."

"I am well, with gratitude to the excellent servants you have provided. Tsurugu-sama, Kaworu-kun, and Hanae-san all came to my aid and fought for my safety." She did not mention that Tsurugu had been the one to betray her. Kaede-dono was a pearl of great value. "I should like you to meet my husband, the *oyakata-sama*."

The *daimyou* looked at the *kyuubi*. Kaede must have told him who was in his house. He made a precisely-calculated little bow. "Naka no Yoritomo *de gozaimasu*."

"Midorikawa Kurou Akimasa *de gozaimasu*." Midorikawa returned an equally precise bow.

Naka no Yoritomo-dono took a breath. "You are welcome in my house, for the service you have given my wife." He looked around the room with the air of a man who has found himself among enemies, but knows honor holds him safe for the moment.

"Your wife is a woman of strength and honor, and service to her is only just."

Naka-dono gave a rueful smile. "To my shame, I am only just learning how true that may be."

The *kappa* stirred and sat up, rubbing its eyes. It blinked at the room, and then it rolled forward and bowed, spilling water from its skull. *"Kyuubi-dono."*

"*Kappa-san.* I have you to thank for the life of my son?"

"I believe so, *tono*. That is, I believe he will survive and heal now."

"Then I thank you most sincerely." He looked at Tsurugu. "Where did you find him?"

"I did not bring him."

"I came with the boy," the *kappa* answered. "He bartered with me to do what I could for this one."

"Which boy?"

The *kappa* considered. "He was one of those who don't like to be spoken of."

"The nephew of the warrior the *oyakata-sama* lost,"

Tsurugu supplied to Midorikawa-dono, an explanation and subtle warning in one.

"I thought he must have been sent by the other one, as they don't like to come out often. Seeing two shadows caught my notice." The *kappa* poured more water over his scalp.

"Who was the other?" asked Tsurugu.

"He was barely alive — not broken in the same way this fox-boy was, but he had enough arrows and blades stuck into him that he was more a prickly bush than a man. His own village had done it, he told me, when they learned he'd betrayed their *oyakata-sama*. He'd barely gotten away." He chuckled. "He told me all of it, once he got enough *sake* into him that I could work. He wouldn't stop talking."

"He betrayed the *oyakata-sama*?" It was Gennosuke, in the doorway. He glanced across to Naka-dono and dropped to the floor. "Please forgive the intrusion. But I must know. Who was this man?"

The *kappa* shook his head. "It wasn't one of yours."

Gennosuke's simultaneous disappointment and relief were palpable. "My — my uncle is missing. I thought this man might know something about it."

The *kappa* shook his head. "His *daimyou* was Sanjuu, or Santou, or—"

"Sanjou no Takeo." Naka no Yoritomo's voice was clipped and bitter.

"That's it, the same. But he had taken orders from Ayumu someone or other, to kill the *okugata-sama* and leave hints it was the fault of — in truth, of Naka no Yoritomo-dono." The *kappa* nodded sagely.

"Ayumu-dono." Naka no Yoritomo's lip curled into a snarl. "He has long walked a knife's edge, and now he has cut himself. And Sanjou with him." He lifted a hand. "Gennosuke-kun, you—"

"If I may, Naka-dono." Midorikawa's eyes had brightened to an unnatural golden color. "I should very much like to look after this myself. In the end, it is my people who were harmed by these, even more than yours."

Naka no Yoritomo looked at the *kyuubi*. "Midorikawa-dono, this man has attempted to kill my wife and myself. This cannot be paid with tricks, and *kitsune* do not generally kill."

"No. But we can make men wish they were dead."

The room was quiet for a long moment, and then Naka no Yoritomo nodded. "I look forward to hearing of your work, Midorikawa-dono."

CHAPTER FORTY THREE

MURAME hesitated a moment, watching Kaworu's slow breaths, and then she rose and withdrew with the light. The *kappa* had pronounced him well enough to last the night, and Murame's vigil had left her exhausted, and anyway Genji was sleeping beside him.

Kaworu wanted only to sleep, as well, but one thing remained. He stayed still, counting for each breath to keep them slow and steady as if in sleep, and waited in the dark. He did not wait long.

Only a faint brush of cloth announced Gennosuke's entrance. "Kaworu-kun?" The whisper was hardly audible, even so near the *futon*.

Kaworu opened his eyes, but the darkness was complete. "Gennosuke-kun."

"I saw your gesture — or what I thought might have been a gesture. So I've returned." The shadow-boy flattened himself to the floor so their voices did not need to carry. Beside Kaworu, Genji woke, but he did not stir.

"I want to tell you." Kaworu swallowed, his throat thick with pain and *sake* and reluctance. He could not tell Gennosuke everything, but he was *kitsune* and half-truths came easily to him. "About your *oji-san*." And Gennosuke deserved a half-truth perhaps even more than the truth.

Gennosuke made no sound, but Kaworu could sense the coil in his muscles.

"I knew your uncle was dead, because I saw him die."

Gennosuke's voice was thick. "Tell me."

"He died protecting the *oyakata-sama*." Kaworu licked his cracked lips. "Not from us. We were no threat. But he died in his duty, outside the *okugata-sama*'s room. No one else ever saw."

Gennosuke made the faintest of noises, a sob or breath snuffed to silence. "He — did he meet another of Ayumu-sama's assassins?"

"I did not see the start of it. I don't know how it came about." He blinked, trying to catch Gennosuke in the darkness. "But you should know he died honorably, and you should be proud of him."

"I am." The words were hardly there, and yet they were granite. "Thank you."

Kaworu nodded once, though they could not see each other, and there was silence. Then Gennosuke rolled away and slipped into the night.

Genji moved in the dark, and a hand touched Kaworu's shoulder. Then it withdrew, and they slept.

狐

A figure in soft grey slid from the wall and into the yard, moving silkily past the sleepy guards. He ducked beneath the floor of the *tai no ya* and crept beneath the building to the rear, where he turned and began to climb. The roof was thatched, as

Ayumu no Sadamu's funds went to furthering his ambitions rather than enhancing his home. The thatching absorbed the soft footfalls and the grey figure moved in silence.

Over the *shinden*, the figure descended again, and a tiny pearl of light appeared in his hand as he slipped inside, illuminating the space where the *samurai* slept. He knelt inside the door. *"Tono."*

Ayumu no Sadamu snorted and shifted on his *futon*. "What? Who is it?"

"*Tono*, I have come with an urgent message."

The *samurai* sat up on one elbow. "Eh? Oh. Why are you here? What is it?"

"You know me, *tono?*"

"Of course I do."

The figure in grey bowed and moved nearer the bed. "It is known that one of Sanjou-dono's shadows betrayed him."

Ayumu sat up sharply. "He has — but then, does he know who bought you? Does he—"

"Do not fear, *tono*. The traitor has already been dealt justice. Sanjou believes he has only loyal servants now."

Ayumu squinted at the grey figure. "Then you are...?"

"No, I am not the man you hired, *tono*." He lifted a hand, palm outward, to stay Ayumu's reach toward his sword. "But I am not sent by Sanjou-dono, or I would not have woken you to speak with you."

"Fair enough," Ayumu allowed. "What is your purpose, then?"

"I am here to warn you from your purpose." The man leaned forward. "Leave the house of Sanjou-dono alone."

The *samurai* scowled. "It is not your place to—"

"And hear this, *tono*, for this is a dire warning you must not ignore." The figure in grey straightened and stood, speaking over Ayumu's outrage. "Do not reach to the east, where you envy Naka no Yoritomo-dono."

"What are you saying? And how dare you rise—"

"Hear me, *onore!*"

The insult silenced the staring *samurai.*

"Listen, and live. Do not reach to the east, for it is not Naka no Yoritomo's land." The figure in grey seemed somehow taller as he spoke. "It is my land, and I am jealous of it and the people therein. And I will not countenance your meddling or your interference with the *tono* I have allowed to flourish there."

Around them the edges of the room took on an unnatural light, and little tongues of blue-green flame began to run along the lines of the furniture.

"Naka no Yoritomo-dono dwells there by my pleasure, as you live here by my good will. And you have moved against one under my protection."

Ayumu, wide-eyed, reached for the sword beside him. Colored fire leapt from it, bathing the room in blue-green light, and he recoiled.

The eerie light glowed in the eyes of the man who was not one of Sanjou's shadows. "And as a good *tono* will move when his vassal is attacked, I will not permit you to strike at Naka no Yoritomo. You did not understand before, but now it has been made clear to you." His head brushed against the ceiling, and he bent over the trembling *samurai.* "If you reach to the east again, you strike at me. And you will not be warned again."

With a crash of thunder, the man in grey vanished and became a golden fox, fully the height of the room, snarling as its nine tails lashed the room to shambles. Ayumu reached again for the burning sword and a massive paw slapped down on his arm, pinning him to the floor. Fangs the length of a *tantou* snapped before Ayumu's face, bathing him in steamy breath, and he screamed.

Voices answered outside, and a moment later warriors burst into the room. "*Tono!* Ayumu-sama! What is it?"

Ayumu waved at them. "*Youkai!* A *youkai* was here, a great *kitsune*! He threatened me!"

The warriors dutifully looked about the room, seeing neatly arranged furniture, coffers, *tatami*. "*Tono?*"

"He was here!" Ayumu snapped. "He destroyed the room, all was dripping fire!"

One of the servants stepped forward and knelt beside the bed. "It was likely a dream, Ayumu-dono. A very sharp dream."

"It was not." But Ayumu had no further argument to make. He looked at his warriors' carefully blank faces and took a breath. "Return to your posts."

All bowed and began to retreat, filing out of the room. Ayumu clenched his fists and then lay down again, angry and ashamed. That they would think—

"They know they cannot trust you," whispered his pillow.

Ayumu leapt from the bed, shrieking, and the warriors whirled and pushed back inside. Ayumu ripped his sword from the rack and, flinging the sheath across the room, attacked the headrest, hacking at it and shouting. Shards flew from the headrest, scattering, and the warriors and servants stood silent as Ayumu destroyed it.

He straightened. "It was the fox," he said. "It took the form of my headrest."

No one answered.

"It was the fox," he repeated.

A servant hurried forward and knelt, gathering the broken pieces of the headrest. It was no fox, but only a destroyed object. The fox must have changed forms again as he reached for the sword.

Ayumu looked around at the staring eyes. "Enough. Go to bed. This is beyond you."

Again, the warriors began to withdraw. Ayumu sighed and looked deliberately across the room.

"They think you are mad," said a voice behind him.

He whirled, slashing with the sword, but there was nothing. Men gasped at the door, and Ayumu made himself stand still. "Stop!"

They stood in place.

"Fetch me that," he ordered with a nod of his head toward the sheath he had discarded.

A servant scuttled forward, retrieved the sheath, and came to present it to Ayumu with a low bow. As he took it, the servant murmured, "They think you are mad, and they may be correct."

His swordsmanship was perfect, a clean slice which cut downward from the neck through the collarbone and upper chest. The man dropped with a nearly-inaudible gasp, and Ayumu leapt and jeered. "Now, he is a fox! You will see!"

But the collapsed body bled across the wooden floor and remained a man.

A woman's quiet sob drew his eyes to the door, and Ayumu looked at his wife, wide-eyed and trembling. She must have heard the noise. He threw the sword to the ground. "Remove him."

Men gathered the dead servant, leaving a dark stain on the planks. As they left, glancing surreptitiously back at Ayumu and sliding the door closed behind them, he turned to his wife. "And you—" he took her wrist "—stay with me. The fox will not return if I am not alone." He did not know if this were true, but it seemed plausible, and he did not wish to be alone in the room again.

Ayumu pressed her to his *futon*, bracing himself above

her. "You will not turn me away," he said, and it was nearly a question. Humiliation and anger burned in him, and he needed her. "I am not mad."

"You are not mad," she breathed, and he pushed aside her robes. She wore her favorite scent, all pine and flowers.

He lay upon her, feeling the warmth of her, and pressed his face into her neck. She made a little sound, shifting, and he bit her, and his mouth was full of fur.

She laughed.

He threw himself backward, spitting and gasping and grasping for a sword, and she sat up, robes disarrayed over beautiful pale skin. "You are not mad," she repeated. "Not yet."

The sword was beyond his reach. Ayumu sat still, staring.

She smiled. "And you were wrong. That poor servant was not me, not even for a moment. You killed your own loyal man. You heard my voice, and you guessed wrongly." And then she was gone, and there was only a headrest, whole and unharmed. "But other times, you might guess rightly."

He lunged, but the headrest was quicksilver in his hands, and suddenly the dead servant stood before him, smiling above his cloven bleeding torso. "And you will never know, until you have made the mistake. And your wife, and your men, and your servants, and all who see you or hear of you, will think you mad. And you will never know when they suppose rightly."

Ayumu shouted and lunged again, but the servant swelled and became the great golden fox, as large as the room and snarling with teeth the length of Ayumu's arm, and he screamed and ducked away and then all was gone, the room was empty, and there were eyes staring at him again from the door.

"It was she! My wife! It took the shape of my wife!"

The eyes stared.

"She was here! When I kept her, when she came—"

"*Tono,*" one said, his voice unsteady, "*tono,* your wife is in her room, and has been all this night."

"But she was here — you all saw her, when I called for you before…."

"*Tono*, we could not look upon your wife! She has not been here tonight."

Ayumu stared at them, and he knew that while they might yet obey his orders, never, never again would they be his men.

CHAPTER FORTY FOUR

THE spring sun shone brightly upon the garden, and
pink and white blossoms showered upon the pond's artificial
island like a painting in motion. Kaworu stood between his
father and Tsurugu. Genji stood to one side, having protested
with a grin it was important not to risk confusing the bride.

There was little danger of that. Kaworu still moved with
short, stiff strides, and anyway Tsurugu suspected Murame
could not be deceived even by Genji's practiced imitations.

Four small *hitotsu-me-nyuudou* bore a palanquin —
lent by Kaede-dono — across the bridge to the island, settling it
gently upon the ground. The woven curtain was drawn back,
and Murame stepped into the light.

"Hurry, Murame-sama," piped a *kawauso*, an otter. "You
must get beneath the trees."

Murame shuffled forward, awkward in her unfamiliar
and heavy formal garments, and reached the shade of the trees.
Blossoms floated around her in surreal affectation. She bowed
to the *kitsune* and her bridegroom.

"Come, Murame-sama." Midorikawa-dono extended a

fan to beckon her forward. "You look lovely."

Rain came softly across the ground, whispering in the grass and fallen blossoms. They stepped nearer one another in the shade, sheltering from both the rain and the sun.

Beyond Tsurugu's concealing *kekkai*, making the island appear uninhabited, servants working elsewhere in the garden muttered and shielded their burdens. "A sun-shower," one called to another. "A fox must be marrying."

One of the *hitotsu-me-hyuudou* giggled.

Tsurugu stepped away, making room for Murame to join Kaworu. She bowed once more to Midorikawa-dono.

"And to *ani-ue*," prompted Kaworu. "He is *chichi-ue's* heir now."

"Leaving the better aid to Kaede-dono." Genji smiled. "I could not have illusioned that *oni* away from Naka-dono."

"You'll have time enough to praise one another at home," Midorikawa-dono said with mock impatience. "Now, Murame-sama, will you walk or ride?"

She flushed, laughed nervously, and then covered her face. "Forgive me! I am only unaccustomed to being addressed thus."

"Murame-sama? And how else should you be addressed?" Tsurugu wanted to touch her shoulder, to give her encouragement as he might have once, but now he could only smile and nod. "Here Kaworu-kun played the servant, but in his father's court he is Akitane-sama, and as his bride you must be no longer a servant, either."

Murame smiled, embarrassed and happy. "Here they will think me *kamikakushii*, stolen away by *youkai*."

"But you come freely." Midorikawa nodded toward the palanquin. "Greet your husband, and then into the palanquin if you will ride. We have a long way to go."

Murame looked at Kaworu, trying to restrain her smile.

He took her hand, their fingers lacing for just a moment, and he turned and escorted her to the palanquin. The *hitotsu-me-nyuudou* shouldered their carrying poles and prepared to bear Murame to her new place.

Outside, the sun-shower passed, and no one observed the foxes' procession as it moved into the east.

Thanks for reading *Kitsune*-Mochi! Did you enjoy it? Please leave an honest review; I read every one, and I'd really appreciate it!

To learn more about the world of *Kitsune Tales* –What frightened Murame on her way down the mountain? What about sunshowers and fox weddings? – check out the ebook or visit my blog at **www.LauraVanArendonkBaugh.com**. You can sign up for news, sneak peeks, and pre-release specials, too!

Other books by Laura VanArendonk Baugh:

Kitsune-Tsuki

Smoke and Fears

Fired Up, Frantic, and Freaked Out: Training Crazy Dogs from Over-the-Top to Under Control

About the Author

Laura VanArendonk Baugh was born at an early age and never looked back. She overcame her childhood deficiencies of having been born without teeth and unable to walk, and by the time she matured into a recognizable adult she had become a behavior analyst, an internationally-recognized and award-winning animal trainer, a costumer/cosplayer, a chocolate addict, and of course a writer. She works in animal behavior by day and haunts Japanese culture and anime conventions by night.

Find her at **www.LauraVanArendonkBaugh.com**. She tweets at @Laura_VAB, too!